A LESSON IN APPRECIATION

Aaron eased around, facing her. Janelle's exotically beautiful eyes always captivated him, but in the moonlight tonight, they didn't look real. They were something of a fantasy, a dream, and maybe he had dreamed her. "Thank you for coming. You're incredible."

Perusing the breathtaking portrait that was his face, she held it by the sides. "I couldn't be anywhere else at a time when you needed me so much."

"Life is so short, Janelle. That's what this experience has taught me. It's short and we have to make the most of it. We have to cherish the good times and hold on to them as if they might pass away. We have to hold on to all the sweetness." His finger glided torpidly across her lips.

Feeling her body's need for him, she stared in his eyes, while accepting his finger in her mouth. "We have to be thankful for those things that are *so good* in this life." She was whispering.

His eyes never leaving hers, Aaron nodded. "You're good." His gliding finger wound down from her lips and stroked her neck. "You feel so good."

LOVE SO
TRUE

LOURÉ BUSSEY

Pinnacle Books
Kensington Publishing Corp.

http://www.arabesquebooks.com

PINNACLE BOOKS are published by

Kensington Publishing Corp.
850 Third Avenue
New York, NY 10022

Pinnacle, the P logo and Arabesque, the Arabesque logo are
Reg. U.S. Pat. & TM Off.

First Printing: January, 1999
10   9   8   7   6   5   4   3   2   1

Printed in the United States of America

CHAPTER ONE

Aaron Deverreau sat at the bar in Hart's Restaurant, smiling about what happened earlier in the dining area. As he enjoyed a meal with a fraternity brother, who he hadn't seen in years, an attractive woman in her thirties invited herself to their table. Flirting with Aaron, she eventually told him he looked delicious, and she could *be* delicious—that night—at her place if he dared to come for a taste. She was bold, he thought, with an even bigger smile, then shifted his muscular frame on the bar stool. Although, she wasn't the only one who had come on to him, probably assuming he was after one thing—one thing she was more than willing to give. His buddies considered him lucky to have such enticing offers. They were always teasing him, calling him "the sexiest man alive." And Aaron had to admit, it was a nice feeling to be perceived as attractive and desirable. Beyond the image, he also knew his sexual desires were strong. He loved thoroughly pleasing a woman he cared about, and loved being pleased in return. However, going to bed with everyone he encountered was not his idea of being a man.

The movie star looks his mother prided her middle son as having, emitted a false reputation. None of those who presumed he was a ladies' man could understand how deeply he could love. So deeply that after nine months, he couldn't fall asleep at night without first wondering about the one who broke his heart. What was she doing at that precise moment? The one who made it impossible to fall in love with anyone else. Wherever she was, was she feeling guilty for what she did? To this day, Aaron hadn't personally known anyone whose heart was destroyed the way his had been. The breakup was so vicious, he never divulged to anyone the truth about why they divorced. Not even his brothers and sisters, or best friends. It was almost as if uttering the words aloud would force him to relive every sensation of that unforgettable moment.

Recalling it all, Aaron's smile disappeared. He had to let her and the memory go. Intending to seal his promise with a toast to himself, he motioned to get the bartender's attention. He had a taste for Grand Marnier, his favorite wine. But a woman walking in the door made Aaron forget his thirst, and remember hunger.

It was something Janelle Sims didn't expect. She was walking by the bar area in Hart's Restaurant with her best friend and colleague, Sherry, after work on Friday. They were talking about an interesting phone call she'd received at her office earlier. That's when in their path to a table, a pair of eyes grabbed hers so forcefully, the man seated at the bar not only conveyed she was *extremely fine* with his burning look, but teased her so that she had to peruse the rest of him. Every lusciously masculine inch caused her gaze to linger. Afterward, she backtracked to eyes blazing with such a stare, it was all his own. All hers too. Those eyes and everything else about him aroused sensations Janelle thought she'd never experience again. She was turned on. *Very turned on.* Turned on like when she had her first taste of how sensually alive a man could make her feel.

Not since Janelle was a teenager, fighting the spells of good-looking boys with no-good intentions, had she been so floored by a man's appearance. If she hadn't known better, the warmth and tenseness suddenly in her body, the untamed rhythm in her heart and tremor in her legs, would have made her forget the promise to herself to never pay any attention to a drop-dead gorgeous man. Hadn't what happened showed her what could happen if she did otherwise?

She wanted what was real in a mate, maturity, honesty, dependability, faithfulness, ambitiousness, and someone who would be a positive force by her side as she reached for her dreams. Mitchell Broussard, who she'd been introduced to at Sherry's husband's birthday party seemed to possess some of those qualities. In getting acquainted with him that night, he certainly made it clear he was ambitious, as well as financially comfortable. There was a definite interest, too, when Janelle expressed her desire to start her own business, a dress boutique featuring her own designs. All that was not so appealing was his abundance of ego. That was revealed the more they talked.

Egotism, being what it may, was much easier to handle than the affairs that were likely magnets to a seductive creature, like the one who hungrily stared. He definitely knew his affect on the opposite sex, Janelle was sure. Steamy moments was all he could offer her. Nothing more. His type would never make a real commitment to a woman, or plan a future with her, and she didn't dare imagine love anywhere near him.

Her own potion of wisdom, nevertheless, couldn't control Janelle at that instant. With her shapely body wrapped in a black silk suit, she stepped along a red, carpeted aisle that separated the bar stools from the dining tables, and couldn't look away from him. She was only lured deeper inside the sensual brown depths that beckoned her eyes to travel elsewhere. A broad chest and thick arms filled his navy blue suit. Neatly fitting slacks covered long legs. His lips were plump and appeared ready to taste something he starved for, while his hair was short, and shimmering black under the club's candlelight, shimmering like his neat brows and mustache. Accentuating all of his handsomeness was skin hued in sweet chocolate. Nonetheless, it was his eyes, unspokenly promising, *Oh, what I could do to you,* that captivated her most.

When Janelle was finally so near the stranger that a whisper of his spicy cologne swept over her, piercing the vapors of hot, spicy food, their eyes met up close. Her heart's patter against her chest became stronger. With his lips pressed together, he tempted her further with a gentle smile. Feeling somehow foolish, Janelle slightly curved her lips too.

Seconds later, as Janelle and Sherry became comfortable on red, velvet cushions, placing their jackets over the chairs' backs, Sherry noticed Janelle's full lips curling.

"What's so funny?" Sherry asked.

"You."

"Me?" Sherry's thin lips tipping up at the corners, she slid her chair closer to the table. "You're thinking about what I said earlier when you said Mitch called you?"

Janelle couldn't help succumbing to Sherry's stinging humor, just as she couldn't stop the growing urge to look over at *him.* Resisting, she held her head firmly in front of Sherry. "Now why do you have to talk about the man like that?"

"But it's true. His old girlfriend did tell me she nicknamed him minute man, because he made love for a minute. And did that minute like he was a mummy bouncing."

Janelle was tickled again, but the funniness of the words waned when she recalled how nice Mitch was to her on the phone earlier. "No, seriously. He and I weren't talking about any dating or sex or anything like that." She surrendered to temptation, letting her attention wander to the bar. *He* was watching the video monitor. She looked back at Sherry. "He wants to meet with me and talk about my business idea."

Sherry was peering in a compact mirror, fluffing an auburn curl. "He wants to meet with you all right." She snapped the compact shut. "To talk about that *minute* business." Gazing steadily at Janelle, she placed the mirror in her purse. "I saw how he was checking you out."

"No, he's really interested," Janelle insisted.

"In getting you in bed."

"In hearing more about my boutique. And I'm so grateful he is." Her expression became intense like her tone. "You don't know what it's like."

Sherry looked confused. "What are you talking about?"

"I'm talking about wanting to do something with your life so bad you can taste it. But every time you try to do it some obstacle always gets in the way. The devil always throws something in your way. But then finally you meet someone, some *angel* who understands how spectacular what you're trying to do is and they try to help. Then you know all your prayers have been answered. It makes all the difference in the world."

Sherry thrust a cautioning hand forward. "Now hold up. Don't put all your hopes in Mitch."

"I'm not. But he did give me *some* hope." Sadness crept in the beguiling curve that was almost her smile. "Do you know that on every morning of the seven years I've worked at Mozelle Designs, I've woken up and wished to God I didn't have to go there? Go there and work my butt off marketing someone else's designs, when I'm aching to have a boutique selling my own designs.

"Sometimes it seems like I started well before my graduation from college. It feels like I worked there my whole life, and I'm never going to be able to leave. So many days when I'm in that office, I feel like I'm missing so much. I feel there is something else out there for me. Something exciting. Something that will give me so much joy. My life wasn't supposed to turn out like this. After graduating, I was supposed to have my own business, get rich and help little girls and boys, who went through ... who went through what I did. But between the house I bought my mom, her other expenses and my own, I just can't save enough to get my business going."

"Did you ever try to get a loan from banks or investors?" Sherry asked. She was watching a platter of lobster being placed on another table. She returned to Janelle. "They have special loans for women and minorities you know."

"Yes, I've applied for them all. My less-than-perfect credit and small savings don't grant me much collateral. As for investors, some are reviewing my business plan, but I haven't heard from anyone yet. I'm entrapped." She couldn't help being drawn to the bar once more. *He* was watching her. Nervously, she brought her gaze back to Sherry. "I ah ... I ah ... What was I saying? I must be getting old."

Sherry glimpsed the direction where her friend's stunning brown eyes had roamed. Now seeing what was so fascinating, she studied Janelle. Her rich, brown complexion suddenly had a glow that Sherry knew didn't come from a cosmetic bottle. "You said you were entrapped."

"Right. I don't know where my head is right now." She wrapped her long silken hair behind her ear. "But the point is, Mitch expressed a *real* interest in investing. And what if he is interested in me on a personal level? I wouldn't mind getting to know him better. I'm not in a relationship and he has some of those qualities that I look for in a man."

Sherry saw Janelle's attention drifting toward the bar again. When Janelle looked back at Sherry, Janelle saw the most suspicious look.

"What?" Janelle asked. "Why are you looking at me like that?" Scowling, she reared back. Yet, she could tell that Sherry caught her salivating over a man that was extremely good-looking, the kind of man she was always preaching about not wanting any part of.

Sherry leaned forward. "I think you noticed there's something mighty pretty in here, and I'm not just talking about the decor."

"I don't know what you're talking about." Janelle moved her chair in some so a couple could pass by.

"Oh, you know," Sherry accused, scratching the corner of her mouth with a burgundy nail. "Some things just make a woman's day. Put that spice in it. Give her something juicy to think about in bed at night, and that's one right over there." She paused, shifting her interest in his direction. "Blue suit, near the end of the bar." Smiling, she switched back to Janelle. "But I don't have to tell you that. You know who I'm talking about. You're not fooling me. I see that eye action between you two."

Janelle fought giving him another glimpse. She picked up her menu and began browsing over it. "A man like that can't give me what let's say Mitchell Broussard could. Mitch could offer a woman something real and solid. Now a man like that . . ." As much as she longed to take another glance, her gaze remained on the menu. "Now he's probably only good for some hard breathing."

Sherry raised a high arched brow. "Hard breathing is not a bad thing if it's for the right reasons. And I've already told you what Mitch's ex-girlfriend said. Mitch needs some *serious* lessons on how to make a woman breathe hard."

Janelle waved her hand at Sherry. "Oh, stop. Sex isn't everything."

"I know it's not," Sherry agreed. "But I've known Mitch a little longer than you have. And he doesn't score too high in other areas either."

"So why did you invite him to your husband's birthday party if he's so undesirable?"

"Because he's his boss and everyone else in their department had been invited." Sherry sighed. "Look Janelle, in the three months that I've worked at Mozelle with you, I feel like I've known you forever, and I've really come to care about you. And you've shown me how much you care for me too. In such a short time, we've become more than friends. We're sisters. And sisters should want each other to be happy. That's why I don't think you should get involved with Mitch for business or anything else. He's been over to our place often, and from what I've seen, he has a cold streak in him. You should hear how he bad-mouths his own brother. And the way he brags. *Please.* You're a good woman. You deserve a good man."

The waitress then appeared, interrupting Janelle from commenting, whisking her into thoughts as Sherry ordered her dinner. As much as Janelle loved Sherry, she disagreed with her frequently when it came to men. From Janelle's perspective, Sherry didn't understand what a good man was. Proof of that was Sherry's own choices in love, Janelle believed.

Sherry, a thirty-nine-year-old administrative assistant was married to a handsome man, who was eight years younger. Christopher was a consultant at an accounting firm, and often took long-distance business trips without her. So many times, Janelle wanted to tell Sherry to wake up. She wanted to shake some sense into her, screaming that Christopher wasn't going away on company business, and if he was, he wasn't going *alone.* Though there was something that always stopped her elixir of wisdom. It was knowing Sherry's rebuttal. Janelle had heard it many times before. "You're letting the past haunt you, Janelle. You're letting the past twist your view of men. Not all good-looking men play around on their ladies. Leave him in the past. *She* probably has."

When the waitress finished scribbling their orders, Janelle watched her until she was well out of hearing distance before assuring Sherry, "Don't worry about me so much. I can handle Mitchell Broussard."

Hours later, they had changed the subject. Laughing about a funny play they had seen, they feasted on lobster, shrimp, clams, pasta salad, and French bread. Janelle regretted that the time went so fast. She guessed it always did when you were loving someone's company. Tonight, as much as she resisted it, there were two people whom she enjoyed. On the way to the exit, bypassing the bar, she prepared herself for one last look at the handsome man. More than a look, however, she was soon excited by a voice that brought to mind a sexy late-night disc jockey, or a baritone rhythm and blues balladeer.

"Good night, beautiful," he said, as their eyes met up close again. "Hope you have a nice evening." He sounded as arousing as he looked.

"Good night to you too," Janelle responded demurely, though sensuously as she suddenly felt. "Hope you have a good one too."

When Sherry and Janelle reached outside, Janelle was wondering about the guy so much, she was barely aware of anything. Much the opposite, Sherry was scanning the bustling avenue. Since the stores were closed at that hour, she thought the brightly lit downtown Philadelphia area, combined with the comfortable September air, was perfect for window-shopping and walking.

"I heard how you spoke to that guy," Sherry remarked, as they began strolling.

"What do you mean you heard how I spoke to him?" Knowing she had purposely sounded cuter, Janelle laughed at herself.

Sherry was smiling too. "Sounded real sexy."

"You're trying to say I was flirting?"

"You didn't sound like that when you were talking to me at the table, and you don't sound like that now either."

"I'm only interested in one thing," Janelle declared, swaying her head to some music coming from a club they were sauntering by, "and that's talking business with Mitchell Broussard."

They had made merely a few steps past the club, when Sherry looped her arm inside Janelle's guiding her back toward Quincy's. It was the new after work club everyone at their office was chattering about. Happening music, along with its state-of-the-art design made their coworkers return to it again and again.

"I think I better get home," Janelle said, though she was tempted to venture inside when they stepped up to the entrance. Up-tempo music was rocking the packed club.

"Why?" Fascinated by the full dance floor, Sherry was popping her fingers, and bouncing her round hips. "Do you have some *hot* man waiting to give you some *hot,* buttered love at home?"

"No," Janelle replied with a grin, and swayed her body, along with her head. Of medium weight like Sherry, she was also roundly endowed in the buttocks, but more self-conscious of it. Nonetheless, tonight, she didn't move that way. Janelle was in the mood for dancing.

"So let's work it a little bit," Sherry prodded, bouncing harder, and tugging Janelle toward the ticket booth. "My man is working late and we finished another week at that godforsaken place."

Janelle was convinced. No sooner than they entered the club, both of them were centered in Quincy's, shaking their bodies to the funky and hip-hop beats. Some time later, with the music mellowing to slow jams, they decided to head home. Since Janelle's moves worked up a little sweat, she wanted to freshen up in the ladies' room before leaving. Making her way by several guys standing near a wall, she turned down dance offers and drinks, and had just politely told a guy she couldn't give him her number, when she made another step and there stood the unexpected. Her heart did a jolt. It was the stranger from the restaurant.

"Are you following me?" he asked. Smiling, his eyes traveled between her eyes and lips.

Janelle showed no signs that her heart was banging in her chest. "I don't think so," she answered, then made a step to proceed where she was headed.

Gently he touched her arm, drawing her gaze up into his. "Can I dance with you? When I'm on the plane going home tomorrow, I want to close my eyes and remember the best time I had in Philadelphia. And if you would feel how hard and fast my heart is beating right now . . ." He glanced at her hand as if he wanted to place it against his chest. "Then you would know that, that time would be with you."

A pleasant warmth flowed through Janelle, but she restrained from letting her lips show how good he made her feel. Neither did she succumb to the desire to touch his chest and confirm if his heart was beating wildly like hers was. She revealed only the tiniest smile. "And where is that plane taking you?"

"To Arizona. Phoenix, actually."

"You're a long way from home."

"Home is where the heart is, they say. I can be at home right now if you indulge me in one harmless dance."

Janelle vied to ignore the longing she felt to get closer to him, to touch him, to know who he was. "I'm sorry. I was on my way to the ladies' room and then my friend and I are leaving." She went around him.

A moist hand clasped firmly around her, forcing her to look over her shoulder. She froze. Held by his stare, a sweet ache of aliveness grew inside her.

"Just one dance . . . please."

The weakness in her body, which radiated in her eyes, acquiesced before the light nod of her head did. Before long, a stronger grip on her hand led her to the one empty space on the dance floor. There he placed his hands just above where the curve of her hip began, with just enough pressure to make her wonder what else could he touch so perfectly. As he tantalized her with this simple motion, a group on a soulful ballad crooned, "Am I dreaming? Or am I imagining I'm here in your arms?"

"I must be," Janelle whispered under her breath.

Slipping her arms around his broad shoulders, she was so excited by the hardness of his chest. More rousing, she was so stunned by the untamed beating within it, she stiffened. Was his heart really racing that fast and hard just like hers was? Or was her mind making her feel what she wanted to happen?

"Am I holding you too tight?" he asked in response to her tensing.

"No, not too tight."

Silence floated between them when their legs and hips began to move. Loving the way he held her, loving his closeness, loving his sexy, masculine presence, Janelle heard above the music, "What's your name?"

"Janelle."

"Janelle is a pretty name. It fits you. I'm Aaron."

Feeling his heart's rhythm matching the wildness of hers, Janelle smiled awkwardly. "Thank you. Your name is nice too." She didn't know what was happening with her and this stranger. Keeping a conversation going made it easier to deal with. "Are you visiting family or friends here in Philly? Or are you in our fair city on business?"

"I did meet with a frat brother earlier," he answered, his voice losing its strength, but none of its seductiveness. "I used to go to college here at Wharton. But my visit wasn't merely to catch up on old times. We were discussing business. I'm a real estate developer in Phoenix." His stare roamed to her lips, then probed lower, and so much lower it appeared like his eyes were closing. "In fact, I'm happy to say my company just added another complex to our commercial property acquisitions."

Janelle was in awe. She didn't miss being mentally undressed either. As well, she couldn't stop the fervent surge it stirred through her. Even her assumptions about him, the ones that hovered around them, warning her that a man so gorgeous couldn't be trusted couldn't thwart the growing desire. What was she doing? Added to it all, his career intrigued her.

"That's interesting, what you do," she commented.

"And what about you, Janelle?"

"I'm a marketing analyst at a fashion company right now, but I really want to open a dress boutique and sell my own designs."

Boyish exuberance swept over his face. "Beauty and talent." His smile gleamed in his already vibrant eyes. "I knew we had a connection. From the instant I saw you, I knew it. I'm always looking for good investments. Always! Show me an outstanding business plan, and if it's truly outstanding, you can come to Arizona and open your business there. I'll set you up in one of our finest properties."

Uncertain if he truly meant what he was proposing, Janelle half smiled. "I can't go to Arizona."

"That's too bad," he said, unsmiling, and taking in every exotic feature until he stopped at her eyes.

Staring back at him, in that crazy moment, Janelle could have gone anywhere with him—a complete stranger, a likely player. She was also wondering what he would have been like if she could have gotten to know him better. There was just something about him. Something that made him seem like he was more than his looks portrayed him as being.

Though suddenly feeling foolish, she eased her eyes away, and tried to relax. Yet, a calm, unemotional exchange between two dance partners wasn't what existed. Feeling her breasts pressing into this hard-bodied creature, she felt them and her entire body becoming more sensitive with each intoxicating movement of their exquisitely blending limbs. Tighter he held her. Reflexively, Janelle did the same. As if his heart had invited her near it, she laid her head against his chest. Before long, she was floating in a provocative other world, one where she was even more dazed in the sensuality of this dreamy creature.

Closing her eyes, Janelle glided her cheek to where his top shirt buttons were opened and a portion of his chest was revealed. Its hardness, and the frizzy hairs of it brushing her skin would have thrust out a moan if she hadn't bit her lip. Longing for more, Janelle caressed her nose across his heated flesh, and she realized most of his cologne had faded. The sweet scent of him pleasantly embraced her senses. Loving his natural smell, she ached to kiss his chest. Although, deep down Janelle knew she couldn't have been so reckless with a near stranger; she also knew she wasn't the only woman who felt like this about Aaron. How many other women had he worked this same spell on?

Janelle couldn't be one of them. This was not her type of man. A glance around the room at all the women checking Aaron out, showed her why he couldn't be. Though feeling Aaron's pleasing, uneven breaths heating her face, and her hands burrowing into his back, and his chin mashing into the top of her hair, and the occasional lust-drugged stare into each other's eyes, she couldn't deny he was becoming something to her.

He made her feel so erotic, and with each luscious motion of their mingled hips, she felt more passionate. They were so close she couldn't escape his hard excitement for her, and she was certain she wasn't imagining it. But why was she letting him do this?

She knew it was wrong to feel like this, to dance like this, to be charmed like this by the kind of man she always avoided. Yet, her heartbeat in perfect syncopation with his attested how much she loved it and wanted more. It all stirred the most intensely pleasurable fullness down inside her, which ached to be satiated. In some way, fully clothed they were making love. When was the last time life sent her something that made her feel so good?

"I haven't danced slow in so long," he whispered lazily across her ear. "It was worth the wait."

Janelle raised her head, beholding vulnerability in his

piercing eyes. "I haven't danced slow in a long time either."

Several songs played with their bodies never separating. Janelle's thirst was all that drew them apart. Aaron hurried away to get her a drink. As he did, she remained seated to ensure they had a table. The club was getting so crowded people could hardly move. Janelle didn't even see Sherry. However, as Janelle relaxed waiting for his return, her mind was working like her raging heart. What was she going to do when Aaron asked to see her again? Because he definitely was. If only her answer could have relied on how he sent her emotions into a frenzy. More entrancing, he just seemed so wonderful. But a man like that, one so handsome, wasn't he trouble? Janelle should have known that better than anyone.

When it seemed Aaron was taking too long to get her pineapple daiquiri, Janelle worried if something was wrong. Hence, she weaved throughout the crowd, heading toward the bar to find him. Spotting him a good distance away in an interesting situation, she halted her steps and gawked. Now she knew what was delaying Aaron.

CHAPTER TWO

A group of professionally dressed women were huddled around Aaron. While clutching a drink, which Janelle presumed was hers, he was laughing and talking with them. After observing for a moment, Janelle couldn't watch anymore. With the disappointment in him weighing heavily in her chest, she sauntered in another direction far from his view. She eventually stopped nearby the dance floor, her vision blurred by thoughts, which were only interrupted by Aaron's overpowering presence appearing beside her.

"I went to our table and saw a couple there," he said, while debating if he should explain about running into his four friends from college. They detained him with updates of their families and careers. Deciding that would bore her, he certainly knew who wouldn't bore him. Glad as he was to chat with his old buddies, he couldn't wait to get back to Janelle. "I thought you had left for a moment there. That would have broken my heart."

Wondering why every sweet thing he professed sounded like he sincerely meant it, Janelle smiled weakly. "I wouldn't want to break your heart." *Even if you could so easily break mine.*

"If that's true," he went on, handing her an icy drink, "then can I see you? After tonight?"

Knowing she couldn't trust him, and scouring for a reason to say no, which didn't make her seem possessive and insecure, Janelle mused on her response. Doing so, she accepted the frosty drink he'd carefully wrapped with several napkins, merely saying, "Thank you."

"You're welcome. But you didn't answer my question." Was he wrong in assuming she enjoyed his company too? Straightaway, he answered himself no. Something was happening between them. It was as real as the air they were breathing. Every time those exotically beautiful eyes gazed in his, it was all the confirmation he needed that she felt it too. "It's no trouble for me to fly back and forth to see you. Can I have your number so we can talk about it, and just talk period. Janelle, I think we can really enjoy each other. I mean *really* enjoy each other."

Janelle thought so too. Knew so. Sipping the fruity pineapple taste of her daiquiri, while he stood silently watching her, the heat in his eyes penetrated to that essence of her that was purely woman. Even so, picturing him with his gathering of admirers arrested its addictive effect. Not even their starting to dance again could shatter the image. "I really don't give out my number just like that," she replied, feeling it was a reasonable excuse. "Not to someone I meet for the first time in a club." But as she spoke, Janelle wished her actions could have been firm like her words. Her head was ordering her to run away from this man. Much the opposite, her body couldn't resist getting closer, swaying slower and slower with him to the song's provocative rhythm.

"I can understand what you're saying," he agreed, although he didn't want to. He couldn't bear never seeing her again. "I could be anybody. A real nut. A serial killer. But I assure you, I'm not."

Just then, Aaron was distracted by someone behind Janelle. Curious about what was capturing his attention, Janelle looked over her shoulder. Seeing Sherry, she ceased dancing and swerved around fully.

Grinning, Sherry was looking from Janelle to her dance partner. "I'm sorry to interrupt. But I wanted to let you know I'm going to be heading home. Chris is probably home by now."

Through all the magic of the night, Janelle hadn't realized how late it was. Sherry's husband was probably home by now. "Oh, I'm sorry to have you waiting, Sherry." Janelle then looked uncomfortably at Aaron. "This is Aaron. Aaron, this is my best friend Sherry."

A bright smile greeted Sherry as he shook her hand. "You have good taste in friends. It's nice to meet you, Sherry."

"Same here, Aaron." Sherry's tiny lips curled.

"We ah . . . better get going," Janelle suggested, then gazed at Aaron. "It was fun dancing." She retreated a step.

"It was more than fun." Desperate to see her again, he granted her a lingering look, all the while hoping she would change her mind about giving him her number. Though, he couldn't come on too strong, pushing to get it. That could turn her off. "You can call me whenever you like," he said, removing a business card from his pocket. After writing his home number on it, he handed it to her. "If . . . if you're looking for an investor for your business, or property for it, or if you need anything else call."

She accepted the blue, engraved card, trying not to lose herself in his stare again. Janelle knew Sherry was watching her so closely, she probably knew how many times she blinked. "If I need your help, I won't hesitate to call you. It really was nice meeting you, Aaron."

"It was more than nice meeting you. You're unforgettable."

Wondering again why everything he said to her sounded

like he really meant it, when he couldn't possibly have, Janelle treated herself to one last stare. Seconds after, she headed to the exit with Sherry.

Aaron Deverreau watched her disappear beyond the gold-trimmed glass doors, and continued watching that direction several minutes after. Realizing Janelle wouldn't miraculously reappear inside the club, he turned his head toward the dance floor. Slow gliding bodies crammed every space. Nonetheless, Aaron was scarcely aware of them. Everything was obscure except for what happened moments ago. "Man," he said to himself.

After running into his four friends again and spending time with them, Aaron started feeling lonesome a few hours later. He was lonesome even in the midst of all the joy of reminiscing about some of the best times of his life. The reason being, he knew none of those times compared to the moments not long ago with *her*.

The way she looked when he first laid eyes on her at the bar made him stare boldly, foolishly, lustfully as if he didn't possess the sophistication and self-control he prided himself as having. But Aaron couldn't help himself. Everything about her made him want her. *Bad.* What's more, when he was fortunate enough to have contact with her, the desire multiplied. The soft, but intelligent way she spoke made him want her. The way she smelled like coconut made him want her. The way she carried herself with a combination of sexiness and grace made him want her. The way she moved her body so erotically against him as they danced made him want her.

Even the way she made him feel when she looked up at him with those eyes made him want her too. To say she made him feel good was an understatement. The feeling was something Aaron couldn't do justice in describing. He could only experience it, savor it, and God knows he wanted to feel it some more.

Aaron was still pondering about her as he left the club, strode down the block to the garage, then drove his rental car out of it en route to his hotel. Driving down the brightly lit avenue he wished he could have taken her home. It was undeniable that he yearned to be as intimate as possible with Janelle. However, knowing that was unlikely, he would have also loved simply relaxing and conversing with her in a private atmosphere. He longed to know everything he could about her. Who was she? Who was she besides one of the most physically blessed creatures he had ever seen in his life? What did she like to do in her spare time besides visit clubs?

Waiting at a red light, his two fingers dallying with the hair along his chin, Aaron took a deep breath and decided he had to get her off his mind. At least momentarily. At least until he knew if she was going to get in touch with him or not. That way if she didn't, he wouldn't have worked up his emotions and wouldn't be so disappointed. Yet, as Aaron was about to drive off with the light changing to green, a heart-stopping sight made him question if he was seeing a mirage. Poised at the corner across the street, Janelle was alone and flagging for a taxi.

Some slick, swift maneuvers of Aaron's vehicle succeeded. Soon after, the silver Town Car came to a screeching standstill before her. Aaron leaned toward the passenger door and quickly rolled down the window.

"Aaron!" she declared, with all the surprise revealed in her face. She approached the car and inclined downward to better view him.

Aaron bent more toward her. "What are you doing out here? I thought you would have been home by now. I assumed you were driving back."

"We were. But I had car trouble."

"Tell me about it." He hurried out of the car and came around to her side, quickly opening the passenger door. "I'll take you home."

Fearing she'd fall under his spell again, Janelle looked

off pondering on what to do. Finally, she gazed in his eyes. Like when she first saw him at the bar, they again promised, *oh what I could do to you.* "I . . . I don't want you to go out of your way. Really, I can hop in a taxi. It's no problem."

Aaron's lips tipped at the corners in a grin, even if his expression somehow displayed hurt. "You're not making me go out of my way. And I know you made it clear you don't want to give out any personal information to strangers at clubs, but again, I swear to you, I won't hurt you. I just want to take you home safely. Look at me. What do your instincts truly tell you about me?"

They tell me you're driving me crazy, making me want you to feel you close again, her mind whispered. A moment after, her lips tilted up in a little smile. "All right. I live on Chestnut Street, right off the bridge."

As Aaron set the temperature levels in the car for her comfort and located a slow jamming radio station, Janelle watched his large hands as she explained, "Sherry and I parked our cars in different garages. So when my engine died—"

"Oh, no, not your engine?" Shaking his head, he removed his hands from the green illuminated dials and placed them on the steering wheel.

"Yes, my engine of all things." Janelle slid a strand of hair behind her ear. "Several blocks after I drove it out of the garage, Sherry was gone home and didn't know what happened to me. I called a service to pick it up and they came promptly. And when you saw me, I was trying to flag down a cab. They all had passengers. I appreciate your offering me a ride."

Aaron looked over at her, his gaze slipping slowly over her features. "It was no trouble, Janelle." He forced his attention back to the road, occasionally glancing out his side window. Multicolored lights from towering buildings set against the obsidian were strikingly in his view. Aaron didn't see any of the magnificence. All he could see was the woman beside him even when he wasn't looking at her. "Though I am sorry about your car, this will at least give us a chance to get more acquainted."

"Uh, yes, it will."

With the soulful, slow songs of various musical artists flowing as a background for their voices, they talked about their careers, with Aaron again expressing interest in investing in her business if he found the proposal exciting and profitable enough. Moreover, it would have been advantageous if Janelle was willing to relocate to Arizona, establishing her boutique in one of his commercial development properties. Elaborating more on their goals, it became obvious to both of them how important the other's dreams were.

Janelle was so impressed with Aaron's accomplishments. Equally, he valued how dedicated and determined Janelle was to make her dream come true. Her passion about the boutique was contagious, affecting him so, he was practically sold on financing the enterprise before seeing any plans on paper. What's more, the way Aaron saw it, because he had been so blessed with his dreams coming true, it was his responsibility to ensure others experienced the same.

Chatting further, Aaron asked what had been on his mind all along. "So what do you do when you're not working at your nine to five, or home designing outfits for your boutique? I know you can't work all the time." This was an easy way for him to find out if they enjoyed the same things, as well as if someone was in her life. "Do you go to the club often?" He lowered the radio volume.

"That was my first time at Quincy's."

"Well, you sure weren't acting like it. You were burning up the floor like it was yours. You *owned* that bad boy!"

Janelle laughed. "I like dancing."

And I like your smile, Aaron thought. Staring over at her full, glossy lips, he loved the way they curled so innocently and sensuously at the same time. "I can see you like dancing. And the fellows sure liked you.'' Aaron recalled how the men in the club were ogling at her. Hunger blazed from their eyes. Aaron guessed it was probably the same way he looked when he first saw her in the restaurant. ''Those guys were like wolves. Before you danced with me, I was checking out all of them. They were willing to do anything to get close to you.''

With her eyes aimed on the fleeting streets outside the window, but really seeing none of them, Janelle laughed again. ''They just like dancing too.'' She glimpsed Aaron's handsome profile, then peered back out beyond the windshield. ''They wanted to get into the music.''

''They wanted *you*. And I can't blame them.''

Something impassioned in his tone enticed Janelle's gaze from the hazy images beyond the glass and across at Aaron. If they had still been driving, he would have had an accident staring at her so long and hard. Fortunately, he had just parked in front of her building.

''This is the place,'' Janelle remarked, feeling so uncomfortable she switched her gaze toward her building.

''Don't go yet,'' he pleaded, tapping her arm.

Janelle twisted toward him, a chill running over her from the faintness of his touch. ''All right. I'd like to sit here a minute . . . with you.''

''I'd like that too. Because I want to know more about what you like to do and simply things about you.''

Their conversation resumed, luring them into sharing the activities they enjoyed and tidbits of information about themselves. Each was amazed how much they had in common and how much they thought alike. Janelle was also surprised to learn that Aaron was born wealthy. As one who grew up at the opposite end of his financial spectrum, she didn't want to depress him with harsh realities that she had survived with. Hence, Janelle merely shared part of her childhood. She shared the love she was showered with from her mother and siblings. The rest—the rest that she fought every day of her life to forget was never mentioned.

Becoming more and more engrossed in each other's exciting conversation, the time passed quickly. Although, within its hastily moving seconds, they did do more than talk. They felt something. It was something as potent as when they danced. It was a feeling that breathed with life, which neither could get enough of. Janelle could have talked to Aaron all night. Aaron could have done the same with her. Eventually, those prospects did come true. The red, yellow and marine blue of sunrise began stroking the sky's blue with a hint of light.

"And I like to travel too," Janelle mentioned, noticing for the first time that night was turning into day. Knowing she would have to leave Aaron, she gazed back at his face, absorbing all the lusciousness she would miss. "Though I haven't been to any exotic or foreign places. My dream is to go to the Caribbean. Bermuda is first on the list."

"Bermuda will take your breath away," he said, enthusiastically. "I've been there three times and on each visit, I discovered something I missed before. Bermuda is just like being with a person you love being with. The more you're around them, the more you *have to* be around them. You're addicted to them." Pausing, he brushed a wayward strand of hair off her cheek. "You have to go there one day, Janelle." *One of these days with me!* "I assure you, you won't be disappointed."

She smiled, while again feeling a tingle from his touch. "I can't wait to go. Your enthusiasm makes it sound irresistible."

"Will you be going with someone?" he then asked, and afterward hoped he hadn't crossed that border of intrusiveness.

"By someone, whom do you mean?"

Scraping a finger on his chin out of awkwardness, Aaron reared back further in his seat. "A man."

"I don't know." Shrugging her shoulders, Janelle was

secretly amused that he just didn't come out and ask if
someone was in her life. Nevertheless, she felt like playing
it cool. That is until she knew more about his intentions.
Every pleasurable second around him, Janelle was finding
it easier to forget those women that surrounded him in
Quincy's. Perhaps they were acquaintances he already
knew. After all, when they danced he had mentioned going
to college in Philadelphia.

Aaron lowered the radio volume again. They could
barely hear Uncle Sam crooning "I Don't Ever Want To
See You Again." "I ah . . . I don't have anyone in my life
that I want to take on a trip like that right now. I would
like to take someone special there though. That's not the
kind of place you just take anybody to. It's like magic, and
you have to take a person there who you feel magic with."
Pausing, he stared at her wide, sparkling eyes. "I haven't
been there since I've . . . since I've been divorced."

Her wide eyes widened with shock. He seemed like the
type to marry only when he was an elderly man, well after
his wild oats were sowed. "How long were you married?"

"Long enough to know I made a big mistake."

"Any children?"

"One."

"Breakups are really hard on children." She knew that.

"Having parents whose marriage is hell is hard on children too. But I don't want to talk about it." Although,
even at that moment, Aaron couldn't help envisioning the
unthinkable atrocity his ex-wife committed against him.
Forcing the nightmarish image away from his mind's eye,
it was easy to concentrate on the beautiful woman beside
him. "Right now, I want to move forward with my future."

"Have you been enjoying your single life?" Janelle asked.
It was a sly way of finding out what she wanted to know.
Was he sleeping around?

"It's been fair," Aaron responded. "I date. How else can
one move on with their life without meeting new people? I
have dinner or a movie sometimes with someone. But I

don't have a girlfriend. I haven't really met anyone I con-
nect with. That is . . . not until tonight."

The lingering look in his eyes, which hung through a
sudden silence, combined with those last words made
Janelle feel ecstatic. If only he meant it, she wished. If only
his definition of a date meant the same as hers. Sure, she
would go out with a guy, talk, eat and attend an entertaining event with him. That being as it may, afterward, she
would return home, occasionally granting him a peck on
the cheek as they parted.

Of course, in the past she was in committed relationships
where there had been more. Nonetheless, a date was
merely a date to her. Could his dates have been so innocent? Had she really made an unforgettable impression
on him? Or was he playing with her head, playing a game
he had mastered so many times before? Was the chemistry
she felt between them really there? Or was she imagining
it because he turned her on so? To make sense of it all,
examining the situation sensibly and unclouded by her
overwhelming attraction to him, Janelle knew she had to
get away from Aaron. *Fast.* Otherwise, she may have never
left him. She may have wound up letting him . . .

Across from her, Aaron took his time perusing the soft
features of the woman he hoped he would see again and
again. He had noted her hand on the door lever, and her
repeated glimpses out the window. It was as if the dawn
was her signal to leave him. Aaron missed her already. He
knew the instant she left him, the air around him wouldn't
even feel the same. All the life she made him feel the
entire night would vanish. Worse, he had no control over
ever feeling it again. It was all in her hands.

"I have to go, Aaron," she announced, still wondering
about his definition of a date. "I didn't even realize it was
morning."

"That's because we had so much to talk about."

"True," she agreed.

"It's so rare to meet someone you can simply talk to for

hours and hours. In a sense you feel like you've known them forever. In another sense, it's so exciting getting to know them because you know you have so much to learn about them. So much that you instinctively know will bond you with them even more."

Janelle nodded, while struggling to avoid his eyes. Looking at the door lever, she soon gripped it. "It was so nice ... tonight was. All of it. The dancing. The ride. The stimulating conversation."

"So will you call me?" He hoped he didn't sound like he was begging, even if he was.

Debating her answer, Janelle found the lever safer than his eyes. She couldn't think straight when she looked in them. She couldn't remember that she avoided men like him her entire life. But abruptly Aaron lifted her chin, guiding her sensual features toward him. Janelle had no choice but to gaze in his eyes as deeply as he looked in hers.

"I'll call you," she promised, her voice uncontrollably dropping to a whisper. "I will."

As she began to open the door, Aaron ached to kiss her good-bye. He grew warm desiring to discover what her lips, tongue and mouth tasted like. He longed to feel her body close to his like when they danced. Nonetheless, knowing he had to contain his impulses with her, he merely reached for her hand. Caressing it, he held her with his stare. "I'll be waiting for that call."

Janelle merely smiled. She couldn't even express how much she wanted to talk to him again.

Not wanting Aaron to know she thought about him when she went inside her apartment, when she laid down in bed, when she got up the next day, when she worked, when she left work and when she did anything and everything, Janelle waited four days before removing his card from her purse and dialing Aaron's home number. In calculating the three hour time zone differences between Pennsylvania and Arizona, he should have been home.

Wild drumming beat inside her chest as the number rang several times.

Finally, a young, pert woman's voice answered on the other end, "Hello?"

Speechlessness overcame Janelle. It had to be the wrong number, she assumed. It was 10:00 P.M. on a Thursday night in Phoenix. Aaron should have been answering his own phone. Janelle examined the card, only distracted from it by the ultrafeminine voice uttering again, "Hello?"

Janelle decided she must have dialed it wrong. "I'm sorry. I have the wrong number," she replied. After hanging up, she carefully dialed the home number on the card again.

"Hello?" the young lady said once more.

Yet, this time Janelle couldn't respond. The haziness that disappointment had swept her into solely allowed her to place the receiver back in its cradle.

Late on a Thursday night, her mind echoed as she gazed at Aaron's name on the business card. Purposely, Janelle had waited late to call him because she wanted to ensure that he was home. During their magical encounter, he informed her he sometimes went to the gym after work. However, he claimed that by 10:00 P.M. he was usually settled in. Janelle just didn't count on female company settling in with him. Did the soft voice belong to one of his dates? But why would a mere, harmless date answer someone's phone?

The answer curled Janelle in a knot on her bed. Conclusions about him circled her mind, only relieving Janelle when her own phone rang.

"Hello?" she answered.

"Janelle?"

"Yes." Not recognizing the masculine voice immediately, she uncurled her limbs and sat up straight. She could better tune into the caller that way. "Who is this?"

"Mitch. I hope you don't mind me calling so late. But I remembered you said, you went to bed late, even on weekdays, like I do."

"Mitch?" she repeated, then after a second realized who he was. Because of the charms of Aaron Deverreau, she'd almost forgotten meeting someone decent, who didn't care about being the playboy of the decade.

Miles away, Aaron Deverreau hadn't forgotten. He hadn't forgotten the woman who made him feel so alive, he couldn't get her out of his mind. When he woke in the morning, when he worked, when he came home, when he did whatever he had to do during the twenty four hours of the day, Janelle was always there in his thoughts. Their chemistry was so right. So good he couldn't understand why she hadn't called. Was it because she had a man? After all, Aaron didn't really come out and ask her that question, not specifically.

Every time someone called him at work or home, his chest raised with the hope that it was her. Hearing the phone seconds ago, tonight he felt no different.

"Who was that?" he asked his little sister. Aaron had come out of the shower and entered the guest bedroom where Lenora lounged on the bed. With her thick, black braids spilling over the shoulders of her floral, silk pajamas, she was painting her toenails in fuschia. She needed some pampering after what she'd been through.

Lenora was spending time with her favorite brother the last few days. Aaron always knew how to make her feel better after she broke up with a boyfriend she was madly in love with. So many times she had come to him with this problem. Lenora fell in love every few months.

"It was just some chick with the wrong number," she answered.

CHAPTER THREE

Nine months later

Entering Mitch's penthouse, Janelle tossed her purse on the couch, kicked out of her pumps, slid off her jacket and let her coffee-hosed feet ferry her quickly to the bathroom. Turning the Jacuzzi's knobs until she felt warm water, she then poured in bubble bath, before the rest of her clothing tumbled onto the lush carpet. Janelle couldn't wait to dip herself in the scented bubbles, inhaling coconut. Soothing her body within the bubbles would help her calm down from the change that dawned with the day.

It was almost unbelievable that she handed her boss a resignation letter, stating she was about to be a business owner. Deeply she was indebted to Mitch for making that possible. He believed in her enough to become her business partner. He made her feel secure in the personal relationship they had as well. There wasn't any passionate romance existing between them, which Sherry felt Janelle deserved. Rather than that, Janelle believed they shared more meaningful things.

Like Janelle had always yearned for, Mitch was dependable, mature, faithful and one who believed in her, despite the downside of his character that could often be selfish, conceited and cold. Negative traits were in everyone she often explained to Sherry. In fact, this was her reasoning to herself when it seemed Mitch was becoming unbearable to live with anymore. The truth of that belief pointed no further than herself. How could she ever forget what happened not so long ago?

At moments like this, when she was alone, she was always reminded of what she'd hidden for the last six months. But what she couldn't understand was why did it make her feel so bad, as if she'd done the scandalous thing? *She* was the one who was betrayed. She had nothing to feel ashamed about.

Lifting her smooth legs into the mint-colored tub, then melting her naked skin into the white foam, Janelle tried to will her mind away from her secret. She forced her mental workings toward exciting thoughts like Mitch accompanying her tomorrow to look for space for the boutique. Though exhilarating as it was to get her business off the ground, there was something more pleasurable always lingering in thoughts. It was the image of Aaron, a near stranger she'd met months ago.

Ashamed as it made her, even being in a relationship hadn't stopped her from thinking about him. The memory of that woman answering the phone hadn't stopped it either. Long ago Janelle realized that woman could have been anyone, a relative, an employee, a housekeeper. Unfortunately, by the time the realization came, it was too late. Janelle was already involved with Mitch.

She always carried Aaron's business card in her purse and looked at it often. That night he had turned her on so with his body and his mind, that even at this moment, she desperately craved more of whatever his presence drugged her with. Dancing with him was a scene plucked straight from her fantasies. She enjoyed the way he moved, the way he looked down at her, the way he held her, the way his voice sounded, the way his words made her feel like an incredibly desirable woman. Mingled with it all, there was a warmth and down to earthness about Aaron that Mitch never could possess.

When he drove her home, it was magical too. In getting acquainted, Janelle discovered he was as big a dreamer as she was. Sure, his wealth had likely provided him some assistance. In any case, she knew it couldn't grant him the spirit she felt from him. It couldn't stir up the passion for his work. It could inspire the hunger to achieve even more dreams. All those characteristics had touched her. Yes, they dreamed alike, and as the night went by too swiftly, it revealed they thought alike too. And combined with the way he was looking at her, and how he felt against her body when they danced, and how he made her feel inside, it all made it seem like he'd been heaven sent to her.

Janelle was certain he needed no lessons on how to make a woman breathe hard. Closing her eyes, she envisioned how he would do this. He would start by whispering across her ears sexy words, as he traced her body with his pinkie, working her senses into a frenzy, until before she knew anything, she had surrendered herself, leaving all her love in his capable hands. For seemingly endless hours, he could make such sweet love to her, that she would believe there was another heaven, which wasn't in the sky—but in his arms.

Opening her eyes, however, the water began to grow cold as the reality forming in Janelle's mind. After all the loving, the tenderness, the honeyed words, then he would leave her, leave her with tears that forever glazed her eyes—glazed them like Janelle's mother's eyes. Everyone always thought Maya Sims' eyes just looked that way—mournful. Janelle knew better. She knew about tears that came from such pain, they wouldn't allow her mother the relief of flowing from her eyes. They merely sat there, held behind her lids, sitting and sitting even through laughter.

Except they couldn't hide from a daughter. They couldn't lie to her that she didn't care that her handsome husband left her for one of those women who were always after him—the ones who he stayed with three and four days at a time. Finally, one day he announced to her mother that he was leaving for good. With his packed bags standing by the front door, he also planted a little kiss on Janelle's forehead. Kneeling down to gaze in her frightened eyes, he promised he would always be there for his pretty baby girl.

She never saw him again—not alive. He never sent her a birthday card, or a Christmas present, and he didn't call. He never sent her mother money that she so direly needed for the five children, which he helped conceive. What's more, he never gave her mother back the love, which Janelle was sure Maya would have returned if he had just shown up again on her doorstep.

When he died, Janelle entered the funeral prepared to call him "Jerk" aloud in the church. Trivial as it was, it was her way of paying him back, for her mother's pain, her pain and the poverty that robbed her childhood, replacing it with grown up struggles. Except the word didn't come. Instead, she cried and didn't understand why.

It was Janelle's vow to never fall prey to men like him. Not to the pretty ones, with pretty words, who could make the prettiest love because they had mastered the art with too much experience. Women were always throwing the gift of themselves at them, and like her daddy, they weren't turning down any presents. Her mother had never known true passionate love. She had never experienced the joy a wonderful woman deserved. Those realities were all the justification Janelle needed to try to forget Aaron, and cherish Mitch. Unless a miracle happened, Mitch would never fill her with passion. On the other hand, he wouldn't fill her with pain either.

"Hi, there."

Startled by the unexpected voice, Janelle flinched at the sight of Mitch in the doorway.

Thick bubbles still clinging to her skin, she sat up straighter. "Hello. You surprised me."

His polished, wing tip shoes squashed into the carpet as he walked toward the Jacuzzi, settling his slender frame on the side of it. "Hope you were thinking about me?"

"Maybe a little." She studied his beige face, lagging at his wide mouth. For once, in their time of living together, she wished he would have greeted her with a kiss. "How was your day?"

"Fantastic!" His small, fleshy eyes brightened. "I met with a college buddy. We had a good time. But there was something big that happened before that."

Janelle raised up a bit. "Tell me? What happened?"

"I was told I could make partner. It's between Renauld Pierson and myself."

"That's great!" she said with a laugh. "Work harder, and you'll have it."

Mitch began loosening his tie. "It's not a matter of working harder. I'm a lot smarter than he is, and I have to let the higher-ups know that. Smart people don't have to work harder. They work smarter. I didn't get to the position of top senior manager at the top management consulting firm in the country by working my buns off. And I didn't get a multimillion dollar stock portfolio that way either. I'm a genius. That's why I'm where I am." He tossed his tie aside, then began unbuttoning his shirt.

Her head slightly tilted, Janelle observed his cockiness a moment. "Yes, intelligence does get you a long way. But who said working hard isn't smart? To be successful you have to think, then execute with action. And that includes attending to all the details, putting in all the sweat you might call working your buns off. I'm going to always work hard when I start my business and when I'm at the top of it. The same thing it took you to get there is the same thing you're going to need to stay there—and that's the best talent you have to offer. Plus, if you're working at something you love, it's fun. It doesn't even seem like work." Pausing, she smiled at him. "I know you put in some elbow grease somewhere along the way. You're lying if you say you didn't."

Mitch didn't find anything funny. "No, I didn't. I'm just the smartest man alive."

"If you say so."

"I know so." His gaze lowered from her face to the bubbles dissolving from her body.

Janelle caught the lust blazing in his eyes. Despite it, before any intimacy, she wanted him to ask about her day. Since he didn't, she announced, "I did it. I told Mozelle I'm opening my own business, and I would only be working at his company a week longer."

"Good for you." Mitch's wandering eyes grew more ravenous, until his middle finger swiped bubbles off her breast, exposing a nipple. "You look so good."

Janelle ignored his obvious desire. "You should have seen Mozelle's face when I told him."

"Forget, Mozelle. Let me help you get out of that tub."

"I don't feel like getting out." She wrapped a damp hair behind her ear. "Get in and I'll finish telling you how my day played out."

"I don't want to hear about your day right now. I want some loving." He stood, extending his hand to her.

Looking up at him, Janelle didn't budge a finger. "Join me in here," she invited him.

"You know Jacuzzis aren't what I like. I like the bed."

"Be wild and crazy sometimes."

Mitch laughed. "I'll show you wild and crazy." He started unbuckling his belt. "I'll show you all right."

You never showed me before, Janelle wanted to say. Instead, she took a deep breath. "No, really, Mitch. Let me tell you about what happened. I feel like telling you in here. It'll be fun."

"You told me. What else is there to tell? You resigned. End of story."

She disliked how he spoke to her. He was treating her triumph like it was so insignificant. "Are we still going tomorrow to find a location and register the boutique?"

"Yes, we're going to meet with the attorney, who'll handle registering it."

Janelle looked alarmed. "What about the location?"

"I already found one."

A tinge of anger colored her features. "Why did you go find a location *for me* without bringing me along?"

"Because I know about business. I'm the expert. I thought you would be happy." Aggravated, he rubbed across his eyes, before gazing sternly back at her. "If I had known you would have reacted like this, I wouldn't have tried to surprise you!"

The word *surprise* made her feel guilty. "Where . . . Where is it?"

"In Rottingham Square."

"How does it look?"

"Like a store, of course. It was a three room antique shop before. And just like you wanted, there will be one room for the three seamstresses, one for customer alterations and the front display area of course. And the rooms will have major renovations done to your specifications."

"I didn't mean to sound ungrateful," she apologized, feeling bittersweet about what he'd done. "I just had this vision for my boutique and I thought you wouldn't understand it."

"I know everything, Janelle. Everything there is to know, I know it! Believe me, you're going to love it. And it's going to be very upscale. Is the amount we agreed on for the start-up capital enough?"

"Yes, it is. I appreciate it so much Mitch."

"Now, no more talk about the boutique. Come to bed with me."

* * *

Fragrant coconut candles shaded the two-tiered bedroom as Janelle eased on top of the mauve satin sheets. Slinking beneath them, she disenchantedly watched Mitch disrobing and hoped this time their lovemaking would be different. She longed to be looked at like she was everything in the world to him. She ached to be kissed like he could never get enough of the sweet nectar from her lips. She desired her flesh to be caressed and titillated with slow gentleness, but at other times with the fire a woman often hungered for. Amid all this, she needed to hear him passionately declare he loved her.

The impassioned profession of love didn't come. Neither was there a kiss, or a tender caress. Much the contrary, swiftly Mitch's frowning face buried itself in the curve of her lengthy neck. Doing this, he clumsily rotated his hips against hers, entered her body, moved stiffly, speedily, then after a spasmatic motion, exhaustedly flung himself aside.

Hardly able to catch his breath, he managed, "That was so good. Whooh." Shaking his head, he faced the ceiling. "You're too much. Just too much."

Janelle turned her back to him. Like always, he made her feel like she wasn't there. Selfishly, he had been so consumed with his own pleasure, in spite of her repeatedly making him aware of his lack of warmth as a lover. She felt used, degraded, cheated, and like she was gas that filled up an empty car before it drove off to its destination.

"I know nobody can make you feel like I do," Mitch boasted, amused with himself. "No man alive."

Oh, shut up, Janelle screamed in her head.

Soon after, she heard him breathing. Glad he was sleeping, she turned around to watch him. With his modest features and physique, he was a decent-looking man. More significant than that, he was kind to her—much of the time at least. Better than her other boyfriends. There were various conflicts with those characters, ranging from one who was possessive, another who was a mama's boy, and another who had an aversion for employment. Compared to them, there was nothing maddening enough about Mitch to abandon their relationship.

Sure, she wasn't enthusiastic about his unromantic nature, or his ego. Contrasted against what she was accustomed to, however, Mitch was a dream. So why didn't he feel like one at a moment like this—when he was right next to her, but she felt so alone?

During a quiet time like this, when Mitch slept contentedly, Janelle often laid awake wondering—wondering a range of things. Wondering if there was more. Wondering about the scandalous secret that became part of her since she became part of Mitch's life—the secret he could never know about. But most of all, she wondered about the man she couldn't forget—Aaron. Aaron Deverreau according to his business card. If he danced so sexily with her that night, how would he make love? What was he doing at this very moment? Was he somewhere thinking about her too? Or was he laying somewhere thoroughly satisfied after loving his latest conquest senselessly? Why wouldn't he get out of her mind?

"Hi, there," Mitch mumbled, waking up.

"That was a short nap."

He took several breaths, then stretched. "I couldn't help dozing off. You do that to me. You knocked me out." He propped himself up against a pillow in a sitting position. "I had a dream. I can't forget it."

"What about?"

"Us. Going down the aisle, standing before the priest."

"That's an interesting dream."

"It could be reality."

Janelle just looked at him. Was he really implying what she thought? That would mean . . . *forever*. Forever feeling like she did with him. Forever not feeling anything else other than what they had. "Are you talking about us getting . . ."

"Exactly! I can't think of anything more perfect. We enjoy living together. We get along well. We're going into business together with the boutique. And it would look good for my making partner if I had a wife."

"Now the truth comes out!" Seething, Janelle snatched the covers high on her body and flung her back to him. "How wonderful! You want to marry me for a career move."

"No!" He clutched her arm, tugging her back around. "It's not that. I was just giving you little reasons for considering all beneath the bigger reason."

"What reason is that?"

Sincerity colored his features. "You know how much I care about you. Haven't I shown you? Haven't I? Look at what I'm about to do for you. Would your father have done such a generous thing for your mother?"

Janelle regretted sharing her past with him. He always used it against her in an argument. "No . . . I . . ."

"Because that's what a man does when a woman means everything to him. He gives her the world. No cost is too high."

It seemed like she was given the world months ago, dancing and just being with . . . and it hadn't cost a thing. Those feelings he filled her with seemed like the world. Those incredible feelings. She could have been near him forever and been so happy.

"So what's the answer? Will you marry me?"

CHAPTER FOUR

"Aren't you wondering what you'll be missing?" Sherry asked Janelle as they took a Saturday stroll through the mall, shopping for items for the engagement party Mitch was throwing.

Knowing how much she thought of Aaron Deverreau, Janelle shrugged her shoulders. "It's a woman's nature to wonder."

"For instance, that guy you met at the club last year," Sherry went on. "The one you danced and rode home with. In Quincy's, I was watching you two a while before I came over. No way in the world you can tell me he didn't get to you."

"He probably *gets to* everybody."

"How do you know?"

"Because I do." Slowing up, then stopping at a bookstore, browsing the romance titles through the glass, Janelle assured, "Mitch is not going to mistreat me."

Sherry joined her in admiring the display. "He's not going to give you what you need either. You two are not compatible, personality wise, and you know how else." Emphasizing her point, Sherry raised a brow.

"I wish I wouldn't have told you that."

Sherry laughed. "Too bad. You did. Now let's hear it. Has he gotten any better?"

"Yes," Janelle lied.

"No," Sherry countered playfully. "You're saying that, but there's nothing in your face that shows you mean it. I want you to have a man that makes you wake up in the morning humming, or a man that makes you smile because you can't stop thinking about how good he treats you, and how good he makes you feel in the bed, and out of it."

"Mitch treats me well," Janelle protested. "That's what's important. I've been searching so long for a man like him. He gives me everything I want. And as far as happy . . . I'm—I'm happy."

Then why did she have to constantly repeat how happy she was, Sherry questioned. It was a constant phrase with her, like she was brainwashing herself. For that matter, Sherry wanted to know if Mitch was so fantastic, why couldn't Janelle share with him what had been mentally tormenting her for the last six months?

After purchasing some books, they were strolling throughout the mall again when Sherry asked, "So for the rest of your life—*the rest of your life*—you're never going to experience the magic of falling in love?"

Janelle stiffened. She didn't know what was worse, the somberness in Sherry's voice, or the tense way her words made Janelle feel. "You're too dramatic sometimes."

"You might as well say you're not," Sherry insisted, and eased over to a shoe store. After a glance in the window, she continued walking beside Janelle. "If you marry him, it's not going to be because you're in love. So is it because he can provide materially? Janelle, you don't seem like the type to marry for money. If you do, you'll be paying forever, just like they say."

"I never said I didn't love Mitch."

"You're not *in love* with him."

"I'm not marrying for money. I just don't want to wind up . . ." She searched for the right words.

"Like your mother."

Silently, they continued walking.

"I bet Roxanne is not going to like Mitch and I getting married." Janelle broke the quiet.

Puzzled, Sherry frowned at her. "His sister-in-law? Why do you say that?"

They entered a department store.

"Because lately I've been getting these vibes that Mitch's dutiful, grieving sister-in-law has designs on him."

"Really?" Sherry's eyes widened.

"That's right. And I've always sensed she never liked me."

"Did she ever do anything to you?"

"Nothing obvious." Janelle picked up some perfume, sprayed her wrist, then sniffed the violet-like fragrance. "Just sometimes I'll catch her giving me an evil stare and other times, there's these other little signs." She put the perfume back and eased around the counter. "I go out of my way to be friendly to her, but it's not reciprocated. Basically, I just sense she doesn't like me."

"Do you think she knows?" Sherry's eyes locked with Janelle's. The secret they shared was the unspoken message between them.

Janelle was held to the gaze a moment, then looked off silently. Her expression became so sad Sherry wished she hadn't asked the question.

"I don't think she knows," Janelle answered finally. "But I know."

Roxanne Broussard patted her short, sandy colored hair and aimed her large, hazel eyes at the closed door ahead. A gold-trimmed nameplate on it read: Mitchell Broussard, Senior Manager. Ecstatic to have recently become her brother-in-law's secretary, she was further thrilled to merely to spend time with him. Successful, rich and generous, he was the type of man that impressed her. She wished his brother, Lawson, had possessed those qualities.

Although, when she met her now deceased husband, she believed differently. He wined her, dined her and took her on a monthlong trip to Paris, all the while presenting the facade of a prosperous businessman. Months after marrying him, the truth fell hard. Lawson's struggling antique car dealership was on an upsurge during their courtship. When the business plummeted during their newlywed days, and Roxanne couldn't afford the extravagance her husband had lavished on her, he was far less appealing. All in all, Lawson was a loser from Roxanne's perspective, and not at all a real man like his identical twin.

"Guess what magnificent news I have?" Mitch asked, as Roxanne strode through the door.

His wide, bright smile drew out hers. "From the way you look it must be something big."

"Bigger than big."

"I can't imagine." Her hazel eyes sparkling with excitement, she eased down in the chair before his desk. "Don't keep me in suspense."

"I'm getting married."

Wind somehow swished around her head. "Married?" Her hand started trembling.

"Can you believe that?" Mitch was so tickled his skin reddened. "Janelle and I are finally doing it."

Roxanne was smiling, but Mitch was too happy to notice how sick her expression really looked.

"Wow, this is sudden," she remarked with a weak laugh.

"After seven months of living together, I don't think so." He looked down, fumbling through his jacket pocket. Not finding what he sought there, he searched the top of his desk for the elusive article.

"Congratulations."

"Thanks," he replied, not looking up. He was too preoccupied in opening a drawer, continuing to ferret out something he desperately needed. "Where is it?"

"Where's what?" Roxanne forced herself from the dismal fog this news swept her into. He had to be joking. He couldn't get married, before she . . . "What are you looking for?"

"My checkbook. I had it here somewhere." He was tossing everything out of the drawer. "I need to write out a check for . . ."

For me? she asked herself. "For a bill?" she asked aloud.

"Actually, it's for Janelle. I probably forgot to mention it to you, but she's opening a dress boutique. I need to write a deposit check for the space and some renovations we're planning."

Roxanne's head began to throb. "She's opening a boutique? That sounds like an expensive venture."

"It is. But she's determined to do it. So what can I say? Besides, a fringe benefit is we'll make a lot of money from it. She's pretty good. Well, I don't have to tell you. You've seen the outfits she's designed. She's always wearing them."

That cheap crap. "Yes, I have seen them."

Roxanne was so upset, she didn't feel like going to work when she woke up the next day. Calling in sick, it wasn't heartening either to hear Mitch prattling about an engagement party on Saturday night. Throwing things and curses followed hanging up the phone. With her rage, she imagined removing Janelle from this earth in the most violent ways.

After pouring herself a cup of black coffee, she stretched her long, slim legs out on her beloved chaise, then took a few sips. Calmer now, she took a coherent inventory of why Mitch marrying Janelle bothered her so much. One reason was that her opulent future depended on getting Mitch's millions by getting Mitch. The other reason was that she simply disliked Janelle. Roxanne was nauseated by the way she flaunted her looks as if she was a goddess. Roxanne felt she was better looking and far more exciting too. She couldn't see what Mitch, or Lawson, for that matter, saw in her.

Yes, Lawson had seen something too. Roxanne wasn't blind to the gleam in her husband's eyes. Neither could she deny the gentleness in his tone and manner whenever Janelle was around. Added to these, the two were always laughing and having lengthy conversations. Was their friendship getting out of hand? Roxanne thought so, even if she never argued with Lawson about it. She simply allowed him his delight. As Lawson and Janelle dug themselves a hole, Roxanne wanted Mitch to see what she saw. To her frustration, Mitch was too busy merely seeing Janelle.

That being as it may, after Lawson's death, Roxanne counted on Mitch being her ticket to a life of luxury. As long as Mitch wasn't married to Janelle, nothing of significance was shared with her in Roxanne's view, namely his bank statements. Being rich was her dream since growing up middle class—middle class, while moving in wealthy circles, where she felt teased by that lifestyle. Now the dream was gone.

By midweek, however, when Roxanne still felt too sick to go to work, she was in for a big surprise. Answering her ringing bell, she faced a postman with a certified package. After closing the door and seeing that the manila envelope was from a bank, Roxanne recalled them phoning her to pick up Lawson's effects from a safety deposit box. Since he was virtually bankrupt when he died, Roxanne was uninterested in claiming his possessions. She believed he owned nothing of value. Now curiosity nudged her fingertips to open the envelope. A tinkling sound coming from the package made her more curious.

A rip of the paper and Roxanne soon beheld a rare-looking diamond ring. Breathtakingly, a huge stone was beset by slightly smaller jewels. After several moments of screeching her delight, Roxanne paid attention to a letter enclosed with it. Joy swiftly drained from her upon discovering it was addressed to Janelle. Far worse, in scanning a bit further, she learned the ring was Lawson's grandmother's and was intended to be a token of love—for Janelle. Roxanne was strangling-*mad*.

When she read the rest, astonishment and outrage masked her features. That is until the significance of the letter overshadowed the betrayal. The piece of paper was such a gift Roxanne started laughing. Hysterical, shoulder shaking sounds bombarded the air, and when she stopped, a scheme formed in her mind. Straightaway, she picked up a pen and pad, and sitting at a desk, began copying the letter her husband wrote, copying his handwriting as well. Only her version, complete with anguishing embellishments, would be the one for Mitch's eyes. Humming her satisfaction with her completed workmanship, Roxanne laid her pen aside to dial Mitch. As soon as possible, he had to see the letter.

Finding out he was out of town until Saturday, the day of the engagement party, didn't make her happy. Even so, each time Roxanne reminded herself of the power she now possessed, a smile curved her dollish lips. The expression returned again and again, especially when she finally reached Mitch an hour before the party, convincing him something was so urgent he had to come over—immediately.

"So what's the emergency?" Mitch asked testily, stepping in the door. "My guests are going to be arriving soon. My boss, my colleagues, some family and friends. I hoped you would be well enough to come too. What is it that couldn't wait?"

Guests were already cramming the spacious penthouse when Mitch returned home. Shrimp appetizers were being served. The band was playing the ninth song in the compilation of music Mitch requested, an instrumental of "The

Closer I Get to You." Looking pleased about the turnout, Mitch circulated around the suite with the unflagging energy of a young child. In fact, Janelle thought it was peculiar the way he behaved: constantly moving, talking loud, making wild hand gestures, laughing when nothing was funny and dancing rather friskily when he never danced at all. Strangely, throughout all this socializing, he didn't call her over to introduce her to any of his friends she had never met. Sadder, each time she came near him, he seemed to deliberately move away. Or was she imagining it?

"What has Mitch been smoking?" Sherry asked at one point. Standing next to Janelle, she was observing him dancing like his feet were naked on hot coals. "Something has really wound him up."

Hoping he would give her the slightest look, Janelle's eyes narrowed on her fiancé, while she commented, "I don't know what's going on with him, but he sure is making me feel invisible."

When Mitch's boss gathered everyone to toast the couple, touching words were expressed for a devoted employee and his bride to be. On the heels of his speech, he then suggested that Mitch say something mushy to his lovely fiancée. At that invitation, finally Mitch stared at Janelle. Everyone surrounding them smiled.

"Janelle, oh, my Janelle." Pausing, he stared at her even more intensely. "Janelle, I . . . I—I can't pretend like this anymore! Janelle, I wouldn't marry you for nothing in this world. You're not good enough for me! I must have been out of my mind to ask you to be my wife. But now I'm clear as day. I'd rather burn forever than have to live with the sight of you every day of my life!"

There was suddenly a monster in Janelle's presence. One so terrifying, he made her heart beat so fast and strong it shook her entire body, beating amid a silence so potent, she swore the whole world was holding its breath. Janelle attempted to tell herself Mitch hadn't tortured her that way. Such degrading words weren't spoken to her in front of a gathering of people they knew, and if Mitch had said, he was joking. Except the stunned expressions circling them attested there was nothing funny. The coldness in Mitch's eyes guaranteed it further. The look also imparted that she was in the midst of a nightmare.

"Excuse me and Miss Sims," pierced the hush and astonishment of everyone. Mitch grabbed Janelle's arm, ushering her into the kitchen.

She jerked from his grip as the dining room door swung shut. "What in the world is going on with you?" she shouted. "How dare you humiliate me like that!"

A vein in his temple bulged as he leered in her face. "It's not me who had something going on!"

God, please don't let him know, she cried inside. *He can't know. He can't. I was tricked. Tricked so cruelly!* "I don't know what you're talking about."

"Liar! *Did you sleep with my brother?*"

Nausea knotted in her stomach. "Who—who told you that?"

"Lawson did today! I wouldn't have believed him, except I couldn't get out of my head how close you two were, always huddled together in deep conversation. Now I know what all that talk was about—sex. Yes, he told me all of it."

"You're talking crazy!"

"I read a letter my dear departed brother wrote to you. It was in his safe deposit box. Never got around to mailing it I guess. It was accompanied by my grandmother's ring. He was going to give it to you. I guess for services rendered."

"Don't talk to me like that!"

"How should I talk to a slut?"

"I'm not a slut!"

"What else is a woman who sleeps with her boyfriend's brother?"

"I have to explain it to you. It's not what it seems like. It's *not at all* what it seems like."

"It's pretty clear to me! Did you sleep with Lawson or not?"

"It's not that simple. I—"

"Did you sleep with Lawson, *my brother*? That's all I need to know."

"Yes, but—"

Mitch stormed out of the kitchen. Pursuing him, winding throughout their still shocked guests, Janelle found herself outside of the suite and in the corridor. Catching up to him, she grasped his wrist, forcing him to turn around and look at her.

"Mitch, I thought he was you that night. Lawson tricked me. My God, you two were identical twins. I wanted to tell you. But you—"

"Did he trick you all the other nights too?" His small, fleshy eyes burned across her face.

"What?" As if it would help her understand what he was talking about, she reared back with a frown. "What other nights?" *What is he talking about?*

So enraged he was, Mitch almost threw his hand back to strike her full force. Instead, he pushed her away, hurrying to the elevator. Soon alone in the hallway, Janelle stood motionless in a haze of disbelief, only waking when Sherry came toward her with her arms outstretched.

It took hours before Janelle convinced Sherry that she would be all right if left alone. At last, nestled beneath the blue velvet covers of her bed, absorbed in the soundlessness of the empty penthouse, Janelle could hear her thoughts. Initially, they were all about Mitch. Where was he? It had been hours since he left. What was he doing? As well, she needed to know why this letter gave him the impression that there was an ongoing affair between her and Lawson.

Would he forgive her if he knew the whole story? It wasn't how it seemed. Lawson wasn't what he seemed.

Facing a coconut scented candle on the dresser, Janelle gazed into its soothing light, and let her mind drift back to when she befriended Mitch's brother. Compassion was what she felt toward him because he was a warm hearted person, who no one believed in. It was his dream to expand his antique car dealership to phenomenal success. Many cautioned him it wouldn't work, primarily Mitch. In love with the security of the corporate structure, he presumed Lawson's career path was not a solid one. Faithfully, Mitch discouraged Lawson, often embarrassing him by comparing the fortune he amassed to the near paucity Lawson approached several times.

Janelle treated Lawson differently. As one with dreams of having a business herself, she understood that often those who became great endured struggle before achieving their hearts' desire. She encouraged Lawson to never, ever give up on his dream. In the same way, he encouraged her. For hours, they could discuss their aspirations, losing themselves in a secret world understood solely by the other.

Mitch was the first to detect that Lawson had more than friendly feelings for his girlfriend. Privately, he argued with Lawson about it. Vehemently, the accusation was denied. As well, he warned Janelle about keeping her distance from his twin, claiming one day Lawson might mistake her kindness for more. She dismissed it with her sincere belief that Lawson regarded her like a sister. Sisterly is certainly how she felt toward him.

Then came the night. Janelle believed it was Mitch arriving early from the office one Friday evening. He had been putting in extra hours for several weeks and seeing him at such an hour meant they could spend some quality time together. She also believed it was Mitch, who kissed away her clothes on the living room floor and made the sweetest love she had ever known with him.

Only after their intimacy, when he continued to kiss her

so passionately did she start to feel something was awry. Mitch never kissed, never caressed, never told her how much he loved her, unlike the man whose arms she filled. He couldn't stop telling her how much he loved her. He couldn't stop stroking her so tenderly. Soon after, her funny feeling grew to madness as the truth thrust to the core of her consciousness, and all she could do at first was cover her mouth, holding in the sickness.

"I knew it would be like this," Lawson professed. "I always knew you would feel like that, and we would make each other feel the way we just did. I love you, Janelle. I had to show you how much."

Her screams exploded through the air. They were curses of how much she hated Lawson for deceiving her and how much she wished he was dead. After throwing him out, she nervously waited for Mitch to come home. During those seemingly endless hours, she struggled with how she would explain what happened. She also grappled with how she would interpret the lurid circumstances to the police. Guilt gnawed at her. Would anyone believe her? Lawson could have alleged it was consensual sex, and there would be no evidence of bodily injury or struggle to confirm otherwise. Atop all this, Mitch forewarned her about Lawson's intentions.

What would stop him from saying she deserved what happened, or even worse, wanted it? A few times, he had went as far as implying that she was leading Lawson on, and was enjoying doing so. All in all, the blame seemed to aim her way. Nevertheless, several hours later, before Mitch arrived home and before she had a chance to go to the police, Roxanne phoned crying. She demanded to speak to Mitch. It turned out that Lawson had suffered a massive asthma attack.

Warm tears strolling down Janelle's cheeks prodded her back into the present and into wonder. Where was Mitch? Wherever he was, what was he thinking? Planning? What did that letter mean to her future? Was the wedding really off? Was the business partnership off? Was this devoted man, so unlike her father, out of her life forever?

Janelle reached for the tissue box, finding it empty. A handkerchief was in her purse on the end table, so she raised up to get it. Mingling her fingers through some caramel candies and various trinkets, she eventually touched the flowery cloth. At the same time, a business card dropped from the clutter onto the carpet. Janelle picked it up and read the name inscribed on it: Aaron Deverreau.

"Want some of this, Aaron?"

Aaron swerved around from a mountainous landscape that spellbound him and faced barbecue ribs smothered in a thick, sizzling sauce. Macaroni and candied yams graced each side of the meat. Feeling hunger pangs rising from the pit of his belly, weighing against his tongue, Aaron's gaze then ran beyond to the person offering the sumptuous meal.

Dimples the size of grapes greeted him. Yet, when he found his way to Nikki Richard's round, glittering eyes, he knew her generosity extended beyond the food. A newcomer to Phoenix, she was also one of Aaron's latest tenants, the owner of a posh, skin-care salon. Both had been invited to a barbecue given by their mutual friends Demarre and Chantel Gracen.

"I think I will have some," Aaron accepted, returning the smile.

Locked to his eyes, she handed him the steaming plate. "Is that all you want?"

"That's all for now." He dabbed the corner of his mustache. "Thank you so much."

"You're welcome. I'll be right back. I think I'm a little hungry too." Nikki walked out of the backyard onto the veranda, and then within the house.

Turning back around to the picturesque view that fascinated him before, Aaron reached for a rib first. Chewing its tenderness, he savored the mouthwatering flavor, while thinking to himself how nice Nikki was. In the limited encounters he had with her, she appeared considerate, pleasant, and was lots of fun. She was even pretty. So why wasn't he interested—interested in seeing much more of her?

Ever since meeting her, she had hinted that he should show her around town. Now coincidentally, they wound up at this barbecue together. Card partners, dance partners, cooking partners, Aaron had a good time with her during the day. Thank God what his ex-wife did to him, hadn't turned him off to women completely. He could still enjoy their company, and no way could he live without sex. It was just that *feeling something* was what he couldn't do anymore. *Feeling something* in his heart. There was always respect and caring for any lady he was involved with. But when would he again feel something that even closely resembled love?

The strongest emotion that consumed him was with that beautiful creature he'd met last fall in Philadelphia. *Janelle, Janelle, Janelle, God bless you,* he thought, envisioning her sultry image. Desperately, Aaron wished she would have called him. In his fantasy, she would say she was moving to Arizona to open her boutique there. Greatest of all, she would confess she wanted to be near Aaron.

In reality, Aaron knew she wouldn't call. First of all, she might have been involved with someone. Secondly, they lived too far apart. Third, he had come on too strong. She probably knew he followed her from the restaurant to the club. She probably also believed he was following her when she left the club. Not impressive either, Aaron practically begged her to open her business in Arizona when he hardly knew the woman. Lastly, he was so physically excited by her, she might have thought he was a pervert. He wasn't.

There was just something about her. Whatever it was, it touched his body, touched his spirit, touched his mind, and he ached to know if it could touch his heart. After all this time had passed, he still couldn't quench the longing to know her much more. The fact that she was opening her own business showed her ambitiousness. Aside from that, she seemed as sweet inside as she looked outside.

In his mind, Aaron had stared at Janelle a million times, memorizing that beautiful face and her body that made him think of one thing. Her scintillating, brown eyes had an exotic upward slant at the outer corners, and a way of looking at Aaron, which made him feel that she had never looked at any other man in such a way. Much lower were lips that weren't small or large, but full and shaped so sensuously they made him ravenous for their taste. Extremely luscious, too, was her dark skin, a potpourri of caramel and chocolate. So smooth it was, Aaron wanted to close his eyes, kissing her slowly from head to toe. He craved to feel her hair as well. Skimming her shoulders, its glimmer made it look like black silk.

Equally unforgettable was her body. Dancing with Janelle so closely, it took all Aaron's self-control not to touch her all over. Remembering her, he could smell the coconut oil faintly brushed over her skin. He could even hear her soft, very feminine voice reverberating across his warm neck, caressing his ear. If there was ever a moment he could have held on to forever, Aaron knew that dancing with Janelle that night was it. Just being with her was it.

"Aaron?"

Nikki's voice tugged him from his musings and around toward her. She was standing in front of him with a plate matching his.

"I guess I'm not the only greedy person around here?" he teased.

"No, I can be greedy, too, when I have something I really like." Staring into his eyes, she bit into her rib.

Aaron cleared his throat. "So are you having fun today?"

"The best." Dimples graced her cheeks. "But I know how the night could be better."

"How's that?"

"If you showed me around the city tonight to experience the nightlife here. I know for a fact you're not going home to any particular woman. Chantel told me you're a divorcé, and you're not seeing anyone right now. And I'm single, and I . . ." Taking a deep breath, she closed her eyes, then opened them. "And I find you very attractive. What do you think about me?"

"I—I think you're attractive also." He was taken aback by the question and it showed.

"Did I come on too strong?" she asked, somewhat embarrassed by his discomfort. "I didn't mean to. I—"

"No. I'm flattered."

"I don't mean to come off as super-aggressive. Normally, I'm much more laid back with men. But you're so interesting and so exciting and so attractive. What's the harm in two unattached people of the opposite sex spending a little time together?" She laughed. "We might really like each other. Who knows?" She laughed again.

Nodding, Aaron's plump lips curled contentedly. "You're right. Who knows?"

"But if you feel there's someone else you would rather be with tonight, I'd understand." Behind her back, Nikki crossed her fingers.

Straightaway Aaron looked off to the view only he could see, seeing again the woman he couldn't get out of his mind. It was foolish to think he would ever see her again. Even if she had lost the number, she could have tracked him down via his company. Aaron focused back on the woman before him. "No, there isn't anyone I'm planning to be with tonight. Sure, I'd be glad to show you around town."

CHAPTER FIVE

Janelle's heels crushed into the corridor's royal-blue carpeting as she strode up to the penthouse door. Searching through an oblong, beaded bag for her key, she prayed Mitch's disappearing act was over. Sunday he hadn't returned home, and as soon as sunrise peeked through the blinds on Monday, she was overwhelmed by his absence again. Worried, she contemplated waiting around the house for him, except handling some of her mother's financial obligations drew her outside, running her about until late afternoon.

The key was having trouble fitting the lock when the door swung open.

"It won't fit," Mitch announced. Like torches, his eyes blazed across at her.

"You're wrong about me, Mitch." She took a deep breath, hoping it would temper her racing heart. "I didn't want to be with Lawson."

"I read that letter! I know about all the times, all the places, all the ways you *did it,* all the things you said to each other, all the plans you made with him."

Janelle couldn't hide her shock. "Something is wrong here. That letter couldn't have possibly been written by Lawson. If it was, he was lying. We were together once. *Once,* and only because of his deceit!"

"Do I look like a fool to you? You know who I am." With his thumb, he pointed to himself. "I'm the smartest, richest man to ever cross your path and you thought you could use me. Sorry, game is over. You lose."

"I wasn't trying to use you." *God is my witness that I wasn't.*

"You were!"

Listlessly, she was shaking her head. "This is unbelievable. Where did you say you received that letter from? The bank?"

"It doesn't matter."

"It does! There are lies in it! All I know is that Lawson pretended he was you one night." She could hardly talk for the emotion strangling her voice. "Let's go in and I can tell you the entire story from the beginning." She started inside. Mitch blocked her entry.

"Your things were sent to your mother's."

The shock drew her hand to her chest. "No, don't tell me you did that."

"Oh, yes, I did it. So if you want them, they're in New Jersey. There's no reason for you to ever come to this house again. There isn't even a reason for you to call me again. And don't even think about going near that joint bank account. I withdrew everything. And as for that boutique, I have my deposit back for the space and renovations. Now get out of my sight and I hope you enjoy the view at the bottom. You belong there."

The door slammed.

Secluded in Sherry's guest bedroom, Janelle peered out of a window covered in white chiffon curtains. Beyond it, the orange-yellow glow of sunset cast over the trees, lawns and colonial-styled houses lining the street. Janelle couldn't appreciate any of the scenery. Ponderings blinded her of everything but what her mind permitted her to see.

It was actually over between Mitch and her. The most solid man that ever shared her life wasn't in it anymore. The fact that she couldn't easily dismiss the hurt wedged inside her proved she loved him. Yes, Janelle did love him. *In their way.* Not with passion. Not by feeling *in love*. Not with hugs, kisses and caresses. But with friendship, mutual respect and devotion to each other. It was the kind of love her father never gave her mother. Now it was gone. How was she supposed to keep on without it? How could Mitch so easily let it go?

The more she thought about the tumultuous events of the last hours, the more that anger started seeping in the cracks of her broken heart. Not only was she livid at Mitch for treating her so horribly, but she was more furious with herself. Even if Mitch was out of her life, it shouldn't have affected her livelihood. Now opening her own dress boutique, featuring her own designs, was merely a dream again. Her individual savings were practically nonexistent, since most of her salary was dispersed among her mother's mortgage, along with her mother's new Lexus payments and the refurbishing of her mother's home.

Being so secure with Mitch had persuaded Janelle to do all that. He promised her she wouldn't have to fret about finances any longer, because her name was on his most sizable bank statement. How had she become so comfortable with his generosity? Greed wasn't in her nature. Most importantly, she had never depended on a man before. What was she going to do about surviving? About her dream? Her replacement had already been hired at Mozelle. Worse, it would take months to land another position and years to save up for the business. As far as bank loans, she was rejected before. As for investors, they took their sweet time. She couldn't even ask her brothers and sisters to help her out. One of her brothers had his family to take care of, the other was paying his dues in an advertising career and her two sisters were both in college studying law.

Why had she handed her strength and power over to someone else? To Mitch? All of her life, she stood strong and tall on her own. The Newark ghetto she was raised in hadn't killed her because her spirit always guided her away from the bullets and gang fights on the way to school and back home. Her spirit carried her above the drugs, alcoholism and prostitution that so heavily plagued her neighborhood. Her spirit kept her together—kept her from losing her mind—when her father abandoned their family, and the ache of hunger and near homelessness, dragged her into its dungeon for years, until from somewhere a light emerged that led her out.

It was a blessing from God. She could draw, design and sew clothes so exquisitely, her talent helped Janelle pay her way through college. The scholarship she was awarded for her brilliance in fashion design, recompensed the rest. For countless hours, Janelle could create her artistry, losing her soul in the joy of performing the work, and later the euphoria of seeing and holding the finished product. Easily as breathing came to her, she knew this was her purpose.

More than ever before, she also knew that now was the time for this dream to come true. If not now, then when? She ate with the desire, walked with it, laughed with it, breathed with it, woke with it, slept with it, did everything and anything with it—always feeling it so deep in her heart. And what about the other heartfelt dream she had? The one to give grants to children from underprivileged homes, so they wouldn't grow up the way she did? God knows, she couldn't throw it all away now.

Moving away from the window, her bare feet paced back and forth along the length of the small room. With each step, there was a question about her unknown future. With each question, she grew more desperate. There had to be something she could do. What?

Unable to deal with harsh reality anymore, she reveled in fantasy. Often it was her indulgence over the last few days to relax. Closing her eyes, she imagined so many wonderful things: a successful business, a trip to a lush, Caribbean island, relocating her mother to a mansion, and even the gorgeous vision of a man: Aaron Deverreau. However, in conjuring up his handsome presence, she couldn't help remembering him stating that if she had an exciting and profitable business plan, he would be interested in financing her business and providing property for it. The sole catch would be her relocating to Arizona.

Dialing his number, Janelle knew what she was thinking was crazy. On the other hand, desperation was unfamiliar with reason. After nearly a year had passed, she was going to call this man asking for money and property for her business. With all the women who probably threw themselves at him, he wouldn't remember her. *Hang up fool,* a nagging voice ordered. Janelle was about to comply. Stopping her was a professional sounding woman on the other end of the receiver.

"Aaron Deverreau's office. May I help you?"

"Ready for lunch, brother?"

Bald and husky, Demarre Gracen entered his business partner's office and sat in a gray, velvet chair before him, waiting for an answer. Another partner in Deverreau, Gracen, Hall Development, Brett Hall, sauntered in behind him. Unusually tall and slim, he chose to stand, biting on an apple.

"Give me five minutes," Aaron told them, straightening items on his desk. "This morning was a hectic one."

"Tell me about it," Demarre added, and picked up a picture that sat to his right. A curly haired boy of about seven or eight stared back at him. "This is the latest picture of Kyree?"

Aaron glanced at the photo and smiled. "That's my little man."

Brett bent down over Demarre's shoulder to admire the

photo. "That is one good-looking little guy. Gets better looking with age too. He looks like his mom."

Demarre nodded his agreement. "But he's definitely going to be the sexiest man alive like his stepdad."

Aaron flung a rubber band at him. "What did I tell you about calling me that?"

Smiling, Demarre placed the frame back down on the desk, and gazed across at his friend. "You're still planning that trip with him in August?"

"Of course." Aaron opened a drawer, placing diskettes inside. "Last summer we had a good time. My brother came and brought his boys too."

Speculating, Demarre rubbed his fingers over his slick head. "I wouldn't mind taking my son to a basketball camp like that. Maybe I'll join you guys."

"You won't want to leave, man," Aaron enthused, closing the drawer. "That's how much fun it is."

Demarre nodded. "I'd love to play basketball all day. That sounds real sweet. You're right, I might not want to leave."

Biting into his apple, Brett shook his head. "No way. That would kill my knees."

"But then again," Demarre went on, "I have my woman to get back home to." He winked at both men.

Brett grinned. "Marre is whipped. He's totally whipped."

Demarre waved him off too. "Get out of here. You're just mad because you're tired of trying to be a player. And I stress *trying*."

Aaron chuckled. "Easy on him. You're one of the lucky ones. Marriage is not for all of us. Enjoy your freedom, Brett. And don't be so quick to give it up."

Demarre waved him off too. "Now what's your problem? When was the last time you talked to your ex anyway?"

"I talk to Kyree. He's the only one I need to talk to."

"You sure?" Demarre studied him. A fraternity brother, as well as a business partner, he'd known Aaron a long time and knew him well. Whenever his ex wife was mentioned, he noticed the tension. Was love still there? If it was, he wanted Aaron to have it. He was one of the best men he knew. "Don't you miss her? You two seemed so right together."

Not meeting his eyes, Aaron opened another drawer. "You don't know anything about it." He placed a folder inside a compartment. "You don't know her like I do."

Demarre leaned forward. "Well, tell me. You never told us why you two divorced."

"I did tell you. Irreconcilable differences," Aaron replied.

Brett watched Aaron gathering the last batch of diskettes. "Marre is right. You never told us what really happened. One day you two were a together couple and the next you didn't exist anymore. Something happened. Something big."

Aaron stood, straightening his tie. "Are you guys ready for lunch?"

Demarre and Brett looked at each other. Moments later, they walked ahead to the elevator, while Aaron stopped at his secretary's desk to browse through his messages. Flipping through the pile of pink slips, there weren't any urgent calls that needed returning. That is until he saw a message that raised his head back. He read it twice to make sure he hadn't read it incorrectly. Janelle had called. *Janelle*. She wanted to see him.

CHAPTER SIX

Feeling the butterflies that hadn't swarmed inside him since he was a teenager, Aaron walked from behind his desk to answer the knock at his office door. Gripping the doorknob with one hand, he tugged his tie straight with the other. He was expecting his three o'clock appointment: Janelle Sims.

The door opened, and Aaron contained his excitement about seeing the woman he couldn't stop thinking about. He had imagined her so much, building her sexiness in his mind, he assumed when he saw her again that it would be impossible for her to be as beautiful as his mind made her out to be. After all, he only saw her one time. Months ago, too, the day before his thirty-seventh birthday. As memories blurred, he knew it was easy for an imagination to put someone in a prettier package. This time, however, imagination didn't do reality justice. Aaron couldn't stop looking at her.

"Janelle, it's so good to see you again. Please, come in."

"It's nice to see you again too," she said, stepping inside the office. She almost touched her chest to check if her heart only felt like it was plunging through its skin. "I appreciate your agreeing to meet with me on such short notice." She went toward a chair in front of his desk.

"I know your business is important to you and I want to help." Watching her walk, loving the way the creamy, white suit clung to her round hips, hugged her tiny waist and showed off her curvaceous legs, Aaron forgot to close the door. With a Lord-have-mercy shake of his head, he did so when she sat down.

Afterward, he faced Janelle from across the desk. "So you said on the phone you would like to acquire a commercial property and possibly open your boutique here in Phoenix?" He tried not to linger on the sultriness of her skin. She glowed like she was sitting amid tropical sunshine, rather than fluorescent office lighting. "Well, we have plenty of properties available and one of our agents will be glad to show them to you." Wishing his heart would stop racing, he handed her a packet. "This is a listing of our commercial units. Their various sizes, locations and cost are indicated."

"Great," Janelle remarked, not knowing what was making her more nervous, seeing him again, or what she had to tell him. Contemplating how to explain her plight, she faced her lap, then gazed back up at the face, which her hands and lips were quivering to touch. "Look, Aaron, I have to be straight with you." Gnawing on her lip, she twisted nervously in her seat. "I . . ."

"I what?" He noticed furrows spreading across her forehead. "What's so hard to say to me? I won't bite."

She looped a wayward hair behind her ear. "I need your help."

"What can I do?"

"It's a business proposition." She felt her bones constricting with her discomfort. "And I give you my word, I'm not trying to hustle you. I'm a very hardworking person and I plan to give my all to achieve my goals."

"You made that clear the night I met you." *You also told*

me you would call me, but you didn't. "What is it, Janelle?"
Crazy as it was, he would have done anything to keep this
stranger near him. Besides, he always sought interesting
opportunities in which to invest his massive fortune.
"Come on, tell me."

She took a deep breath. "I *really* want the space for my
boutique, but I can't give you any payment until profits
come in."

Aaron nodded. "That's fine."

"It is?" Shocked he didn't need to think about it, her
eyes widened. "Thank you, Aaron."

"It's my pleasure." His eyes lingered across at her.

Warmed by them, she felt her heart speeding even faster
than it had when he opened the door and she saw him
standing there after thinking she would never see him
again. But now she came to the next part of her quest. "I
remember you saying you were always looking for good
investments."

Aaron nodded. "I did say that to you and meant it. But
first I have to know what are your investment funds like?"

"I have to be honest with you. I don't have any financing.
I have a hundred or so designs that I've managed to make
over the last year, and that's it. I don't have financing
for more materials, equipment and other costs, including
hiring seamstresses."

Suddenly quiet, he stared openly at her for a moment.
"Are you good?" he asked.

Half smiling, she knew he couldn't have been suggest-
ing . . .

"I mean talent wise, as a dress designer," he clarified.
His voice was somewhat lower and his eyes lowered on her
as well. "Did you design the outfit you're wearing?"

"Yes." Janelle watched his seductive brown eyes slowly
tracing over her body, as far as her sitting position allowed.
She felt like he was undressing her, and ashamed as it
made her, Janelle knew she couldn't have been any more
turned on if he was. What was he doing to her?

"You are good," he complimented her. He continued pretending to inspect the exceptional detailing of the glamorous design, all the while knowing it was what filled it and what the sexy lines exposed, which made him warm. He wound his gaze back up, meeting eyes spun straight from a man's fantasy.

Eyes always told a story, his elders had enlightened him, and if he was reading hers correctly, she was feeling the same thing he was. He had to get to know her better. He had to find an entrance into her life. He hoped her prospects on paper looked as good as the ones on her.

"Did you bring your business plan with you?" he asked.

"Yes," she said, hurriedly reaching into a portfolio she'd been carrying. "Sketches of the designs are enclosed with it too." Smiling, she handed the thick document to Aaron.

Reading the first few pages, Aaron nodded without looking up. "It may take a little while for me to go over this. So bear with me."

"It's no problem." And it surely wasn't. With his eyes on the business plan, her own eyes were free to just stare at him. What a luscious treat.

Janelle was admiring his lips for the seventh time when Aaron finally looked up. "This is excellent," he said, pointing to the document. "It's going to be a very lucrative enterprise."

Janelle beamed. "I'm so glad you think so. So does this mean you will think it over?"

"Nope."

"No?" Her elated expression crumbled.

"Because I don't have to think it over." Aaron grinned, drawing out hers. "I'm investing in this boutique. I would have to be crazy not to. I'm not letting this get by me." *I'm not letting you get by me either. Not without a fight.*

"Are you serious?" The surprise raised her hand against her chest.

"I've never been more serious in my life. Now all I have to do is get in contact with my lawyer and the bank. And you should get a reputable attorney too. After that, we set up a meeting and get rolling as soon as possible. We'll make it happen.''

She had to be dreaming all this—especially him. The thrill was about to explode from her. She couldn't wait to tell her mother, siblings and, of course, Sherry. "Aaron, I don't know how to thank you.''

"You don't have to. Again, it's my pleasure.''

She began writing some notes on a pad. As she did, he felt free to delight in her exotic, sparkling eyes, her chest heaving with exhilaration and her overall being gushing with aliveness. She was a passionate woman. He loved that. And it made him curious if she took that passion away from someone in Philadelphia. "So I guess all this means you're moving to Phoenix?''

Putting her pad aside, she met his eyes. "It sure does.'' Her russet-glossed lips curled invitingly. "Change is good.''

"That's true.'' He nodded. "Are you . . . are you making the move alone?''

She was still smiling, but Aaron could see her eyes had lost their sparkle with his question. A sadness blew over her. It made him speculate that something had happened between her and a man.

"Uh, yes, I'm moving alone.''

He wanted to sing, dance and do cartwheels. "Well, you won't be alone for long. I'll introduce you to everyone. Phoenix has a lot of good people.''

At that point, they heard his secretary on the intercom. "Mr. Deverreau, I'm sorry to interrupt, but there is a Nikki on line one, and she says she has to talk to you about something urgent.''

"Excuse me, Janelle,'' he said, picking up the phone.

Janelle tried to be polite and not listen during Aaron's conversation. Even so, she could tell the woman he was talking to was not a business caller. It was obvious the nature of her phoning him was personal. Yet, what did she expect? It had been nine long months since they met that night. She had met someone during that time. He had probably met thousands.

Janelle was standing, preparing to leave the office by the time he hung up. He noticed a difference in her expression. Matter of fact, there was a change in her whole demeanor.

"Is something wrong?" he asked. He stood and walked around the desk toward her. "Why are you leaving so fast?"

Fixing her bag over her shoulder, she smiled dryly. "I have to get going."

"You're going back to Philly *right now?*"

"I have so many things to do."

With her back to him, she made a few more steps to the door. Aaron couldn't help touching her arm. When she turned around, they were nearly as close as when they danced.

Glancing down at her body, then gazing up into her eyes, Aaron wanted to be even closer, though he knew this distance would have to do for now. "Can I take you out to dinner tonight?"

Looking up at him, she inhaled the spicy cologne, and realized it was the same fragrance that invigorated her senses before. "I'm catching a flight back tonight."

"That's too bad." His voice was husky with deepening breaths. "I thought we might go dancing afterward. You know, I was in my glory dancing with you that night at that club."

"It was nice," she admitted.

"I couldn't stop thinking about you."

Did he really mean that? She wanted to tell him she couldn't stop thinking about him either. Yet what she couldn't stop thinking about precisely at that moment, was that woman who called. There was someone in his life. As good as he looked, probably many someones. "I really better get going."

"Can I give you something to take back with you? A little remembrance?" Staring in her eyes, he placed his hands on her shoulders, then curved his face to meet the beautiful one before it. His stare unmoving from her mouth, he parted his lips, bringing them toward hers.

Janelle placed her fingers against his lips before they touched her. "I'd rather not."

Certain there was something happening between them, Aaron wanted to ask her why not, or kiss her anyway. However, it became clear he had to go slow with her. After all, it was likely she had just ended one relationship. He couldn't risk scaring her away by being too anxious.

"I understand."

Turning her back to him again, she moved close to the door, then looked back as she gripped the knob. "I'll be in touch with you about the meeting. And again, I appreciate your faith in me. It's going to be a very exciting partnership. You'll see."

"I have no doubt it will be."

The door closed quietly.

Shedding his clothes on his bathroom's burgundy tile hours later, Aaron couldn't get Janelle out of his head. Nine months had passed since he saw her. Nine months, and the feelings she aroused in him back then hadn't lessened at all. If anything, they were intensified. In his office, she was so sweet. She looked so good, smelled so good, sounded so good. There was just something about her, that same something he felt when they met. Aaron hoped his lawyer could set up a meeting immediately.

He ached to be around her again. He ached to just talk to her in a secluded setting like they did that night. Lifting his hairy, muscular legs into the shower, he was so invigorated by the possibility of more nights like that. Feeling the warm stream cascading over his face as his head bent back, Aaron also knew it was a divine blessing that something urged her to come to him with her business proposal.

Attracted to her as he was, he hadn't made the decision to invest based on that.

In reviewing the lucrative plan, the sketches and the sexy outfit she wore, it was evident he couldn't pass up the opportunity. More than that, he couldn't wait to see her dream unfold before her eyes. It would probably seem like magic to her. As magical as the way she made him feel. Aaron longed for her to be with him right then. He wanted her hands all over him. He wanted his all over her. One of these days, Aaron knew it was going to happen. It didn't even matter that she had shunned his kiss this afternoon. He felt something between them. He knew Janelle felt it too.

Riding the airplane home, Janelle laid her head back on the lush, reclining seats and smiled to herself. Her dream was about to come true. After hungering for something for so long, she was about to see what it tasted like. It touched her heart that it was about to happen. Several times, she had to dab at her eyes, as she cried tears of joy. She was so glad she never gave up. In her hard times, she was so grateful to God for giving her the strength to keep on moving. She was so grateful that she had sense to listen to his voice speaking to her soul when she wanted to give up.

Everything was about to change, her career, where she lived, and generally her life. For the first time in her life, perhaps she could be truly happy. The boutique was about to become reality. She would finally have some financial comfort too. That would enable her to completely wipe out her mother's debts and provide her with more luxuries. As well, Janelle could purchase her own home, a dependable car and other items she had always longed to buy herself. Thanks to Aaron, all this was possible.

Aaron, she thought again. Gorgeous, wonderful, sexy Aaron. Now if he was hers, she could add a whole other dimension to the word *happiness*. He looked so good in the office. He was so kind, so considerate, so seductive. It took all her effort not to kiss those delicious-looking lips when they came near hers. It would have been the kiss of her lifetime, just as he seemed like the man of her lifetime—the one who was unforgettable. It almost seemed like God had sent him to her. Not only because he had made her dream come true, but the way he made her feel that night when they met was sheer heaven. The way he made her feel in his office this afternoon, assured her time hadn't taken any of her attraction to him away. Discomfiting as it was, she was more attracted to him.

Greatly, she wished she could have been more to him than a woman he was going into business with. For a second, she imagined being the woman in his heart. The *one* woman in his heart. Except Janelle knew that was impossible. Some woman named Nikki had called him today, and who knows how many others he was involved with.

Janelle had to stop thinking of him *that way*. She had to convince herself that Aaron wasn't the most desirable man she'd ever met. She could only think of Aaron Deverreau as a wonderful business partner and friend. That is all he could ever be to her. She would grant him all the sweat he needed to ensure the business's success. Yet, she would never give him her heart.

CHAPTER SEVEN

In the moments following a highly successful meeting, the attorneys shook Aaron's and Janelle's hands, before leaving them in Aaron's office alone.

Janelle was thrilled about the terms Aaron had rendered her. She owned a majority of the company regardless of his full financial backing. On top of that, he'd granted her an exceptionally generous starting bonus. It would enable her to pay off her mother's mortgage, buy some nice things for herself and make an endowment to a girl's organization she'd read about in Phoenix.

"I can't tell you how happy I am, Aaron," Janelle enthused, staring up in his face. Incredibly, he was more handsome than their last encounter in this office. If he tried to kiss her now, could she resist?

"You don't have to tell me how happy you are." Her glow lit up the room and his heart. Aaron couldn't help moving closer and closer to her. "I feel your happiness, Janelle. You're glowing."

Neither could Janelle keep her distance from him. She eased nearer and nearer. If it was possible, she felt even more attracted to him. "I don't know how to thank you, Aaron. I don't know what I could possibly do to appropriately thank you."

"Oh, yes, you do." They were standing so close to each other, he smelled her coconut fragrance exuding from her skin. It compounded how much she had turned him on during the meeting. It was so difficult to focus on business when he was thinking of much *hotter* things. With the way Janelle was making him feel, he would have given her anything. Anything. Particularly what he wanted to give her most—himself. "Have dinner with my son and me? He's visiting me."

"Is your son the adorable little guy in the picture?" She glanced toward the stunning portrait on his desk.

"That's him all right," Aaron said. His eyes drifted over her body as she picked up the picture and stared at it.

She put it back down and caught Aaron's gaze roaming over her. An intensity filled his eyes that penetrated to the core of her, making her want him even more. "He—he's gorgeous. I was meaning to ask you about him the first time I was in your office, but I was so nervous about asking you for money, it was all I could think of."

"Well, you can make me real happy by dining with us tonight." He was so turned on he couldn't let her out of his sight. Even if they couldn't be lovers, he just ached to be near her. "Please, Janelle. And if you're worried about being uncomfortable around my ex—and—and not that you should be, but she won't be there. We never see each other. Kyree's nanny brings him to me, leaves and returns to take him back home."

"I can't, Aaron," she said, with desire titillating her to the point that she ached for him too. On one hand, she wanted to stop seeing him the way she did. On the other, the emotions he always inflamed in her filled her with such ecstasy it was addictive. He made her feel so good. "I'm looking at houses this evening. I have to have somewhere to live. The agent is supposed to meet me here any minute now."

"Let me handle that for you."

"No, Aaron, you've done enough for me."

At that point, a tall woman donning a navy suit, clutching a portfolio entered via the partially opened door, drawing their attention to her. "Are you Ms. Sims?" she addressed Janelle.

Extending her hand, Janelle approached the woman. "Yes, I am. And you must be Mrs. Porter, the real-estate agent."

After Janelle again thanked Aaron for believing in her and becoming her partner, the two women were heading out the door when he grasped Janelle's hand. Her face still glowing, she looked around at him.

"When you're back home in Philly," he said, "get in touch with me. Let me know where you're going to be living and on what day you'll be relocating. I'll help you get settled."

Smiling, she nodded. "I'll call you and let you know my arrangements. But you've helped me enough. Really. One of these days I'm going to do something for you. I want to give you something that'll really make you happy."

Departing with that promise, Janelle hurried to the hall, catching up to the agent. In the mist that her presence left behind, Aaron mused on her words. She had already done something for him. She made him feel alive again.

Clad in black sunglasses, Sherry drove down a crowded street toward a skyscraper, with hoards of people passing through its revolving doors. Parking her Volvo in front of the building, she began shaking her head. "I say you're crazy for doing this," she said, then looked beside her.

Biting on her lip, Janelle couldn't take her eyes off the building. Why did going inside there make her so nervous? She was merely going to talk to Mitch. Mitch, the man she shared so much of her life with. The man she almost married. "I have to do this. It's going to bother me if I don't."

"No, you don't," Sherry argued. "Let's continue on to the airport so you won't miss your plane. That fine man is waiting for you in Phoenix."

"He is not," she shot as quickly as the tinge of arousal she felt at the mere mention of Aaron. "And as far as my plane goes, I'm four hours early."

"Don't waste it on Mitch. You and I can sit in the airport parking lot and talk. I'm going to miss you, girl."

Gazing at Sherry's auburn curls, her even-toned face and tiny, russet-glossed lips, Janelle became sad that days like this with her friend were about to end. "I'm going to miss your crazy self too," she said with a smile.

"You're not acting like it." Yet, Sherry could see beyond the smile to the sadness in Janelle's eyes. Sure, she knew their becoming long-distance friends caused some of it. The source of the rest of it lay elsewhere. "Don't go inside there, Janelle."

"Sherry, I just have to say what I have to say to Mitch and leave."

"Why?" She sighed, inhaling a whiff of raspberry from the puny fragrant cardboard tree that hung from her rear-view mirror. "You don't owe him anything."

"I have to let him know that I didn't do what he thinks I did."

"I wouldn't care what he thinks after he dogged you out like he did."

"He did that because he believes I betrayed him with his brother."

"It doesn't matter, Janelle. You don't love him."

Pausing, Janelle half smiled, half frowned. "You're wrong. You always thought that. I did love him. I couldn't have lived with him all that time and not have loved him. No, it wasn't that passionate feeling like in a romance novel, or like they write about in love songs." For some reason, she visualized Aaron. "But the love was there. A simple, caring kind of love for another human being who you've shared your life with. That's why I just can't leave with him thinking that I did something so terrible."

Scowling, Sherry scraped a long pink nail against the corner of her mouth. "You're not hoping he'll believe you, so you two can get back together, are you?"

"Of course not. Even if he did forgive me, I don't want to be with him anymore. The feelings just aren't there anymore. I feel so . . . so different." Again, Janelle envisioned Aaron. "I just have to let him know I wasn't using him. It's one of the most horrible things in the world to be accused of something you didn't do."

"I still say you're making a mistake."

Within moments, Janelle took a deep breath and stepped on the glass elevators that were designated for the floors twenty-five and above. Getting off on the thirty-ninth floor, she took another deep breath, before heading up the paneled corridor, which lead to his secretary's desk. A clump grew in Janelle's throat as she pictured how Mitch must have told his sister-in-law about the letter.

What would Roxanne say to her? Janelle knew if she was correct in sensing that Roxanne disliked her, the woman probably wanted to murder her now. What would she say to Roxanne about Lawson? The truth, she answered. That's all she had was the truth. And her truth was innocent.

Roxanne was looking down at the pad she was scribbling on when Janelle approached her desk. Her heels were muffled by the dense, gray carpet. Soon aware of someone's presence, Roxanne looked up. Her bright hazel eyes widened, and to Janelle's surprise, Roxanne smiled.

"What can I do for you, Janelle?" she asked.

"I—I'm here to see Mitch," Janelle replied, baffled by her pleasantness.

Roxanne scanned over her appointment book, then looked back up. "I don't see you in the book. And I'm sorry to be so formal, but these are the rules Mitch has specified since you two aren't getting married."

"No, we aren't. Did Mitch . . . did he—"

"Tell me why the engagement was broken?"

"It was painful, but he did."

With her discomfort making her chest heave, Janelle looked aside, before gazing back at Roxanne. For someone who was facing a woman who she was told was having an affair with her husband, Janelle thought Roxanne was mighty pleasant. "I'm sorry. And I know what Mitch probably told you, but Lawson and I weren't having an affair. He tricked me. He pretended he was Mitch."

With a blank expression, Roxanne nodded. "I really don't want to hear about it. I've put it in the past and so should you. If I don't forgive and forget, who will forgive me when I do wrong?"

Janelle was bewildered. Roxanne was so warm and sincere. Had she made incorrect assumptions about this woman? Or was Roxanne the greatest actress she'd ever seen? A great actress, who was pleased as pie because now she had access to who she really wanted—Mitch.

"I am going to put it behind me," Janelle responded. "But first I must talk to Mitch. Is anyone in there with him?"

"No, but he won't see you without an appointment. Call him and make one."

"He won't talk to me. And I must see him."

Janelle strode to the door.

"Don't!" Roxanne warned her.

Mitch sprung from his seat. "What are you doing here? Get out before I call security."

Janelle couldn't believe he was still so furious at her. She couldn't believe he was threatening her this way. "Mitch, I'm leaving Philly," she said, easing closer to his desk.

"Philly is lucky."

"I wanted to say good bye, and I also wanted you to know that I didn't have an affair with Lawson." She stared in his keen, fleshy eyes, but they were so filled with hatred, she couldn't look in them for long. "He tricked me like I told you."

"Why are you still trying to get in my wallet? I am *not* investing in that business!"

"This is not about your investing in my business. This is about two people who cared for each other. We shouldn't part this way, with so much anger and so much deceit between us."

"You were the one who deceived me!"

"No, I was deceived."

"Stop lying!"

"I'm not. Your brother deceived me."

"I'm not listening to this."

"And someone is deceiving you with that letter." She eased a few steps nearer. "I didn't have an affair with your brother."

"Liar. You're such a liar."

"I'm not!"

"You are! How many other things have you lied about?" With his hands in his pockets, Mitch came around the desk, standing just inches in front of her. "You mean nothing to me anymore. Getting over you was easy as dropping a dime. I'm seeing a lady in my league now. She grew up in wealth and luxury. She went to the finest schools. She holds an executive position in one of the richest corporations in the world. She's pure class all the way, unlike the women I've share my precious time with in the past."

"It's good to know you're getting on with your life. I'm getting on with mine too. I'm opening my boutique in another city."

"Liar."

"I am."

He laughed. "In your dreams."

"I'm telling the truth. But I just couldn't bare you walking around hurting because you thought I was having an affair with Lawson."

With his face reddening with his rage, Mitch chuckled wryly. "It's not working Janelle."

"What? What's not working?"

"This begging routine. But what could I expect? You may have crawled on your hands and knees out of the ghetto and went to college and maneuvered your way into a halfway decent job, but you're still not good enough for me. You're nothing. No wonder your daddy had to get away from you. I don't blame the man for never coming back. I don't blame him one bit!"

Water filling her eyes, Janelle backed away from him. He was a stranger to her now. A devil. "You are so evil. How could you say something like that to me?"

"I'll talk to you anyway I like."

Unable to endure anymore torture, Janelle ran out of his office unaware of Roxanne as she hurried to the elevator. Mitch's door slammed behind her, and Roxanne was free to do what she ached to do the whole time that she listened to them at the door. Throwing her head back, she laughed until her stomach hurt.

CHAPTER EIGHT

Simply lounging on the airplane assuaged the anguish Janelle had been subjected to from Mitch. The plane taking off and fading into the sun-drenched sky signaled the beginning of a new life. The old one complete with all its gloom was behind her.

Regardless of how much Mitch belittled her, she was on the airplane because she was on a mission to fulfill her life-long dream. Added to the magnificence of that fact, a man who'd been extremely kind to her was her business partner. Despite her vowing never to become romantically involved with Aaron, Janelle knew it was a blessing merely to have him play some role in her life. She would have to settle for that.

So hours later, as Janelle glided through Phoenix's bustling airport en route to the baggage claim area, she was already feeling better. Her brand-new life was about to start. She looked forward to settling in the five-room house she was renting. Knowing she had much to be thankful for, Janelle was heading to the baggage claim area when a bald, elderly man with a goatee walked over to her.

"Are you Janelle Sims?" he inquired. "I was given a description of you. And I must say, you are as beautiful as I was told you were."

Leery of him, Janelle was reluctant to answer. "Yes, I'm Janelle. Who are you?"

"Chester Hicks, Jr., your driver for today. Now come with me. I have your luggage."

Her brows flew up with her surprise. "You do?"

"It's in the limo that Mr. Deverreau sent for you."

"Mr. Deverreau?" Suddenly feeling like a princess, Janelle couldn't help smiling. "Oh he did send for me, did he? That was nice of him."

Minutes after, Janelle was escorted to a white limousine with tinted windows. After the driver opened the door, she bent down to slide unto empty backseats. Her movement froze and her heart did a jump when she saw Aaron.

"Hello there," he greeted her.

"Hello there, yourself." They exchanged lingering smiles and looks for a moment, before Janelle coasted her buttocks along luxuriant, beige leather cushions.

Aaron was soon delighted by her sitting next to him. "Bet I surprised you huh?"

"You sure did," she said with a laugh. She couldn't get over Sherry teasing her about him waiting for her and he actually was. "But you didn't have to do this."

"I wanted to. We're working together and we should look out for each other. Don't you think so?" He gazed in her slanted eyes, looking so deeply he saw that they were a much more vibrant brown than other lighting had made them out to be.

"You're right," Janelle agreed, so entranced by the look he gave her that she had to force her eyes to look out of the window. They were driving by a park.

Aaron was like a tour guide as they traveled throughout the city destined for her new home. He made everything sound so interesting and had a great deal of pride about the place he called home.

When the limousine eventually stopped in a posh part of Phoenix, and specifically in front of a two-leveled condominium with a terrace, Janelle wondered aloud, "Is this your home, Aaron? It's very nice."

"No, this isn't my home," he answered, clasping her hand and squeezing it lightly. "It's yours."

Loving the feel of his hand on hers, she shook her head. "No, you've made a mistake. When I was telling you over the phone about the house I was renting, you must have written the address down wrong."

"No, Janelle," he said, wondering if the rest of her was as soft as her hand. "I wrote it down correctly. In fact, I visited the house, inspecting it for you. And what I saw was a place that was much too small for an artist. You need space and beauty so you can create. So I found this place for you."

She didn't know whether to be angry or happy. Angry that he assumed he knew what was best for her and happy because it was a thoughtful thing to do and the house was beautiful. Happiness won as Janelle's hands covered her mouth. In disbelief that she was about to live in such a beautiful home, she gazed at it, then back at Aaron. "Oh, Aaron. That was really nice of you. But I can't afford this place."

"Yes, you can because I own it. It's one of my residential properties and since we're partners, it's not going to cost you anything."

Spectacular as this all was, Janelle knew she couldn't accept anymore generosity. "You could be renting out this place, making a fortune."

"Don't worry about that. I want you to create great designs and I know that somewhere that you feel good in will make you very productive."

After going throughout every inch of the lavishly furnished, twelve room house, Janelle returned in the living room where Aaron was. "It's the most beautiful home I've ever seen. But Aaron, I can't live here. You've done so much for me already." Besides that, she didn't want to feel indebted to him. What if he was doing this to entrap her into a sexual partnership instead of a business one? "I can only live here under one condition."

"Name it."

"That you name a monthly fee for it, and let me pay it all up at some time in the future when the business is making a big profit."

"Done."

"Great. Great," she said and just gawked at him in amazement.

"What is it?" he joked. "Something on my face?"

"No, there's nothing on your face."

"So why are you looking at me like I have two heads?"

"Because," she said chuckling. "You've been so kind to me. Why?"

Aaron stared at her for a moment, restraining the urge to hold her beautiful face in his hands and let her know why with his kiss. "Why?" he repeated. "Why? Don't you know why?"

Silence held the air after the question was asked. Feeling that he had come on too strong again, Aaron thought he better leave. Parting with an discomfited look, he strode down the pebbled walkway, and waved good bye before stepping into the limousine. Janelle watched the vehicle drive away. When she came inside, closing the door behind her, she leaned against it and heard again his question echoing in her head: "Don't you know why?"

CHAPTER NINE

"So how does it feel to see everything finally coming together?" Aaron asked his latest tenant after entering her boutique. They were standing in the midst of pandemonium at Janelle's Designs. Some grumbling, some joking, workmen were putting up shelves, laying down carpet, installing counters and sliding racks, painting and attending to various other duties.

Taking a break from helping them, Janelle looked exhausted, but happy. "I've never been so tired in my life," she said, noting that Aaron wasn't wearing his usual business attire. A black sweat suit and sneakers appeared equally attractive on him. "But it's a fun tired. Where are you off to today?"

"To help out a young lady."

"That's nice," Janelle commented, baring an anemic smile.

"I have to let her see that I have more than entrepreneurial skills." Rubbing his hands together, he scanned the room's activity.

Janelle forced the smile to remain on her face. "You better get going. You don't want to keep her waiting."

"I'm not. Show me the paint and a brush."

She glowed. "You're talking about helping *me?*" She really didn't know he meant her.

"Of course."

Flaunting a genuine smile, she speedily gathered the paint, pans, rollers and brushes. Assisting her in arranging everything, Aaron controlled his urge to gawk at her. Donning jeans and a tank top, she looked hotter than the weather that was roasting the city. He grew warm.

They began with one lengthy wall, which the veteran painters hadn't approached yet. Progress was slow, however, because their conversation was so alluring. During the days they were setting up the business, Aaron made the greatest effort to keep their contact and phone calls of a friendly, but professional nature. There was no way he was ruining his chances of knowing her better by surrendering to his burning attraction to her and making romantic overtures, which she wasn't ready for. Hence, as they endeavored to give the wall a glossy coat of pale pink, they talked about harmless, entertaining topics. Each found it exhilarating the way they sparred and agreed.

Aaron believed Arizona's mountains and canyons were more appealing to a tourist than Pennsylvania's historical landmarks. Liking Phoenix, but loving Philadelphia, Janelle disagreed. Neither did they agree on music. Aaron didn't think the new rhythm-and-blues artists were talented like the older generation, his favorites being Gladys Knight, Aretha Franklin, Marvin Gaye, The O'Jays, Isaac Hayes and other classic artists that he enjoyed even as a small child. Janelle adored them as well, but she was equally excited by new artists, such as Babyface, Mariah Carey, Whitney Houston, Dru Hill, Mase, Puffy Combs, Boyz To Men and so many others.

Her most beloved movies were *Boomerang*, *Soul Food*, *Set It Off*, *Sparkle* and *Waiting To Exhale*, whereas he could repeatedly watch *The Five Heartbeats, A Rage in Harlem, The Fugitive, Devil in A Blue Dress, Malcolm X* and *Boyz In The Hood.* When it came to books, there was some dissimilarity, but much harmony. He loved mysteries, suspense and business reading. She loved romances, women's fiction and fashion books. However, they both shared a penchant for self help and inspirational works. In that area, they discovered they read the same authors, and were in accord in nearly all beliefs expressed in them. For hours, they lingered on this subject.

Humble as Aaron appeared, Janelle was amazed when she learned more about his wealth. He was the son of an oil tycoon. Surprisingly void of an accent, he was born and raised in Texas. Later, he went away to college at Wharton Business School in Philadelphia. She wanted to ask Aaron if he knew Mitch, since Mitch went to the same college and was Aaron's exact age. Yet, she was trying not to think of Mitch anymore. She didn't have to wonder why she never ran into Aaron at her alma mater in the same city, Drexel University, since there was seven years difference between her and Aaron. She also learned that Aaron fell in love with Phoenix during a business trip and decided to make it his home.

In speaking with him further, Janelle also couldn't help comparing Aaron to Mitch. Mitch had grown up middle-class, and was the most conceited person she'd ever met. Much the opposite, Aaron, had been raised in grandeur and seemed to be the most humble person she'd ever met. She hoped he wasn't putting on an act to impress her.

Matter of fact, she hoped he wasn't trying to impress like she tried to impress him. She did this by leaving out details whenever he asked about her family and childhood. It was always heartwarming to reveal the close relationships she experienced with her mother and siblings. Nevertheless, Janelle didn't feel it was necessary to tell him about the poverty and her father's desertion.

By the time, the workmen left for the day, and Janelle

realized the quarter of the wall they coated was all they could do at the late hour Aaron wanted to suggest that they have dinner. Controlling his urge to move fast though, he offered her a ride home instead. Just that simple pleasure was so enjoyable with her.

Having had so much fun with him, it was impossible for Janelle to say no. When had she enjoyed just talking with a man so much? Mitch certainly didn't like to have a decent conversation with her. He liked to talk about himself, and hear himself.

Janelle found Aaron so funny too. The hours had flown by in seemingly seconds. "I'll be right with you," she told him. "I just have to put a few things away." She scanned the room.

"Need any help?" he offered. By then she was already bending over to pick up some tools a workman left on the floor. Immediately, his attention stuck on her backside.

"I don't think so." She stood, then turned around to find him conveniently scraping a dried drop of paint off his finger. Watching him, Janelle couldn't help noticing the glistening of his smooth, chocolate-hued skin. She pondered if it was the extreme heat of the night that made it look like that. Like a sexy, scented oil was rubbed all over him. It lured her into imagining what the covered parts of his body looked like shining that way. "On second thought, I do want your help," she told him. "Could you just put this in your car?" From the counter, she handed him a large plant. "I thought I would start decorating this place. But after today and seeing what it takes to get this place ready, it's clear my poor plant will just get trampled over. Besides, I'll wait until we finish painting."

"We tried," he said with light laughter, drawing out hers. He took the plant and walked toward the door. "I'll meet you outside. My car is right in front."

"Be right there."

Feeling as if she was high off something, Janelle hurriedly tidied things, turned off the lights and hurried to get outside. It was only when she stepped out the door, and saw Aaron next to his car, that suddenly she didn't feel so happy. A woman dressed in African garb was standing by it with him. They were laughing and talking. Once, she even punched him on the arm. Janelle looked away and began locking the boutique. After taking her time to do so, she turned around to find the woman was gone.

"Everything okay?" Aaron asked, as they rode through downtown Phoenix. He had taken the long route to her home, anticipating that she would enjoy seeing the nightlife and all the bright lights of the area. To his disappointment, Janelle seemed unimpressed. She hadn't spoken a word since she sat in the car.

"I'm fine," she said. "Just tired."

He looked over at her. "Would you tell me if something was wrong?"

She gazed straight ahead. "Yes. But nothing is."

I acted so silly. The scolding ran through Janelle's head consistently the next day, as she assisted the workmen at the boutique. Why did she become so miffed because Aaron chatted with someone of the opposite sex? She talked with men. Existing in the world with them, how could she not talk to them?

Further proof of how ridiculous she behaved, was what occurred earlier in the day. The lady in African garb, the one who conversed with Aaron had dropped by the boutique. After introducing herself, Yanna, gave Janelle a small gift. A breathtaking sculpture, it personified the image of an authentic African princess, named Iasia. It was an artwork from her afrocentric novelty store located down the street. It turned out Yanna was one of Aaron's tenants.

In getting acquainted, she even told Janelle that Aaron attended a Kwanzaa celebration at her home the previous year, and her husband and children were still talking about the inspirational speech he gave. The theme of it was: Don't let anyone or anything break your spirit.

Realizing how foolishly she had behaved, Janelle was

inept helping around the boutique. Unable to concentrate, she was clumsy and indecisive about where things should go. By the time the workmen left that evening, she'd decided to stop by Aaron's house. In setting up the business, she had attended a meeting there, and remembered where it was located. To return some legal documents concerning the business would be the perfect excuse to see him. Thereafter, she hoped they could have fun, talking like they had the day before. She had really enjoyed it.

Janelle stepped outside to lock up. A tap on the shoulder startled her. She looked to the side, and a portly, elderly man, dressed in a blue suit, grinned at her. He was waving keys.

"Are you Ms. Janelle Sims?" he asked.

Santa-like as he appeared, she still ogled him suspiciously. "Yes, why do you ask?"

"These are for you." He held out the keys to her.

"What for?"

"For this." Spreading out his arm, he moved aside, pointing to a red, shining Porsche that was in their view. "Mr. Deverreau has provided a rental car for you, at his expense, of course. He knew you didn't have a car, and he knows how dangerous and inconvenient it can be for a lady to travel by public means. And he would like to escort you home himself every day, but his demands as a businessman make that impossible."

Dazedly, moving toward the car, Janelle shook her head. First the condo and now this. "I can't believe this." No one had ever been so thoughtful and considerate to her. Every time she turned around, Aaron was making her feel like a princess in a fairy tale. She had to do something for him.

"Ms. Sims, is it to your liking? Mr. Deverreau said if it's not, you can choose another."

"Oh, no, I don't want to choose another." She glided her hand over the sleek exterior. "This one is so nice, and this is so thoughtful of him. I was already on my way to his house to give him something. Now I can drive there."

With the documents in hand, Janelle practically ran up the elongated pathway leading to Aaron's front door. After pressing the bell, she turned back around to admire the Porsche. She'd parked it in viewing distance, in one of the estate's driveways. Gnawing on her lip from the excitement, she couldn't wait to thank Aaron for it. She couldn't wait to just see him. She hadn't stopped seeing him in her mind since last night.

"Can I help you?"

Janelle spun around to a stranger's soft voice. A young woman greeting her with a dimpled smile, and a yellow, clinging jumpsuit, obviously wasn't the maid.

Janelle ignored the downheartedness she felt at the sight of her, and smiled in return.

"Hello. I'm here to see Aaron. I have something to give him."

Nikki Richards glanced down at the packet, then raised her gaze to the very pretty face before her. Speculating if her relationship with Aaron was solely business, she informed her, "Aaron is upstairs taking a call. But you can come in and wait if you like." Nikki hoped she'd decline the offer. "We were about to have dinner. There's plenty if you would like to join us."

Janelle felt a sickness growing inside her, and she knew she shouldn't have. Aaron and she were friends and business associates. They hadn't committed themselves to each other romantically. They hadn't even kissed, because she wouldn't allow them. He didn't even know how much she liked him, because she was so afraid to admit it even to herself. Hence, there was no reason to feel like this. "Do you know how long he'll be?" she asked.

"No, I don't," Nikki answered, studying the woman's expression, detecting in it something that bothered her. "He's on a long-distance call." She glimpsed the package again. "I can give it to him if you like."

With the offer, Nikki peered across at her, sliding her scrutiny over the seductive slant of her eyes, and on down to the hourglass curves of her figure. Could Aaron resist such a woman if she wanted him, Nikki wondered. Was this woman the reason he hadn't made love to her yet? Or kissed her? Or tried to spend any time with her? Nikki had initiated every contact she had with Aaron.

Janelle was uneasy with the way Aaron's friend was staring at her. Reluctantly, she handed the packet to her. "Thank you. What is your name by the way?"

"Nikki Richards. And yours?"

"I'm Janelle Sims."

Inside the house, Nikki sat on the sofa, tossing the envelope aside. About ten minutes later, Aaron came down the steps.

"Sorry, I took so long," he apologized. He plopped in the chair across from her. "Business. Business. Always business."

"So you'll be even richer?" Smiling, she crossed her legs.

Aaron laughed. "If it happens, it happens. But I'm just having a good time. I love making deals."

"What else do you love?" Nikki uncrossed her legs and walked over to him. "If you're not going to sit next to me, I'm going to sit *on* you." She positioned her bottom to ease onto his lap.

Straightaway, Aaron stood, letting her plop down on the plush cushions of the chair.

"Nikki, I think we have different expectations for our friendship."

"Friendship?" Taking a deep breath, she sat back in the seat. "I thought we were heading for more."

"If I've done anything to make you think that, I'm really sorry. I don't like to play games with ladies' emotions."

"But all you had to do was say that you're not into me like I'm into you."

Aaron had said it. With his words and actions. More

than once, he told her their personalities weren't suited to each other. What's more, his actions were consistent with his words. He never called Nikki, unless he was returning her call. And other than showing her around after Chantel and Demarre's barbecue, he never accepted any of her invitations. As for tonight, she had stopped by unannounced, surprising him with dinner.

Showing Nikki around town that night wasn't easy. Nothing pleased her. As they dined at one of Phoenix's finest restaurants, she complained about everything from the food to the service to the prices to the decor. When they went to a movie, she chattered the entire time, childishly pointing out the physical imperfections of every character instead of grasping what the film was about. When they listened to music inside the car, she brought up only scandalous things she'd read about the recording artist's personal lives. When they returned to her place for drinks, lounging on her couch, she divulged personal and somewhat embarrassing information about her clients at the skin salon.

On the heels of that, she depressed Aaron with one negative statement after the other. There were stories about all the bad relationships she'd had. There were stories about all the family problems she'd had. There were stories about her money problems. There were stories about how jealous her employees were of her. There were stories about people who she couldn't stand. There were stories about people who she thought, thought they were better than her. There were stories about all the people who she'd get back for mistreating her.

Then there was her view of all the ills of the world. It came to the point when Aaron couldn't suffer through anymore. Remembering the phone call he was expecting from his son, he thought it was an excellent excuse to end the horrible date.

Now, many months later, Nikki was still making him miserable.

"Again, if I've done anything to lead you on," he told her, "then I apologize. I try not to do that to women. I wouldn't do anything to a woman that I wouldn't want a guy doing to my sister."

Nikki sighed. "Is it something that I did or said? Maybe we can start over. I do believe if you gave me a chance, you would really, *really* like me."

Aaron hated hurting her feelings, hated that she was making this so hard. Still, he had to be honest. "If it's not in me now, Nikki, it's not ever going to be there."

Nikki stood slowly. "I guess I'll leave now, and I'm not angry at you, Aaron. Really, I'm not. I can move on from here. Good night."

After he heard her car driving away, Aaron started to go back upstairs and relax. It had been a real long work day. A mysterious package laying on the sofa lured him in its direction. When he was on the phone upstairs, he thought he heard someone at the front door. Yet, he believed Nikki would have told him if someone had dropped by.

Aaron picked up the envelope. A smile brightened his handsome features when he opened it. The legal papers Janelle had to sign could have been given to him anytime. He smiled even broader, realizing she had just wanted to see him. He wanted to see her too. Bad. Talking and spending time with her had been so much fun. It simply added more credence to what he felt when he first saw her: there was something about her. He looked forward to learning much more about what that something was.

CHAPTER TEN

An aqua-blue Caribbean sea torpidly moving beneath
the sunset appeared like an artificially enhanced portrait
as Mitch lay on the beach in Bermuda. He wasn't alone.
Angelique Winthrop, the red-haired, slender beauty, who
was now his love interest, leaned her body against his. Her
satin-skinned hands and impeccably manicured fingers
clutched a small bowl of strawberries. She'd been feeding
them to Mitch.

No longer having the taste for the fruit, Mitch turned
over on his stomach, folded his arms beneath his chin and
peered out at the ocean. Life was weird sometimes, he
thought to himself. He was on an exotic vacation, a dreamy
island, accompanied by the kind of woman he felt was
deserving of a refined man like himself. So why was he
wondering what would it have been like to take this trip
with Janelle? Was it because she always expressed that going
to Bermuda was her dream vacation? Was that why he
chose this destination for Angelique and himself? To be
spiteful to Janelle? Mitch didn't understand himself anymore. He hated Janelle. She had deluded him so it sick-

ened him to even utter her name aloud. So why couldn't he get her out of his head?

Noticing that her new love didn't look as happy as she was to enjoy this day at the beach, Angelique placed the uneaten portion of strawberries aside on the blanket, laid on her stomach, then joined Mitch in perusing the sea. "Is something on your mind, Mitch?"

"Something like what?" He didn't look at her. The water seemed to fascinate him.

Angelique sighed, as a whiff of the ocean's fresh salty scent breezed by her. "I don't know. You tell me."

"There's nothing to tell."

"I hope you're being honest with me."

"I am."

"So we can go out tonight? We've been here a week and haven't done hardly anything at all. I'm dying to see what the night-life is like."

"I want to relax in our suite tonight."

Angelique sat up. "Mitch, why did you bring me here if you don't want to enjoy anything with me? We haven't gone anywhere except to this beach. And whenever I want to go sightseeing or shopping or to an entertainment event with you, you act like I'm asking you to cut off a leg. You just hand me a stack of money and pat me on the back, sending me off *alone*. That's not good enough. I came here to be with you. And not just in your bed."

Angelique marched off and far from Mitch, making deep footprints in the sand.

Shortly after, Mitch returned to the suite. Still clad in her red bikini, she was laying on the bed, facing a wall.

"I'm sorry," Mitch apologized.

She turned around to look at him. Distress marred her normally lineless, heart-shaped face. "Do you mean it, Mitch?"

"Yes, I do," he professed, maneuvering on the bed,

fingering the skinny red straps to her bikini top. For a moment a flash of Janelle laying beneath him, waiting for him to love her emerged in his mind. The sexy, innocent way she always looked up at him when he was preparing to love her always intensified his passion for her. It was only after their lovemaking that her gaze wasn't as appealing. That's when she would claim he had been consumed with his own pleasure, uncaring about hers. She claimed he never kissed her, caressed her, never cared if she was fulfilled.

During this vacation Mitch was determined for it to be different with Angelique. Each day her screeches of delight assured him he was doing everything possible to satisfy her. Tonight would be no different. He just hoped he wouldn't close his eyes and envision Janelle during their lovemaking. Not again.

But hours later, Mitch learned that he did more than fantasize about Janelle as he made love to Angelique. Awakening from a much-needed rest, he beheld her standing above him, fully dressed. Her luggage sat beside her.

Alarmed, he sat up quickly, looking from her somber expression to the stuffed suitcases. "Where are you going? To another hotel?"

"No," she said, dabbing at her red-rimmed eyes. "I'm going home, Mitch."

"Why? What did I do now? If it's about going out tonight, I will go with you all right."

"Don't you knock yourself out."

"What is wrong with you?"

"Nothing is wrong with me. I'm just tired of hearing that name."

"What name?"

"The one you called out a few days ago when we were making love. I tried to pretend I didn't hear it. That was foolish. Because you said it again last night."

Mitch disbelieved he could have done such a thing. A mistake as foolish as that, he would have known that he did it. "What name are you talking about? Maybe you thought you heard a name, but I was making some outcry of passion. What did I say?"

"*Janelle.* You never told me your ex-fiancé's name, but I would bet anything that, that what it is. Good bye Mitch. Guard your heart. I should have guarded mine . . . with you."

On a Saturday afternoon when the sun splashed over Philadelphia, Roxanne couldn't immerse herself in the resplendence of the summer day. She cared less about participating in any fun activities or visiting someone she cared about or indulging in something she relished, like listening to music or reading. Her interest was plotting how she could break up Mitch and Angelique.

Sprawled on her beloved chaise, Roxanne couldn't believe she was striving to disentangle Mitch from another romantic relationship. She couldn't understand why he didn't take her on the trip. For that matter, she couldn't understand why he wasn't showing signs of an attraction to her yet. Clearly, in her mind she was a goddess, who could work a spell on any man. So why not Mitch?

Didn't he want to avenge what Lawson had done to him? Furthermore, Roxanne had been the one who consoled him after his broken engagement. Not in the way she wanted to console him, but she had consoled him just the same.

She planned to change everything. Angelique wouldn't last too long with Mitch, Roxanne was sure. She had observed the super-nice, emotional temperament of Mitch's latest love interest. She seemed too needy for him. Mitch wasn't the type to cater to those types of needs and Roxanne would somehow point that out to him even further. No, they wouldn't last. She wouldn't let them. After all, she was victorious in ridding Mitch of Janelle.

"Why are you back so early?" Roxanne asked Mitch as he strode by her desk and into his office on Monday morning. He was supposed to be in Bermuda for at least two more weeks. She arose from her seat, hurrying behind him.

Mitch sat his briefcase on the side of his desk, then grimaced at all the messages in front of him. "It's a long story." He pored over the messages, then tossed them in the trash.

"What happened?" Roxanne feigned such sorrow in her voice. "Is Angelique all right? She didn't get hurt or anything, did she?"

Mitch took a deep annoyed breath. "She's all right physically, but I have no idea how she is mentally."

"Why do you say that?"

"She was disappointed in the trip."

"Aw, that's too bad."

"Anything you want to talk about?"

"No," he said, turning toward the window, but seeing nothing beyond it. "No, there isn't anything I want to talk about."

He didn't want to talk about Janelle. Mitch didn't even want to think about her. If only his mind would obey and do what he wanted.

CHAPTER ELEVEN

Janelle was pushing a bare dress rack to the opposite side of the boutique when one of its wheels detached from it, rolling underneath her foot. Down she started to go. Luckily, the steel-like body she fell backward against broke the fall. Muscular arms, sleeved in gray knit held snugly against her. At the same time, her rescuer's addictive spicy scent identified all too well who he was. Savagely, her heart began to pound, seeming to rip through her chest. Janelle knew it wasn't from the panic of the near mishap either. No, the excitement was that it felt so good for *him* to hold her.

"Easy," Aaron's voice stroked her. Standing behind her, he gently curved Janelle around, letting his hands rest delicately on her shoulders. "Let these guys around here do the dirty work." His glimpsed the workers. "That's what they're here for. And that's an order from your partner. Good thing I decided to stop by when I did."

"Sure was a good thing." Grateful he saved her from a bruised bottom, Janelle's lips curled entrancingly. In that same moment, she felt a tremor of warmth and had to remind herself of a vow not to be interested in him romantically. Sweet as he was, Aaron belonged to another woman. Most likely to another woman, and another woman too. Their relationship had to be based on business and a platonic friendship.

"I received the papers you dropped off the other day," he told her, still holding on to her shoulders.

"I thought you might need them right away."

Aaron noticed some uneasiness in her expression. "The young lady you left them with also rents a commercial property from my company."

"That's nice."

"We're just friends," he volunteered, then debated how she would construe that information.

Janelle refused to entertain why he was telling her this. "You didn't have to do what you did," she changed the subject. "You don't have to rent a car for me."

"We're partners." Unconsciously, he was lightly caressing her shoulders, until realizing what he was doing made him stop. Awkwardly, he lowered his hands to his sides. "I have to keep you safe and comfortable."

She glowed even more from the delicious way his hands had felt, and also because of his concern. "So how can I repay your generosity *again?*"

"It's my pleasure," he confessed, becoming more and more intoxicated by her smile. "No repayment necessary."

"Do you always rent expensive cars for your friends?"

"I'll do anything for someone I care about." His captivation raised to the brown eyes that he caught slyly glancing over his body.

Titillated by his stare and every other enticing thing about him, Janelle was aware of her heart again. So out of control it was, she forced herself away by turning toward the rack. "Could you help me with this?"

"No, I won't," he argued, grasping the cold metal, and telling himself he had to stop looking at her like that. For now, at least. *Go slow, Aaron.* "You relax and let me move it." One shove and Aaron had situated the rack across the room. "Now what else can I do?" he asked, again face-to-face with Janelle.

She had noticed him styling in sweats again, ice-gray ones. "So you didn't just stop by? You're here to help me again?"

"We have a paint job to finish."

"What about your business?"

Knowing he promised his secretary two days off for the headache of rescheduling two weeks of appointments, Aaron replied, "Don't worry about it. We're in business together too. I have an investment here."

"And you will get your money's worth," she assured. Afterward, Janelle picked up a can of paint, and a brush and began strolling over to the wall they tackled coating the other day. Walking behind her, Aaron truly enjoyed the design of her blue jeans. The pockets fascinated him.

Many hours later, a smidgen more of the wall was painted and Janelle was cracking up. Aaron was telling her one last hilarious tidbit from his high-school days. Despite the work taking place around them, all day they had laughed and talked about various subjects ranging from their dreams to past relationships with people they could now see shouldn't have been running around loose. However, Janelle was careful to avoid speaking of her last romantic entanglement. As for Aaron, he would mention his ex-wife, but wouldn't really talk about her. He would just have a hurt expression. Although, he could rave for hours about his son.

Janelle was again careful not to mention how destitute her family was and how her father deserted them. There was something painful about Aaron's childhood, which he avoided too. For him, it was as if dredging it up would make him relive it.

All in all, it was a wondrous day spent together, filled with laughter, insights, fun disputes. Surprisingly much more shared beliefs surfaced, especially on profound matters, which each held dear to their hearts, such as never giving up on their dreams, and never forgetting to hold out their hands to those in the trenches, who were striving to reach their purpose and simply be happy. For Janelle, those souls were the little girls and boys who were like she once was.

At times as they talked about those who struggled Aaron's sensitivity and warmth seemed so genuine, Janelle almost shared what she endured. Further proof of his understanding was a feature article she'd read about him the previous night in one of the Phoenix papers. He had given exorbitant sums of money to several schools.

Much the same, Aaron was enamored by empathetic qualities in Janelle. It made her even sexier to him. He couldn't stay away.

The next day, Aaron came to help her paint the wall again. The subsequent day he returned, and the next. By the time two weeks flew by, and they discovered the beauty outside, was a replica of the inside, each was addicted to the other's company. The craving thrived with each exposure to the other's mind and body. Even so, it was obvious to Aaron that Janelle still wasn't ready to succumb to the attraction they were undeniably feeling.

Each day during those two weeks, after spending hours in the boutique together, and feeling the high of getting to know someone who understood their innermost thoughts, Aaron would ask her to accompany him to dinner, or just let him show her the picturesque landscapes of Arizona. In extending the invitations, not the slightest amorous overtures would be made. Regardless, Janelle always declined. According to her, she had to hurry home and attend to the details of her designs for the boutique's grand opening. The date was fast approaching. She was so busy she couldn't breathe.

Hectic days being what they were, Janelle couldn't forget a promise she made to herself. Hence, one Sunday afternoon she found herself entering the towering wood doors of the Good Girls Of America Club, a group dedicated to inspiring young girls, fostering their talents, encouraging their education and keeping their spirits high.

"I must tell you that the majority of these young ladies come from destitute households," Karah Jamison, the organization's director explained to Janelle.

"Yes, I read about that," Janelle expressed, seated across from the woman whose gray hair didn't seem to match her youthful face.

"And the reason I'm telling you this, is because I want you to know that any donation you make will be so greatly appreciated, and put to excellent use. And you will learn where every penny goes. I'm so grateful you called us about the endowment."

"I'm glad I called too." Smiling, Janelle reached down in her purse, pulled out a check made out to the organization and handed it to Karah.

Karah's deep-set eyes came alive staring at the amount. "You are so generous. God bless you." She switched her gaze to Janelle. "And again, you will be given an account of every penny."

"I appreciate that."

"But may I ask you something personal, Ms. Sims?" Tightening her lips into a circle, Karah leaned forward.

The suddenly earnest expression made Janelle curious. She hoped a qualification to making a contribution wasn't having a pristine family background. She'd heard how some organizations did checking into a supporter's life history. "What do you want to know? Is it about my upbringing?"

Adamantly, Karah Jamison shook her head. "Oh, no, nothing like that. What I want to know is simply something that I always ask our benefactors: why are they making a donation to our cause? In the past, some have done it for purely tax purposes. Others have done it for public recognition. But I'm proud to say most have done it simply because they were led by their hearts. So I have to ask you, why are you doing it?''

Peering down in her lap, Janelle searched for the most honest words to communicate what was in her heart. Gazing back up, disheartenment showed in the curve of her smile. ''I'm doing it because I used to be like the little girls that belong to this organization. I was so impoverished, and I wish there had been an organization like this to make my life a little easier.

''I feel for these children, like no one else can, because I was one of them. What I give to them comes from my heart, Ms. Jamison. From my heart and no other place and for no other reason than to bring a little joy to their lives.''

Karah showed Janelle around the huge facility. There were various activities for the girls to do including computer classes, music classes, sports activities, tutoring programs and college preparation courses. Trips were additionally part of the program, ranging from local ones to those abroad. The girls were allowed in the building during after-school hours and all day on weekends. On this day, there were many girls engaged in an array of activities. Karah interrupted a dance class to introduce Janelle to three young ladies.

''This is Shaquora, Beverly and Gretchen,'' Karah said. ''Girls, this is Janelle Sims. She's the owner of a new dress boutique that's opening here in our fair city. And she's also one of our newest benefactors. She just donated a large sum of money so you girls can enjoy many more of the benefits of this organization.''

''Thank you,'' Shaquora and Beverly said in near unison. Afterward, they excitedly prattled with Janelle about making dresses. While she chatted with them, she noticed the other girl, the thinnest one, Gretchen stayed to herself. Not only that, but she looked like she was about to cry.

''What's wrong with Gretchen?'' Janelle asked Karah

later when they were alone and exploring more of the facility. "She looked like she was about to cry."

"She always looks like that," Karah told her.

"But why? Why would a young girl be so sad all the time like that?"

"Family problems," Karah replied. "Her dad left her and her mom. She can't get over it."

Pondering if her schedule would permit her to spend some time with those girls particularly Gretchen, Janelle left the building and strolled down the sun-drenched street. In speculating about this pledge of herself, Janelle knew that the boutique's opening would make spending the time impossible any time soon. Although, she would spend some time with the girls. Especially Gretchen. No one understood better than Janelle what she was suffering.

As she continued to stride down the quiet street decorated with large homes with manicured lawns and chic doctor's offices, Janelle's peaceful moment of contemplation was intruded upon by the roar of a motorcycle. One that was too close for comfort. She turned around and couldn't believe who was riding it.

"Out for a walk?" Aaron asked her. His black motorcycle slowed up to her pace.

Yet, she couldn't answer the question because she was too busy looking at the gorgeous creature clinging to him. "Who is this handsome little guy?"

The boy blushed, revealing tiny dimples. "I'm Kyree."

"This is my little man," Aaron gushed.

"And this is my *favorite* daddy," the boy added. "This is the nice one."

Janelle was intrigued by the child's statement. Though not so much so that she found it more interesting than looking at Aaron.

He reciprocated the look, capturing the brown highlights the sun exposed in her hair. "I would give you a ride, but as you can see my seat is loaded." He glanced over his shoulder at Kyree, then gazed at her.

"Yeah!" Kyree exclaimed, grinning at Janelle. "But you can ride next. Daddy will come back for you."

Janelle was amused, enjoying the closeness of the two. "It's nice to see a father so devoted to his child."

"I'm not doing that much. We're just riding."

"You're spending time with him. That's plenty. So many children don't have that. I—I just left an organization and—"

"You mean the girls' organization?"

"Yes. I gave them a little donation. Thanks to you I was able to do that."

Extremely impressed, he was in awe gazing at her.

"Why are you looking at me like that?" she asked.

"Just looking. You're wonderful, that's all."

Janelle chuckled. "You're the amazing one. You . . ." She stopped herself, noting Kyree nudging Aaron in the ribs.

"Daddy, I want to ride some more."

"Okay, okay," Aaron solaced him, then mingled his eyes with Janelle's. "I guess I have to catch you later."

"My nanny is coming to take me back," Kyree informed her. "We have to hurry."

Aaron nodded. "His nanny is coming to take him back home tonight. So we better get all the riding out of our systems."

"Yeah," Kyree added.

Aaron flashed her a lingering look, before taking off and soon fading from her sight. But not from her heart. The closeness and affection between Aaron and his son truly touched her heart.

CHAPTER TWELVE

Feeling invigorated from an exciting ride with Kyree and the excitement of running into Janelle, Aaron parked the motorcycle in front of the house and rushed into the house with Kyree. He was sure the nanny would be coming any minute now to pick his little man up. Aaron missed him already.

However, as he entered the house, his normally gleeful housekeeper greeted him with a worried look.

"What's wrong?" he asked her, hoping the lights were working properly. There were problems with the house's wiring lately. Aaron prayed that it wasn't too late to call an electrician.

It wasn't the wiring he soon learned as he entered the living room, smelling the lilac-scented perfume that was all too familiar. The housekeeper fled upstairs to attend to duties, while a pretty, honey-colored woman emerged from the sofa, approaching Aaron and her son.

"Mommy," Kyree squealed, swallowing Tess Haywood's slim waist in a giant embrace.

"Hi, sweetheart," her velvety clear voice welcomed her boy.

"Mommy, did you come to see Daddy?"

Her bare lips parted soundlessly with her confusion about what to say, even if her large, light brown eyes drifted across the room meeting Aaron's angry stare. "I—I came to see both of you, Kyree." Pausing, she exchanged gazes with Aaron. "Hello, Aaron."

"Hello," he returned stiffly.

Tess peered back down at Kyree, tangling her skinny fingers in the lush, black curls in his hair. "Go get ready, sweetie."

Kyree bent his head back, looking up at her. "Where's my nanny, Mommy?"

"She had to take care of her baby. Her son was sick so she couldn't come."

"But he's a big boy," Kyree declared. "He can take care of himself."

"Big boys need to be taken care of sometimes too. He was in a fight and he has a few wounds."

"Is he going to die? Did the person who beat him up try to kill him?"

"No, he's not going to die. And the person didn't try to kill him." Uncomfortably, she glanced at Aaron. His undying hostility forced her concern back to her son. "Now go get ready. We have a plane to catch."

Tess patted Kyree on the bottom. Both watched him speed up the stairs. When he was out of sight, awkwardly their eyes found each other.

"How are you, Aaron?" Tess asked, unsure if she should sit or stand. Nervously, she glanced at the couch.

Aaron folded his arms. "I'm fine."

"You look fine too." Weakly, she curled her lips, as if unsure if she should smile.

"You're looking well also."

"I hope you don't mind me coming here. But as I told, Kyree, the nanny couldn't come.

"It's okay," he heard himself say and almost didn't believe it. But the words came so naturally. Probably because there was something so different about her. More different than the simple flowered blouse and skirt she wore. Glamorous is how he used to describe Tess. "Sit down."

Tess shuffled across the room, tucking her long skirt neatly underneath her as she settled on the sofa. "I know the last person you expected to see today was me."

His countenance softening, he sat in a floral patterned chair opposite her. "You're right about that."

"I hope it's not too upsetting."

"Upsetting is not the word." Aaron kneaded the hair beneath his chin. "It just brings back memories I'd rather forget."

"I can understand that."

"Can you?" He took a deep breath, inhaling lilac.

"Yes, I can."

"Can you really?" His rich voice dwindled with the emotional way he abruptly felt. "How could you do *that* to me, Tess? Sometimes when I think about it, it's unbelievable. All I was doing, was trying to do everything I could to show you . . ."

"That you loved me?" Looking away and then back at him, she added, "You were just trying to make me happy."

"That's all I was doing."

"I know that now."

"I was trying to provide for my family, for our son."

"And I'm so grateful to you for loving Kyree the way you do. It's rare to find a man that will marry a woman with a child, and make the commitment and sacrifices to that child that you have made to Kyree. My heart just wells up when I think of how you treat him, not like your stepson, but your biological one."

"I couldn't help loving him. When I married you, he became my family too."

"And you're always there for him. I'm so grateful that you loved him and do love him like he's yours."

"Then why did you do what you did to me?" His voice raised, but realizing Kyree might hear, he subdued it. "Why did you do that to me, Tess? I couldn't have loved you and your child more. I couldn't have done anymore for you than I was doing."

Tears bundled in her large brown eyes. "I wasn't who I am now, Aaron. I was someone else that I don't even recognize these days. That woman I used to be is dead to me now. She was insecure and jealous. She didn't care that you were out working all the time to make our lives happy. She was just too consumed with what she thought you were doing to her—cheating."

Aaron lowered his head, and soon after gazed back up at her. "And I do take some blame for the relationship's decline. After all, a man shouldn't work all the time and neglect his family. But I told you how things were going to be when you insisted that we get married right away. You said you could deal with them being that way if it was temporary. And I assured you that my working all the time would be temporary."

"I know," she agreed, drying a droplet of water off her cheek with a handkerchief. "I know what you told me, but I wasn't listening. All I heard was my mind telling me you were cheating on me and I had to do something about it. I wasn't going to let you get away with it. So I . . ."

She couldn't even say it. She still couldn't perceive herself doing such a harrowing thing to a man who loved her and her child so dearly.

"Do you know what that did to me, Tess? Do you have any idea?"

"I know it hurt."

"It did more than hurt. For so long, I thought I was never going to fall in love again."

Tenderly, her eyes searched his. "But now you are in love?"

Suddenly thinking of Janelle, he felt a tug at his heart, but didn't answer.

Studying his expression, Tess nodded. "I can see you are, Aaron. It's all over you. I know we can never be together again. *Not that way*. But I want you to have someone who loves you. You're such a wonderful man. You deserve that. If you are in love with someone, she's such a lucky woman. I hope she'll never hurt you the way I did."

"I doubt anyone would do what you did to me. For God's sake, Tess, what were you thinking?"

"I was out of my mind with jealousy. And as I said before, Aaron, that was someone else who did that to you. Someone whose long gone. And she'll never return again. Because I have something in my life that I didn't have before."

"And what is that?" he said, beholding a softness drifting over her face. "What do you have now that you didn't have before?"

"God. I have God in my life."

"Chantel told me she ran into Tess yesterday," Demarre mentioned the next day as he sauntered in Aaron's office. Thrilled at the company's recent growth, he was carrying a report, which substantiated that success. Aaron and he were supposed to go over it.

"Yes, she was in town," Aaron confirmed, without the hostility that Demarre was accustomed to witnessing and hearing when his friend had any discussion about his ex-wife. Aaron was examining a paper his secretary had just typed. "I'll look at the report in one second."

"Take your time." Demarre pulled a chair in front of the desk, and sat reared back in it, studying Aaron. "So what's up?" He didn't understand this calm expression Aaron had. Matter of fact, he looked rather happy.

Aaron looked up. "What do you mean, what's up? Nothing's up. She came to pick up Kyree and that's that."

"That is not that." Demarre's lips formed an elusive smile. "Something is going on with you."

"No, it's not."

"Yes, it is." Grinning, he leaned forward. "Are you two getting back together?"

"No, but I think she's changed."

"Does that mean you like her again?" Demarre unfolded the computer printout they were supposed to go over. "Does that mean you love her again?"

"I'm trying to like her for Kyree's sake. I hold no grudges against Tess. I'm moving forward. It doesn't even matter to me anymore that she tried to . . ."

"To what?" Demarre frowned. "What did she do to you, man?"

"Nothing."

"You're lying."

"Marre, forget it, man. Whatever it was, it's forgotten now. That's what being truly happy does for you. Makes you forget all the crap people tried to do to you."

"So you're happy?" Demarre studied his friend. "Yes, you are. You have been walking around looking silly. It's that woman, isn't it?"

"What woman?"

"This business partner, Janelle, that you keep yapping about. That's why Tess can't get to you anymore. This woman is under your skin. That's why you're always humming. It's that mystery woman. I knew it was something."

Aaron chuckled. "She isn't a mystery woman."

"She is to me." Knowing Aaron was useless today, Demarre began folding the computer printout. "I've never seen her. You never introduced her to anyone."

"That's because we're not an item yet."

"You're dating. How much more of an item can that be?"

"Uh . . ." Aaron scratched his mustache. "We're not exactly dating yet."

"You aren't." Grinning, Demarre shook his head. "So

this is one of those things when you want to date, but she doesn't? This must be a first for the sexiest man alive."

Aaron balled up his fist, thrusting it at him. "Man, stop calling me that."

"I will," Demarre said with a laugh. "You're losing your touch."

"It's not about having a touch. I can tell she just . . . she just wants to take it slow. I think it might have to do with another relationship."

"Maybe you just don't ring her bells?" Demarre kidded him. "You ever thought that?"

"No, that's not it," Aaron said, visualizing the way Janelle sometimes looked at him. If he was certain of anything, it was that Janelle Sims wanted the same thing that he wanted from her—every drop of her heart and soul.

CHAPTER THIRTEEN

Janelle's doorbell was ringing incessantly one early afternoon. Since the refurbishment on the store was completed, she was unsure when she would see Aaron again. So it was a surprise to open the door and see him escorted by three strangers.

"Come with us to the fair?" were his first words.

"A fair?" Janelle echoed, showing shock at his unexpected visit. She looked beyond his shoulder at the people who beamed behind him.

"It'll be fun," he implored, knowing the only way to get her to go out with him was if others were around. He was certain that the closer they became, she was afraid to be with alone with him. "My friends here can vouch for that. We go every year."

"I'm Chantel," a stunning woman introduced herself, stepping forth. Chocolate-colored, and sporting an inch-long afro, she extended a French-manicured hand.

Smiling, Janelle shook it. "I'm Janelle."

Next, a husky bald guy came forth. "And I'm her husband Demarre."

"And I'm Brett," she heard, gaping up at a very tall, boyish, grinning face.

After the introductions, Janelle invited Aaron and his guests into the lavish condo she'd fallen in love with. Inside, lounging on her dark, floral couches, they talked, laughed and sipped on ice-cold sparkling cider. Finding Aaron's friends extremely likeable and feeling like she knew them much longer than she did, Janelle was quickly convinced she would deeply regret missing the fair.

Before long, Janelle was dressed in a white T-shirt, beige shorts and flat brown sandals. Along with the others, she climbed into a silver-blue van, which was flowing with oldies but goodies music. "My Girl" by the Temptations was the first song playing during their cruise down the sunshine-drenched highway. In near perfect harmony everyone sang, swaying their heads and bodies. Mountains, canyons, cacti and desert met them further toward their destination, drawing Janelle's attention out the window.

Singing lowly, and tapping her fingers, Janelle was enthralled by the picturesque landscapes flying by her. Aaron once told her that Arizona had the most beautiful scenery imaginable, and beholding it, she had to agree. But as she started to look across at the reverse window to see what splendor lay beyond it, she caught Aaron in her line of vision. Staring at his face, and now knowing there was a beautiful man inside, she knew undoubtedly where the most beautiful sight imaginable was. It was sitting right beside her.

In a strain hitting a high note of the ballad, Aaron frowned with his eyes closed. Janelle was amused at first, especially since he didn't see her looking—that is until the smile faded away because there was nothing funny about the warmth she began to feel inside.

Hours later, the warmth hadn't faded. Janelle was swept into the enchanted world of the fair. Aaron was enjoying every minute of it with her, having her for a partner to ride every thrilling and dangerous ride there was. A break only came when the men went to get some food.

Janelle and Chantel sat on a bench, exhausted from all the fun.

"I'm glad I came," Janelle admitted. "I would have missed all this. I've been working so much lately, I didn't know how much I needed a day like this. I'm tired, but it's a fun-tired."

"We did have a good time here," Chantel said with a smile. "And I am certainly glad I had a chance to meet you. I was beginning to think you weren't real."

"You were?" Janelle looked puzzled. "Why is that?"

"Because ever since you came to town Aaron can't stop talking about you. He says you were so smart and so talented and so ambitious and so deep and so super-fine."

"Really?" She contained the joy that wanted to burst through her face.

"Oh, yeah." Leaning toward Janelle, Chantel tapped her on the arm. "Now don't tell him I told you that."

"I won't."

"He's a wonderful man," she went on. "One of the best I've ever known."

Janelle could fully understand why she would say that. At the same time, she was tempted to ask her about all the women in Aaron's life. Something told her not to even before she saw Aaron, Demarre and Brett approaching.

After feasting on hot dogs, French fries, fruit punch and ice cream cones, most of the crew were re-energized for more rides. Aaron, however, was determined to show Janelle a special place a good distance away from the fair. Janelle didn't know how she let him talk her into leaving the others, and strolling to an uphill stretch of land, but once she arrived there, she knew why this place was so special to him.

Rows of lush cottonwood trees mingled with wild roses, yellow lupines and bright violets, forming a tunnel-like ambience, which led to greenery splashed with cascading turquoise waters. A small lake filled with swans sat underneath. As the yellow-orange of sunset cast over it all, Janelle felt like she was in paradise.

"Few people know about this place," Aaron said, standing behind her as she surveyed her surroundings.

"Why is that? It should be a tourist attraction."

"Because when I happened to luck up on it, I bought the land and kept it all to myself. Attendants take care of it and keep it this beautiful." With her back facing him, he was staring at her hair wanting to tangle his fingers through its silkiness.

"It's one of the most breathtaking places I have ever seen." She walked farther among the trees and plants looking up and around her.

Scratching at his mustache, Aaron walked behind her. "I come here all the time to think . . . and fantasize too."

"Fantasize?" The sexy way he spoke that word made her warm.

"Yes, about bringing a woman that I loved here, letting her see paradise and *feel* it."

Janelle swallowed the excitement in her throat. "I think we better go." She started walking off.

Aaron stepped in front of her. "What are you afraid of Janelle?"

"I'm not afraid of anything. I just think it's getting dark and we better go back. We don't want to get left." Her heart was racing.

"No." He shook his head. "There is something else you're afraid of."

"I'm not."

"You are."

"What could I be afraid of?"

"Of this." Burning his eyes into her vulnerable ones, he then let them slink down to her lips. Starved for them, his hands carefully held the sides of her face, and with his head bowed, he brought his lips toward hers.

The first press of their mouths, along with his arms

encircling her waist, mashing her body tightly to his, delivered Janelle into rapture she had never known. His probing lips seemed created for the sole purpose of erotically teasing open hers, making a torrent of desire flood her lower body.

Throwing her head back to receive more of the luscious gift, she held him tighter, and was further tantalized by his hardened excitement boring into her covered flesh. Knowing how much she turned him on, turned her on more. And with his appetite for her, she could hear his deepening breaths, matching her own. She could feel her heart's untamed rhythm making hers more untamed.

Tongue to tongue, she tasted fruit sweeter than any other. It swirled so pleasurably in her mouth, summoning feelings that made Janelle ache to have more of him. Her stroking hands slid up and down his back, triggering his to do the same to her until he dared to delve even lower. Cupping her buttocks, he slipped his tongue out of her mouth and kissed her neck slowly and tenderly.

Tossing her head back even farther, she loved the way he touched her. She loved the way his hand moved to the front of her. Closing her eyes, she squirmed with the need to feel him deep inside her.

She gently kissed his chest, his stomach, and when kneeling, heard him moan and felt a strong shudder as she began to unbuckle his pants. As Aaron eased her back against the ground, Janelle realized she was about to make love to a man who'd made no commitment to her—who she wasn't even dating. How many other women had fallen under his spell so easily and made love to him in this very place?

"I can't, Aaron," Janelle said, moving him off her. Once on her feet, she began straightening her clothes.

From the ground, Aaron looked up at her. He prayed she would reconsider. "Are you sure?"

"Yes," she snapped. "I don't want to be ..." She stopped herself from revealing what she truly felt. He would think she was jealous and insecure if she mentioned those other women.

"You don't want to be what?" He raised himself up so that they were face-to-face.

"I don't want to be involved with someone I'm doing business with."

"Are you sure that's what it is?" Aaron noted she was avoiding his eyes, a sure sign of lying in his opinion.

"Certainly." She wrapped a stray hair behind her ear.

He started buttoning his shirt. "I was kind of thinking that maybe you were afraid of getting involved because of your last relationship might have left you with a bitter taste for others."

Janelle almost laughed at that. Because her life was so happy lately, she hardly thought about Mitch. If only that was the problem. "No, it's not the other guy. It's—it's just that business partners like us should be friends and friends alone."

"We can't make ourselves be something we're not." He stared in her eyes, but she refused to meet his. She looked everywhere to avoid them. "We're already more than friends. Look at what just happened here."

"It was this place," Janelle argued. "It was so pretty and paradise-like, we couldn't help feeling that way."

"You're wrong. We can't help feeling this way, because we really enjoy each other. There was something between us from the first night we danced, and it isn't going away."

Wildly, Janelle shook her head. "No, you're wrong, Aaron. There is nothing there. And if you don't mind, please take me back where the others are, and let's forget this ever happened. And I promise it will never happen again."

"Sure," Aaron agreed, to taking her back to the others, but not to it never happening again. There was no way in the world it could not happen again. A kiss would never mean the same thing to him after kissing her. The feeling of ecstasy that surged through him was indescribable and

BUSINESS REPLY MAIL

FIRST-CLASS MAIL   PERMIT NO. 272   RED OAK, IA

POSTAGE WILL BE PAID BY ADDRESSEE

heart&soul

P O BOX 7423
RED OAK IA 51591-2423

WE HAVE 4 FREE BOOKS FOR YOU!

ARABESQUE

FREE BOOK CERTIFICATE

Yes! Please send me 4 *Arabesque* Contemporary Romances without cost or obligation, billing me just $1.50 to help cover postage and handling. I understand that each month, I will be able to preview 4 brand-new *Arabesque* Contemporary Romances FREE for 10 days. Then, if I decide to keep them, I will pay the money-saving preferred subscriber's price of just $16.00 for all 4...that's a savings of almost $4 off the publisher's price + $1.50 for shipping and handling. I may return any shipment within 10 days and owe nothing, and I may cancel this subscription at any time. My 4 FREE books will be mine to keep in any case.

Name _____

Address _____ Apt. _____

City _____ State _____ Zip _____

Telephone ( ) _____

Signature _____
(If under 18, parent or guardian must sign.)   AR0199

so addictive. What a woman, he thought. That fool who let her get away, was probably someone wishing he had one more chance with her.

Miles away and days later, Mitch sat restlessly at his desk, attempting to dictate a letter to Roxanne. When he forgot what he was going to say for the third time, he rubbed his hands over his eyes, and told her, "I think we're going to have to do this letter another time."

"But isn't it important?" Roxanne pointed out.

"Yes, but I . . ."

"You what?" She sat back, positioning herself so that he would notice the cleavage spilling out of her low-cut blouse.

Unfortunately for her, Mitch could only see that which his mind distracted him with. "I just can't get into it. I don't know what's wrong with me."

"Is there anything I can do?" She slid to the edge of her seat, then torpidly wet her lips with her tongue. "Just ask me, Mitch. I'd do anything. You've done so much for me."

Mitch shook his head. "There isn't anything you can do. I must be crazy but I just can't . . ."

"What? I know something's been on your mind. You made partner and everything and you don't seem happy."

Mitch sighed. "Oh, I might as well say it out loud. I can't stop thinking about Janelle. I can't stop wondering where she is and what she's doing."

"After what she did to you?"

"I know it's crazy. And I—I can't stop hearing her saying that she was only with Lawson one time and that he tricked her. But the letter . . ."

"The letter told the truth," Roxanne insisted. Leaning forward, she leveled her eyes at his. "You need time. And you need to relax. Here, let me help you do that." Roxanne laid her pen and pad aside, and before long stood above Mitch.

He looked uncomfortable when she started massaging his shoulders. Even so, he let her do so anyway.

"How does that feel?" she asked.

"Uh, uh, not bad."

CHAPTER
FOURTEEN

The magic of Janelle's dream finally coming true touched her heart as she gazed up at the sign with the inscription Janelle's Designs. Once inside the boutique, the euphoria surged throughout her again during an inspection of its surroundings. Rich, thick, fuschia-pink carpeting dusted with raspberry potpourri covered the main area, complimenting the pastel pink walls.

Portraits of African American heroines further enhanced the ambience. Company to it, were tastefully arranged bronzed shelves. The shelves were embellished with perfumes, bath oils, powders and flower-sculptured soaps. Nearby them were racks gracefully draped with the highest quality bags, scarves, belts and other accessories. Two velvet, hot pink chaises were more treats for patrons who wanted to relax.

A smaller suite was taken up by a dressing room. The other, equal in size, was comprised of state-of-the-art furnishings for the four seamstresses, which included computerized sewing machines. Amid all the luxury, there were

Janelle's exquisite designs, ranging from sportswear to evening gowns.

Janelle stood in the midst of it all, examining everything until she had to simply stop moving and thinking. At that point, she thanked God for this blessing. She couldn't wait for her mother and Sherry to come for a visit and see it. Who would have thought that poor, fatherless child from the Newark ghetto could accomplish this? *Daddy, I really didn't need you after all,* she whispered to herself.

Customers entering the boutique in hordes heightened the magical feeling that dawned with the day. All complimented her on the lovely clothing and the boutique's interior decorating and assured her they would return. By the end of the day her receipts exceeded her projections. For that, Janelle was extremely grateful.

Locking up for the day, setting the complex alarm system, she smiled from the bits of lingering excitement and hoped that, that something, which was seeping through the cracks of her joy all day would stay away. Keeping busy with the boutique, staying immersed in the high of it, had helped her fight it. Now that something was fighting full force to make her feel disheartened. It was winning. The something was Aaron's absence.

After showing her discontent with him nearly seducing her, they rode back home from the fair in silence. Demarre, Brett and Chantel constantly asked each one was something wrong and what had happened. Each denied there was a problem. Thinking back, Janelle wondered if she was too hard on him. Moreover, she knew the reason why she was. It was because he made her feel so good. Never had a kiss touched the essence of her, urging her to surrender her good sense and make love to a man who she had no commitment to.

It was the sweetest feeling she had ever known. If only he was hers and hers alone. That would have made all the difference in the world. So knowing that he wasn't, why was she still missing him so much? And why was she wondering what loving him would have been like?

She would never know, Janelle thought, as she finished setting the alarm and swerved around. Her heart jumped seeing Aaron leaning against his parked car, holding a bunch of red roses. They strolled toward each other.

"Hello, Janelle."

"Hello, Aaron."

"I—I wanted to come by today for your grand opening, but I . . . I didn't think you wanted to see me after what happened."

"I did want to see you. I wanted you to see what a success it was." She was fighting the yearning to feel his arms around her like they had been in that place—in that paradise. "And it couldn't have happened without you."

"I'm glad your first day was a success. And you're wrong. It was you that made it happen. It was your dream, your designs, your unstoppable will."

In contemplation, she looked aside, then gazed back up at him. "Can we start over? I think I was too hard on you yesterday."

"And I think I came on too strong. I'm sorry. It's just that . . . that . . ." He tried not to stare in her eyes to hold back all he wanted to say. For whatever reason, she wasn't ready to hear it. "These are for you." He handed her the flowers. "A little celebration gift."

Taken aback by their beauty, she accepted them. "These are so nice. Thank you, Aaron."

"You're very welcome."

"They made my day."

"I'm glad." He smiled, and again stopped himself from staring. "Are you headed home?"

Inhaling the refreshing scent of the roses, she nodded. "That's exactly where I was headed."

"How about a little dinner with me? A celebration dinner."

"I better head home."

"Sure. Another time then." Hiding his deep disappointment, he then looked beyond her toward the alarm. "I've been meaning to take a look at your security system. I want to make sure your big dream is protected. Can I?" He threw his head toward the alarm.

"Certainly."

Aaron moved past her to examine it. Watching him from a position that was behind but to the side of him, there was a sudden sadness about him that made Janelle feel guilty. What was the harm in dinner? They would be around others. Besides that, she craved his company like her lungs craved air.

"Aaron?"

He peered over his shoulder at her. "Yes?"

"Is a girl allowed to change her mind? I do want to have dinner with you."

From the side of his face, she saw his cheeks raising into a grin.

An array of seafoods was enjoyed with exhilarating conversation at the Mountainview Restaurant. With dessert's arrival, Aaron was reminiscing about a little speech he gave at Kwanzaa celebration about not letting your spirit become broken.

"Yanna told me you were really good," Janelle said, sticking her fork into a slice of pineapple cheesecake.

"I was glad everyone got something out of it. But at times, it was painful to talk about."

"Why is that?" She began chewing.

"Because it was personal. A teacher once tried to break my spirit."

"A teacher?"

"In elementary school. It was a private school, which consisted of mostly middle-class children. A very good school, too, which is why my parents believed I should attend there. Anyway, this teacher knew who my father was, and he made sure he let everyone know rich people weren't his friends. He always let the class know that in his opinion they were wasteful and shallow.

"He always found fault in the slightest thing I did. Always embarrassed me in front of the class. And whenever we had essays, he loved that. Because that's when he could give me the lowest grade possible, because grading essays can be so subjective. Otherwise, he knew I would excel on any other exam. As we approached our graduation date, he told me something one day after the class left. It really stuck with me.

" 'You're a rich boy, and you're never going to amount to nothing, because everything has always been handed to you. You're going to fall on your face out there in that world.' "

Frowning at the pain this teacher could still bring to Aaron's handsome face, Janelle hated this stranger. "How could he be so cruel to a child?"

"He was cruel all right," Aaron went on. "Not long after I learned he had a big problem. I represented all that he wanted so deeply, but believed he could never have. So he was angry, spiteful, jealous. But sometimes you can learn from your enemies as well as your friends. You can take their rage toward you and turn it into a positive for yourself.

"I learned from that teacher, that no matter what, I wasn't going to be what he said. I was not going to be *nothing*. I was going to stand on my own—and stand tall on my own. And I did. I went on to high school working my butt off. Went on to college and grad school, working my butt off. Went on to open one of the most successful realty development firms in the country, and I did that working my butt off, and I'm still doing it.

"Yes, my dad paid for my college tuition, but the rest I did on my own. I got a job upon graduation and saved, then paid for grad school myself. After that, I did a dynamite business plan, put up some of my money that I saved and started my business.

"And the thing about it is, while I was doing all that,

and while I am doing what I'm doing, I'm really having a good time. I enjoy my work immensely. So I can honestly say that although I may have wanted to show that teacher something, I really accomplished what I did on my will. With my own determined spirit. I didn't have to prove a thing to anyone but myself. Don't let anyone ever break your spirit, Janelle. Promise me that." Trying to forget how her lips tasted, he watched them trembling.

"I promise." But she was trembling because the story had touched her so. It also made her aware that the more time she spent with Aaron, the more they seemed to have in common. It all made her so comfortable with him. Exciting as he made her sexually, he also made her feel warmth, and like he truly understood her down to her soul. Before she knew anything, she heard herself revealing, "A situation tried to break my spirit."

"What happened?" He leaned forward.

"When I was a child I was very poor." She couldn't believe she was telling him this. Yet, there was something about him that put her at such ease. "Some days we didn't even have food. Some days my clothes were so worn the children teased me. Some days I didn't know if I would have a home to live in, or would be out somewhere on the street."

Seeing her beautiful features masked with sorrow, Aaron was shocked hearing this. She always talked about such fun in her childhood, he never would have believed there was such pain. He wanted to know the circumstances. How did her parents allow things to get so bad? However, he didn't want to pry. He hoped she would tell him on her own.

"But I made it out," she exclaimed her face brightening with a smile. "I survived. And I didn't let hi—" She stopped herself. One subject she wasn't ready to talk about was her father.

"You're a strong woman, Janelle," Aaron complimented her. He wanted to say a beautiful one also—one who he wanted to hold and kiss her pain away. He wanted to give her love so pleasurable, it would make up for all the pain in her life.

Feeling as if she might get too emotional and discuss her father, Janelle changed the subject. Before long, they were discussing dreams, God, money, fake friends verses real friends and so many areas, which showed them how much they had in common. Sometimes when one was talking, the other felt like they had opened their soul and taken the feelings from it.

This time they shared together was emitted such a high, it was hard to drag themselves down to the low moments, like when two women Aaron knew stopped by the table to say hello and were obviously flirting with him. Dampening everything also, was seeing Nikki Richards, Aaron's so-called friend. She stopped at the table, said hello to Aaron and Janelle, updated him on the success of her skin-care salon, and then went on her way.

Her innocent behavior even made Janelle believe she was just a friend as Aaron claimed. However, when Janelle saw her in the ladies' room, a few moments later, her behavior was odd. Both were looking in the mirror, touching up their makeup, when Janelle complimented her on her lipstick shade. Not saying a word back, Nikki looked over at her and harshly rolled her eyes.

Seated back at the table with Aaron, Janelle was still wondering about Nikki's hostility. However, she was determined not to let it spoil her night. She was beginning to see that she had misjudged him. As warm and wonderful as he was, he was beginning to seem like he could be faithful too.

"I had a great time with you," Aaron said at Janelle's doorstep.

"Me too. But I always have lots of fun with you."

"Hey, the same with me," he said, glancing at her lips,

but willing his eyes back up to her eyes. But there, too, he felt unsafe. He was so tempted to kiss her, to stare at her, to feel her like he had that day in paradise.

Looking at him, and not wanting to give up his company just yet, Janelle offered, "Would you like to come in for a little while?"

He was pleasantly shocked. "I'd love that."

Inside, Janelle put on a CD filled with love ballads, then went into the bedroom to kick off her pumps and rest her bag. While she was out of the living room, Aaron browsed her video collection, her books, trinkets, browsing until he noticed a familiar sculpture.

He was holding the African inspired piece when she returned. "Did you get his from Yanna's shop?"

"Actually, she gave me one, which I display in the shop," Janelle said, coming over by him. "And I loved it so much I bought another for home. Isn't it nice?"

"Yes, I have one just like it. She gave me one too. Do you know the story behind the Princess Iasia?"

"Not really. I know she was a real African princess, but that's about it."

"Yes, that's true she was a real African princess. She had everything so it seemed. Money, beauty, the love and respect of her tribe. Yet as much as she had to be happy about, she wasn't. She came to her grandmother one day, the wisest woman she knew, and she told her about something that was troubling her. She had no love in her life. Love from a man she loved. Yes, there were men waiting in line to give her their hearts, but there wasn't anyone who she felt was really born on this earth to love her. So her grandmother told her she shouldn't be sad.

"She told her she was a good woman, a good person and that one day that goodness would be rewarded with love. She said that one day, she would look into a stranger's eyes, but he wouldn't be a stranger at all. Those would be the eyes of the one who would touch her heart and soul, like she never knew it could be touched before. There would be something unexplainable about him that would draw her to him.

"And when she learned who he was, she would see that he was a reflection of her soul and their hearts would fit together as one and there would be joy in her like she never dreamed was possible. And one day, true enough, Iasia did look into the stranger's eyes, and sure enough, they both knew they weren't strangers at all. They both knew they were part of each other."

No longer able to control his actions, Aaron stared in Janelle's eyes revealing all his raging heart couldn't contain.

Staring back at him just as desperately, Janelle could also feel her raging heart.

"Aaron I know how that princess feels."

"And I know how that stranger feels," he said in a lowered voice. "I know how both of them feel, because when I first saw you, when I first looked in your eyes, I felt something I had never felt before. There was something connecting me to you. I can't even describe it fully."

Janelle nodded. "I know what you mean. I felt it too. I'm always feeling it."

"Do you feel it now?" Whispering, he was bringing his face close to hers.

"Yes," she acquiesced, not moving away. "And I want to feel more. I want to feel you."

The sensual invitation made Aaron's breaths erratic. "Are you sure?"

"Yes. I want you," she said, telling herself there was no other woman in his life. How could there be when she could feel all that was so deeply between them? "I want to make love to you. I have never felt so . . ."

"I know." He bent his head, gazing at her lips. "There aren't words for it."

Aaron's mouth soon captured hers, hungrily seeking its sweetness, beckoning their arms around each other. A hoarse, virile intake of breath escaped between them. Harder his lips crushed hers, with his body obeying the same will of desire. Surrendering to the ocean of longing for him that flowed down inside her, Janelle held him tighter as well. His rigid masculinity prodded so forcefully into her, arousing her so, she couldn't get enough of his lips.

An interlacing of her fingers over the back of his neck enabled her to draw his mouth deeper into hers. His body shuddered at her inflamed tongue tasting his lips before thrusting beyond them to his nectar inside. His breaths grew louder. His kisses more demanding at the pleasure her untamed tongue was lavishing on him. He couldn't get enough of it. He couldn't feel enough of the erotic madness surging through him, awakening him to feelings that he'd never ever known.

Out of breath, Aaron raised his lips from hers and in a passion-drowned voice begged, "Please let me inside you. Please Janelle." His half-closed eyes slipped down her body. "Let me love you."

Looking up at him, caressing the sides of his handsome face, she nodded. "I want to love you too. I want to make you feel like you're in heaven."

Effortlessly picking her up, Aaron carried her down the hall and into her bedroom. Like she was breakable crystal, she was laid on the bed while he stood above her. His eyes never leaving hers, he removed his jacket and afterward his tie and shirt.

Shimmering muscles and a broad, dark chest whipped her heart into a frenzy. Her arms couldn't wait to feel him as he eased on top of the bed. Eagerly, as he embraced her, it was clear he couldn't wait to feel her again either.

Simply enjoying a strong embrace for a moment, they

soon couldn't resist each other's lips again. Dazed in the unbelievable bliss, Aaron's fingers soon found themselves below the V neckline of her blouse. Excitement caught in a breath in his throat at the delight of discovering she was braless. Squeezing an erect bud between his fingertips, he kissed her even deeper, before freeing her completely of the silken fabric.

"You're so beautiful," he moaned, his hands becoming bolder, covering her huge mounds as much as they could.

Throwing her head back and arching her back for him to feel them better, Janelle wondered if it was possible for him to make her more turned on than she already was. She was bursting with ecstasy. Bursting with erotic sensations she had never known. Fortunately for her, when his head lowered to her chest, she was acutely aware there was more to come.

Caress after caress, and taste after taste of her breasts, catapulted her over that cliff where she ached with the desire to feel him so deep inside her. Pleasuring her more, he tugged her skirt beyond her ankles, his fingertips grazing her shapely legs as he did. After tossing it aside, he then retraced his movements, stopping at her hips. Her panties were soon shed too.

Kissing each one of her thighs inside and out, she couldn't wait when he kissed, touched and played with her moist femininity, making her scream for his love. Freeing him of pants and shorts as urgently as she did, rendered him no doubts of what she wanted.

Their naked skin felt like one as he climbed on top of her. Gazing in her eyes, he uttered, "I won't ever hurt you, Janelle. I just want to make you happy."

"I want to make you happy, Aaron."

He reached down below his hips lifting his throbbing hard love, easing it inside her.

"Umm," she panted, as he moved gently and slowly, the sweet feeling of him absorbing her in its heat.

"Oh, you feel so good," he cried, before his lips found hers.

Kissing her deeply, he moved his hips with wilder and wilder erotic motion. The more he felt her, the clearer it was that his millions of fantasies about her couldn't compare to what she was making him feel. It was a moment so pleasurable it seemed he had lived his whole entire life for it.

Eager to return the joy he was filling her with, Janelle swayed her hips with all the emotion she felt inside. Never in her life had lovemaking been so unforgettable. It was almost unreal, it felt so good. The way he moved, the way he looked at her, the way they felt so perfect together, the way they held and touched, it was as if each was the most precious gift to enter the other's life. She never wanted it to end.

Before long, it was impossible to hold on to the bliss that screamed to free itself. Kissing her even more savagely, Aaron finally let go of the agonizing joy he couldn't hold on to any longer. His dramatic tremors matched hers as they reached that highest plateau of love. Afterward, he planted kisses along her forehead, while putting his arms around her so snugly, Janelle never wanted him to let go.

Well after midnight when all the candles and lights were off in the room, Janelle was awakened from a nap by covers being pulled off her and soft kisses being caressed over her already warm body. "Oh, Aaron," she moaned, feeling the sweetness of his lips stroking over her body. "Oh, Aaron, that feels so good."

"You taste so good," he groaned breathlessly through his kisses. "I just had to have you again. Your body was made for mine."

He delighted her from her toes to her thighs, torpidly

loving her with his mouth, until his hands joined in. A shudder fired through her as he touched her thighs, kissing them, separating them with his fingertips and gently probing her inner warmth.

"Oh," she moaned again, raising her hips as his fondling raised her desire to a fever pitch. "Oh," she screamed again, as his eager fingertips traveled higher with his kisses, meeting her stomach, ribs and taut breasts.

Circling his tongue around her sensitive nipples, Aaron soon was thrilled by her hands all over him, especially what so greatly throbbed for her love.

"Don't stop touching me," he groaned, dividing his kisses between her breasts, neck and lips. "Don't stop loving me."

"I won't, baby," she said, gazing in his eyes, then closing her own as she grasped his back, then slid her hands down to his buttocks. Squeezing them, she became more and more turned on, craving to do much more to him.

Aching for her to do more to him, Aaron soon turned over on his back. Janelle straddled herself on top of him. Feeding him the succulence of her breasts, she rubbed his muscular arms as they tried to reach around her. Loving him further, she eased lower, her lips massaging into his broad, hairy chest and lower to his rippling stomach, and far lower to where his love was ready.

Sliding her soft hands over it, she heard him cry out in that tone that told her what she was doing was unbearably pleasurable. Over and over and over she titillated him, until her own desire was reaching the brink of hysteria. Easing up higher so that their lips met in a deep, lingering kiss, Janelle took his love and led it deep inside her.

Rocking her hips slowly against his, Janelle knew nothing felt more pleasurable than his delicious movement within her. The rush of sensual fire it sent through her couldn't be fully described. It could only be felt as he sped and deepened his strokes. Shivers of delight coursed through her blood, exploding in her lower body, raising her hips higher to meet the increasingly erotic dance of his. Also deepening his tongue's thrust against hers, Aaron squeezed and played with her buttocks, which only heightened her joy. But soon both of them were at the mercy of the height of ecstasy that erupted, flinging their exhausted bodies apart.

Awake from a heavenly, much needed sleep, Janelle uncurled herself from Aaron's embrace to turn on the lamplight. Her own personal waterfall was ordering her to go to the bathroom. After staring at how gorgeous Aaron was even when sleeping, and re-creating the sweet love he made to her, feeling so high from it all, she stood and felt nature urging her to answer its call. Clumsiness stalled her when her fingers brushed his jacket, knocking it off the vanity seat it had been slung across. Papers scattered along the carpet. Quickly picking up receipts and business cards, Janelle couldn't help noticing a folded paper that opened on its own. It was a check. It was made out to a Tess Haywood. The sum was exorbitant. As for the memo, it read: love gift. It was dated the previous day.

Struggling to open his eyes the next morning, Aaron felt sunlight on his face. But unable to forget what truly warmed him, his lips curled mischievously and he reached his hand across the bed. The firmness of the mattress was all he touched.

"Janelle?" he called. When she didn't answer, he flung his legs over the side of the bed. Soon he entered all the other rooms in the condo. She wasn't in any of them.

"Where is she?"

A note he spotted on the dresser may have had the answer. Snatching it up, he read:

Dear Aaron,

I have to take care of some things and will be out all day.
The front door will automatically lock when you close it.

Janelle

Aaron pored over the short note again to ensure that
he hadn't missed something. Where was the line, *Aaron,*
I can't tell you how much last night meant to me? And the one,
Aaron, I can't wait to be with you again. The same hot-blooded
seductress who had made him feel sensations he never had
before couldn't possibly have been the same creature who
wrote these few bland words. Passion would have blazed
in her every syllable. In fact, she wouldn't even have written
anything. The fact being, there wouldn't have been any
need to. The woman he made love with last night wouldn't
have left. She would have desired to make love all day, just
as he craved to. Something wasn't right with this picture.
It all made him feel strange.

The unwanted sensation intensified in leaving her home
and going about his day. Not knowing her whereabouts
left him at a loss to call her. On the other hand, he did
expect her to phone him. How could she not after what
they shared?

During the evening, he continued waiting to answer a
ringing phone with her luscious voice on the other end.
Though, when his phone hadn't rung by midnight, he
called her. There were four rings before the answering
machine triggered. After leaving a message, he hung up
wondering.

Why hadn't she called him? What had he done? Or was
he making too much over nothing? Perhaps, this aloofness
was simply her style. Perhaps it was her way of protecting
herself after having been in a relationship that went sour.

Hours later, worry managed to let him sneak in some
sleep. Dreams came soon after. At first there was Janelle's
sultry image. Her deliciously naked body was coming
toward him. Beyond turned on, he was going toward her

too. But to his astonishment, exactly as he was about to touch her, she vanished. Replacing her was a giant-size gun. Closer it came, so close its blast sounded like an explosion. Straightaway, Aaron sat up in bed drenched with perspiration. Someone was trying to kill him in his dream. It was like déjà vu.

CHAPTER FIFTEEN

It was the most precious gift of Janelle's life—making love to Aaron. Lounging across her sofa, that was the thought blurring the pages of the fashion magazine she attempted to browse through. Now she understood that feeling Sherry always spoke of. That passionate feeling only that special man—your soul mate could give you. It didn't derive from merely making love either. No.

Aaron gave her that feeling when they were in each other's company, or even when she merely thought about him. She had never felt so connected to any man sexually, mentally and spiritually. The joy he filled her with during their many intimate acts during the night and when he held her so tenderly after was so wonderful, she wanted time to stop. If Janelle hadn't known better, she would have even believed she was falling in love.

That couldn't be, she told herself, as she put the magazine aside, and walked over to the window. Raindrops were pelting against the awning, their dreariness matching the way she felt. She couldn't be in love, because it was too painful to admit after knowing she had been such a fool.

That Tess Haywood, who he wrote out a check to, a love gift, had to be someone important to him. Other than her, Nikki's attitude in the ladies' room, proved she was involved with him too. No doubt there were countless others. Although Janelle did wonder when he had time to spend time with them. He was always hanging around her.

Why had she fallen under his spell? Because he had mastered his game, Janelle answered herself. He was just like her father, a charming, sweet, funny, dazzling womanizer whose good looks attracted women in droves. Except, Aaron was probably worse, because he had wealth. He was able to wine them and dine them in the finest.

No more, Janelle told herself. No more being the fool. No, they hadn't made any commitments, but it seemed as if they were becoming close. That kind of close when the chemistry was so intense it promised you were all the man or woman your lover needed, without them even having to state so.

How could she have been so wrong? It all filled her with an ache that rendered her no relief. When she woke it was there. When she laid down at night it was there. When she went about her day it was there. It was there precisely as that feeling like she was falling in love was. No matter what it took, she would make the ache go away.

Janelle had avoided Aaron since their romantic encounter. She hadn't returned his calls, and had stayed home, leaving one of the seamstresses to run the boutique. She hadn't even went out the door. She couldn't see him now. She was too hurt.

The phone ringing roused her from her musings. After hearing that the voice leaving a message wasn't Aaron, she snatched up the receiver.

"Hi, Chantal," Janelle answered.

"So you are home."

"Just screening my calls."

"Is that so?" She paused, as if contemplating to ask her

why. "Must be so working on those fabulous dresses that you can't take a break?"

"Ah . . . yes. But I'm never too busy for you. What's going on?"

"Something fun. I went by the boutique to tell you about it personally, but you obviously weren't there. So I thought I'd try you at home. I wanted to invite you to my and Demarre's networking party on Saturday night. It's an annual thing we do. We call it our summer sizzler."

Anywhere where Aaron was apt to be was out of the question. "I don't think I can make it," she replied.

"You too? Aw, that's too bad. Aaron can't make it either. He's going to be out of town on Saturday."

"He is?" In her mind, Janelle asked where was he going and who with.

"He's going to be out of town on business," Chantal went on. "But I was really hoping you could come. Some friends of mine are going to be there, and two of them are getting married, and I told them about your boutique and that you design all the beautiful clothes in it. So they were interested in talking to you about designing both of their bridal parties."

That sounded exciting to her. What's more, Aaron wasn't coming. "You know, on second thought maybe I will come. It'll be good for me to get out and get dressed up. What time does it start?"

Dressed in an eggshell mini dress with matching high-heeled sandals, Janelle arrived at the packed event about a half hour later than it started. In considering that she would be courting potential customers of two bridal parties, she wanted to wear one of her most awesome designs. Far too much time was wasted trying to select it. Ultimately, she decided not to dress to impress, but wear what she felt good in.

Chantal introduced her to the two women getting married. Moments later, they had scheduled an appointment with Janelle to see her designs and some fashion sketches of wedding gowns. She was grateful for the potential business. Yet, even with a smile plastered across her face, she couldn't lull the ache inside. When she caught sight of the terrace, she knew it was where she needed to be. There she could be alone to sulk.

Clutching the railing, she looked out over the skyline, before shutting her eyes tight. Why had she been such a fool? Why couldn't Aaron have just been a beautiful man, who wanted one woman—and that woman was her?

"Janelle?" The sensuous manly voice, cushioned with a touch on her shoulder, opened her eyes and spun her around.

Gorgeous, but somehow sad, Aaron stood before her.

"What are you doing here?" Janelle asked, her brows knitting together. "Chantel said you were going to be out of town on business."

"I told her to tell you that."

"You what?" she shot.

"It was the only way I could see you. You've been avoiding me and I have a right to know why."

She swerved back around to the skyline. "I haven't been avoiding you. I've just been busy."

He stepped close behind her. "You're lying."

"Why would I lie?" She felt his palms easing on the sides of her arms. God, why did everything he do to her have to feel so good?

"Because you're hiding something, Janelle. You've been hiding something since you've been here. And I want to know what it is."

"Aaron, we had a good time, and it's over. Let it go. You got what you wanted, like you got with all the others." The last words slipped out.

"What did you say?"

"Nothing. Go."

"No." He curved her around. Staring in her eyes, he had proof she was lying. Amid their sadness, they were almost crying that she still wanted him—wanted him as much as he wanted her. "You said something about others. There are no others."

"Stop! Just stop it!" She didn't want to ever appear insecure, possessive, and jealous, but somehow he was forcing it out of her. "I saw that check to Tess Haywood that night I was with you. It fell out of your jacket pocket. I saw that it said love gift on it."

Aaron half smiled, half frowned. "It was a love gift."

"So there is another?"

"Yes, my son."

"I don't understand."

"Tess Haywood is my ex-wife, who lives in Ohio. I send my son a monthly check to her. I call it a love gift, because it is a gift, and that's better for me taxwise to say that it is. I'm not obligated to take care of Kyree by law because he's my stepson."

"Your stepson!"

"Yes."

"Kyree isn't your child?"

"Not biologically. He has a father. A no-good one. But I couldn't be anymore connected to him if he was mine."

This was amazing to her. "Oh, my God. And you take care of him?"

"Yes, I do. When we divorced, we shared nothing, including financial responsibility for him. The courts located his father and has made him pay child support."

"So you're—you're just doing this on your own?" She was frowning from the astonishment of this. "You mean to tell me, you're just taking care of this child when you really don't have to?"

"When you love someone, you'll do anything for them." He paused, staring in her eyes. "I didn't have anything to do with his birth. But those years that I spent with him and his mother, I took my responsibility as his stepfather very seriously. I wish he was my own, but since that's impossible, I'll love him like he is."

"Oh, God." Janelle felt tears coming to her eyes. Not

wanting him to see them, she turned away. "I'm sorry. I seriously misjudged you." She tried to wipe the tears away before he curved her around.

When he saw them, his eyes narrowed. "Why are you crying like this? What is it?"

"It's me. Selfishly, the story just reminded me of my life."

"How so?"

"You're right, Aaron. There are things I haven't told you. I haven't told you about *him.*"

"Who? The last man you were seeing?"

"No. My father."

With tears streaming down her cheeks, and with Aaron constantly wiping them away, she proceeded to tell him about her father's desertion, his womanizing, and how it affected her. He snuggled her head to his chest when she finished.

"It's over Janelle. It's all over. Look at how magnificent you are all on your own. You don't need him. Let him fade in the past."

"Most of the time, I think I have. But at a moment like this, it's all stirred up again. All the pain. Seeing a good man like you taking care of a child that isn't even his, just makes me think about why he left me and my brothers and sisters without even a penny to buy a piece of candy."

With his fingertips, Aaron raised her chin to gaze in her beautiful face. "Remember the promise you made to me the other night?"

"The promise?"

"About not letting anyone break your spirit?"

"Yes, of course."

"Remember it when you think of him. And also remember it when you think of me. I'm not like him."

She pulled back, staring up at him in surprise. "What do you mean?" She hadn't told him she thought he was a womanizer like her dad.

"I know you were projecting your father's womanizing

on me. You mentioned others. And believe me, I've heard that before. From my ex-wife to be more to the point. She thought I was cheating on her too."

"It's your looks, Aaron. You're such an incredibly beautiful man." She searched his handsome face. "Women are always after the pretty ones. Ones like . . ."

"Like your dad."

"Yes. He was a heart-stopper, just like you. Everywhere he went women were throwing themselves shamelessly, and he couldn't resist."

"I'm not your dad. And what if I thought that way. You're a drop-dead gorgeous woman. One glance in the mirror and that's pretty clear to you. I see how men look at you. I know guys come on to you like gangbusters, but I don't think you're bedding everyone."

"Because you're a man. Men and women are different. Women are accustomed to being pursued. Men aren't, so when they are, they abuse it."

Aaron was tickled. "That's crazy."

He made Janelle smile too. "But it's true."

"It's not. You have to judge us men as individuals. Why do women think like that?" The amusement gone from his face, he took a deep breath and looked over the terrace. "I'm so tired of being found guilty when I'm innocent."

The look and his words brought Janelle back to something he brought up earlier. "You said before that your ex thought you were cheating on her."

"She sure did." He was still gazing off the terrace. "It ended our marriage."

"Just because she accused you of cheating?"

"No, not because of just accusing me. Because of what she decided to do about what she was accusing me of. It was what she *did*."

"And what was that?"

CHAPTER SIXTEEN

Aaron looked off to one side of the terrace, then the other, seeming to grapple with whatever it was he wanted to say.

"Aaron, what did she do?"

Finally, Aaron met her eyes again. He took a deep breath, then unburied the words that he'd never uttered to anyone, but himself. "She hired someone to kill me."

Wanting more seclusion to reveal his greatest pain, Aaron suggested they walk along the grounds far away from everyone.

"I was working a lot," he started explaining as they walked. "Building my business and trying to give her everything. She had made a pretty comfortable life for herself as a successful chemist. But I wanted to give her more from me.

"I loved her. We had met at a tennis party and I was smitten. Our marriage was very happy, and she cherished the fact that I truly loved Kyree. She said that was rare for a man to love another man's child so much.

"But all that appreciation went out the window, when she didn't believe how hard I was working. She noticed how women flirted with me and she never thought I was firm enough in telling them to back off. Then somehow things in her mind became twisted when I had some high-profile business deals with some high-profile women. The press was always after us, publishing our pictures in the papers and such. And I was always working and working. She started accusing me of having affairs. It was so bad that for one whole week I stayed in a hotel. I couldn't take the arguing, and I knew it wasn't good for Kyree to be in that hostile environment. I wanted us both to get some breathing room.

"But the night I came back, no one was home. So I went to bed, and when I woke it wasn't because daylight had woke me. It was because the cold barrel of a gun was mashed into my face."

"Oh, my God."

"I pleaded with the guy not to shoot. Did all the sweet-talking I could. And lucky for me, this guy had a conscience. He even told me that if I didn't tell he tried to kill him, he would go to the police and say Tess hired him to kill me.

"Anyway, when Tess returned expecting me to be dead, and for it to look like a burglar had done it, I was waiting for her. I had sent her friend off with the gun he stuck in my face, facing his. And I told her how evil she was. And how much I wanted to send her to prison for what she did. I could have easily gotten the guy's testimony if I made him believe she was turning him in. But something was making me think about Kyree. It wasn't fair for him to grow up without his mother. Despite how wicked she had become, Tess was a good mother to him. And I knew how it was to grow up without a mother."

"You did?"

"Yes, because my mom was sick for most of my childhood. She had very bad diabetes. She was always being hospitalized. I missed her so much. Luckily, her condition didn't worsen and as time went on, there were medicines that better controlled it and today my mom is traveling with my dad. I didn't want Kyree to grow up without his mother."

"So you let a woman who tried to kill you go free?"

"Sometimes in life you have to make hard decisions, Janelle. Kyree loves his mother like nothing else in this world. He would die if he wasn't with her. He would die knowing she was in prison. It was either let Kyree grow up motherless, or my feeling satisfied that she's behind bars. There was no choice for me."

Later on, in Aaron's bedroom, Janelle felt as though she awaited a king to emerge from his bathroom. Laying across his silken sheets, clad in a black lace teddy, she couldn't wait to feel him moving so deliciously within her again. Knowing he was such a man of integrity, made her desire him even more. God knows, she was blessed. The belief was confirmed when he emerged from the bathroom. Aaron wasn't wearing anything. Not even a towel. Most conspicuous, he was ready. *Really ready.* He was so beautiful she ached to kiss him, touch him, have him. *Oh, yes,* she thought as he came toward her, his eyes intense with erotic promises that she knew his body could keep.

Oh, yes, she thought again as he melted inside her, and she heard the groaning whisper, "I love you."

The warmth of love wasn't what exuded between Mitch and several business people as they sat in Hart's Restaurant. The last time he was in these surroundings, he had met with his fraternity brother, Aaron. They had talked some business, but mostly of pleasure. In comparison, Mitch found no pleasure in trying to negotiate a new contract for his company. He had been wining and dining the executives for days and couldn't wait to settle things.

Excusing himself for a jaunt to the men's room while

the executives reread some documents presented to them, Mitch was walking by the bar when he spotted a familiar face. It was George Patterson, his brother Lawson's best friend. Coincidentally, Mitch had been meaning to call him. He had some questions that George may have had the answers to.

"How are you, George?" Mitch asked, sliding on to the bar stool next to him.

George knew Mitch didn't like him, plausibly because George was an alcoholic. He flashed a mouth full of uneven teeth anyway. He wasn't one to hold grudges. "How you doing, Mitch?"

"Great. Great. I guess we both miss my brother."

"I know I do." George sipped his drink, gazing off into his memories. "Your brother was the best."

"Yes," Mitch concurred, but really disagreed. "I was wondering if you could give me some information?"

"Like what?" George looked over at Mitch.

"Like something my brother might have told you."

"Like what?"

"Like about my ex-fiancée, Janelle."

Straightaway, there was uneasiness in George's face that made him peer down at his drink. "What do you want to know?"

"Did Lawson tell you anything about them?"

"Lawson told me a lot of things. He was my main man." He was still focused on his vodka.

"Did he tell you they . . . they were having an affair?"

George shifted his position on the stool. "The dead should rest in peace," he said, still not meeting Mitch's gaze.

"I want peace more than anything, George. I want peace for my brother."

George met his harsh stare. "What are you talking about?"

"I broke up with her because I found out she slept with

my brother. She said it was *once* because he tricked her. He was pretending to be me. Is she lying on my brother?"

George looked away. "Ask her, man."

"I told you what she said."

"I'm not the one who should be telling you."

"Is she lying? Is she lying on my brother? Was she having an affair with him, or did he trick her into sleeping with him once by pretending he was me? I have to know George."

Undecided about what to do, George rubbed the patchy hairs on his chin. Repeated deep breaths followed as he thought. Patience never being his virtue, Mitch reached in his pants pocket. He groped until he reached his wallet. A hundred-dollar bill was removed and slid along the bar in front of George.

Showing surprise, but no hesitancy, George tucked the money in his shirt's breast pocket. Swiveling his stool toward Mitch, he met his eyes once again. "She was telling the truth. He did trick her. But not with malice to neither of you. He just loved her so. He loved her so bad and he wanted to show her how much." He paused, thinking back. "He was so hurt by her reaction, too, when she realized he wasn't you. She claimed she hated him and wished he was dead. He told me about it. Later that night, he died too. But he just wasn't thinking when he did it. Love had him out of his mind. He just wasn't thinking."

CHAPTER
SEVENTEEN

I love you were three words Janelle heard often as the days passed and she shared them impassionately with Aaron. The words were also the confession she ardently returned to him. From deep in her heart, they came from her, laced with passion, warmth, excitement, tenderness and so many more beautiful emotions too profound to interpret with verbal expression. Like it was the compensation for every wrong that had ever been done to her, the love Aaron filled her with made life a beautiful dream.

They spent every moment they could together loving, laughing, attending entertaining events and even shopping a great deal. Anything her heart desired, Aaron was happy to grant to her. There were even gifts she didn't expect, such as making her the owner of the Porsche she drove, along with the condominium, and the property for the boutique. Aaron was so generous to her with everything he had, especially his love. If only Nikki Richards hadn't tried to turn it all into a nightmare.

She had come into the boutique one afternoon, unresponsive to Janelle's greeting as she strode through the door. Instead, with her nose twisted, Nikki maneuvered throughout the dresses and accessories, occasionally picking up an item only to practically toss it back on the rack.

Vying to be pleasant regardless of Nikki's ill mood, Janelle strolled over to her.

"Hi, Nikki. Are you looking for anything special?"

Nikki glared at Janelle a moment, then jerked her head back to the rack. She picked out a brown knit ankle length dress trimmed with chiffon sleeves. It was shoved toward Janelle. "Do you have this in a leopard print?"

"No, we don't," Janelle answered. "Just what you see. But we do make special orders. We can have this style made in a leopard print."

Nikki didn't respond to that. Wordlessly, she stirred about the boutique, coming to a standstill at a lavender evening gown. Almost violently, she stretched it toward Janelle. "Do you have this one in royal blue?"

"No, but we can also have that made in the color you like."

Nikki twisted her lips sourly, before sashaying toward the purses. A red leather one captured her attention. She slid it off the hanger. Following that, she scrutinized it inside and out. "Do you have this one with a longer strap?" she asked.

"No, we don't," Janelle responded, wishing she would go. By now she knew Nikki didn't want anything, except to annoy her.

Nikki continued to browse. Fed up with her, Janelle attended to other customers and other tasks. In the midst of arranging a scarf around a mannequin's neck, she felt a presence behind her. Instinctively, she knew who it was.

"Your dresses are really not to my taste," Nikki informed her.

So, get out of here, Janelle almost said. Though, she couldn't be rude to a customer. "I hope you find what you want elsewhere," she suggested instead, her back to

Nikki. She was still tinkering with the scarf. "I'm sorry we didn't have whatever it was here."

"I'm sorry too," Nikki added. There was an edge of sarcasm in her voice.

Janelle noted the tone, but continued fiddling with the scarf.

"I'm so sorry about Aaron."

Bewilderment weakened Janelle into turning around. "What about Aaron?"

"You really have no idea what he's doing . . . to you?"

Don't let this woman get you upset, Janelle appeased herself. It was obvious Nikki was envious of her relationship with Aaron. Evidence of that was revealed earlier in the week when Janelle and Aaron saw Nikki at a nightclub. She walked right by them and pretended not to see either.

"What is Aaron supposedly doing to me?" Janelle indulged her.

"Supposedly?" Nikki let out a squirt of a laugh. "Aaron is cheating on you, Ms. Glamour Girl."

"Nikki, I'm sorry Aaron rejected you, but—"

"Is that what he told you?" Her question was laced with rage. Stretching her eyes, she shook her head. "My, my, my, his lies are getting a wee bit pathological. I was the one who told him that I wasn't interested in him as a lover!"

Right, Janelle thought, while elaborating, "Aaron didn't have to tell me anything. Look at you. Look at how you're in here bothering me right now. That in itself proves how hurt you are about something. If you didn't care about him, why would you even waste your precious time like this saying these ugly things about him?"

"Because I want you to know what a fool you're being," Nikki bickered. "You're thinking you have him all to yourself, but you don't. He's playing on you. Playing hard. And if you don't believe it, ask him where he was last Friday night."

Janelle's cool demeanor hid how much her memory

was suddenly working. The previous Friday night Aaron worked late. Real late. She had waited up all night for him. He had come to her house minutes before sunrise.

Armed with a composed expression, she refused to let Nikki see the speculation her accusation provoked. "Nikki, will you leave please."

With a smirk, Nikki folded her arms and reared back. "Afraid of the answer. Well, I'll tell you. He was over at my place. He came over there, pretending to be all friendly, so I said okay you can come in. And for a while, he did pretend like he just wanted to talk all friendly like. But after that, he was all over me. You have no idea how I had to fight him off. I thought I was going to have to call the cops. He was acting like he had never seen a beautiful woman before. He was practically attacking me, telling me you weren't enough for him—and I was."

Shaking her head, Janelle was vying to maintain composure in her voice and appearance. Inside of her wasn't holding up as well. Unfortunately, her memory was working far more. The reason being, she recalled how uneasy Aaron looked when he explained his lateness. For only a second, she had felt insecure, questioning whether he was telling the truth. Moments later, she realized she was misjudging him again. And she refused to misjudge him now. "You're lying," Janelle declared.

Nikki's dimples pinched her cheeks, her lips curling in a crooked grin. "No, Aaron is the one who's going to lie to you."

With that prediction, Nikki slung her slender hips wildly out the door.

"Boy, do I have a surprise for you, good-looking," Aaron raved. He was wearing a mile-wide grin as Janelle entered his house that night for the date they had planned.

Flashing him a weak smile, Janelle soon felt herself being

ushered into the dining room. Once there, she beheld a feast of Italian delicacies garnishing the table.

"This is nice," she commented, nonchalantly.

"I remembered your saying lasagna is your favorite," Aaron gushed and pulled out her chair. After making sure she was cozy, he went around to the other side of the table and moved his seat forward. Noticing a candle had blown out, he relit it. But with the candle glowing again, he looked over at her. Really looked at her. In this light her silky dark skin and exotic slanted eyes, made her look as beautiful as ever. It was the somberness, however, which didn't fit with the picture. Her face aimed downward toward her lap, making her appear faraway. "What's wrong with you, Janelle?"

Awakened by the question, she looked up at him. "Where were you last Friday night?"

Knowing exactly where he was, Aaron looked off trying to think quickly. He didn't want to leave out things again. On the other hand, knowing how hard it was for her to trust, he feared her not believing the truth if he told it. "I told you I was working. Why do you ask?"

"Are you sure you were working?"

"Yes, I was," he answered, looking warily. "Why are you asking me this?"

"Because . . . Nikki came in the shop."

At that revelation, Aaron took a deep breath. "Oh, brother."

"Oh, brother what?"

"I can imagine what she told you." He took another breath.

"How do you know she told me anything?"

"Okay, Janelle, let me explain. There is something I didn't tell you."

The words were all the impetus she needed to bolt into the living room. Aaron caught her arm before she opened the front door.

"Let go of me," she insisted.

"Listen to me, Janelle."

"What for? So you can lie?" She jerked his hand off her. "She said you would."

Aaron reared back, his nostrils suddenly flaring with anger. "Are you going to believe that woman over me? Someone you don't even know?"

"Obviously there is something you didn't tell me. You said so. I can only imagine what it is."

"Will you give me a chance?"

"For what? To make a fool of me again?"

"I've never made a fool of you. Yes, I didn't tell you something. I didn't tell you what happened after I left work last Friday. Demarre and Chantel are also friends of Nikki. During the day, Demarre told me her mother passed away. So before I left work, which really was at a late hour, I remembered to call her and give my condolences. It was then that she started crying about her mom and asked me to come over. Said she was very depressed about it and thinking of taking some pills, possibly even to end her own life.

"So feeling sorry for the woman I went over there. And we did talk for a while, and I was trying to tell her why her mother would want her to go on. Then she got out of hand, way out of hand, and she tried to seduce me. I didn't tell you because you had this thing about men, quote unquote, like me and other women."

When he finished, Janelle just looked at him. Everything about him, from the way he looked at her, to his hand trembling like it couldn't resist touching her, spoke that he was telling the truth. At the same time, she needed some proof.

Aaron's face unexpectedly filling with more anger showed he wasn't about to give it.

"Look, Janelle, I love you more than I have ever loved any woman. I get up in the morning thinking about ways I can make you happy. I go to sleep thinking about how I can do it. I think about you all the time. In the short time, we've been together, you couldn't be no more deeper in my heart than if I had known you fifty years. But all that means nothing if you can't trust me. Good night. You can see yourself out.''

Not hanging around for her response, he hurried up the stairs. Shortly after, she heard the slam of his bedroom door. Whirling in the aftermath of his touching words, guilt started gnawing at her. How could she believe this man was cheating on her when he had become so much a part of her life? Sometimes she felt like she was breathing him.

She was always thinking about him when she wasn't around him. And when they weren't together, each could easily contact the other by phone or beeper. Aaron had assured her to call him anytime. He was always where he said he would be. What's more, on the occasions where she had to beep him, he always returned her call immediately. And look at all he'd done for her, given her? There were so many other things telling her this man could be trusted. Truths that soon overshadowed her projecting her father's bad habits onto him. Because as much as she hated to admit it, that's what she was doing.

Seconds later, she quietly entered Aaron's bedroom. ''Aaron?'' she called.

Standing in front of the window, gazing out into the dark, he didn't answer her.

She walked up close behind him. ''Aaron, I'm sorry. I was acting so silly. I was just confusing you with my father. It's not fair to you, and I'm not going to do it again. I love you so much. I don't want nasty things to come between us. I want to forget it. I won't ever mention Nikki again or pay attention to her. I know she's just jealous because she can't have your love. I hope I still have it. If you still want me, I'll do anything to make it up to you.''

CHAPTER EIGHTEEN

She waited for him to say something or turn around. When he did neither, Janelle panicked. A retracing of her steps and her hand was grasping the doorknob. No sooner than it touched, however, it untouched. In a breath, Aaron grabbed her, reeling her into his arms, and face-to-face with him. "Of course, I still want you. I'm partly to blame for this fight we're having. I should have told you. But I was just so afraid of what just happened. Do you realize this is our first argument?"

A timid smile cracked through her somber expression. "Yes. It was a biggie."

"Yes, it was." Aaron stared in her eyes, then dropped his heated gaze to her lips. "Can I make it up to you . . . in a very pleasurable way?" His voice grew hoarse with his longing.

Her hands slid up the sides of his muscular arms. "Do anything you want to me tonight."

"Don't tell me that." He was still obsessed with her mouth.

"Why?" she asked, her warm breath shivering along his neck, as she planted an upward trail of cotton-soft kisses.

Succumbing to the sweet feeling, Aaron closed his eyes. "Because anything might take all night. There's so much I want to do to you." Slowly, he opened his passion-glazed eyes. They lingered on her face, before his mouth sought the pleasing honey of her lips. Kissing them gently, then more forcefully, his hands unbuttoned her blouse quickly. He freed her of her bra, skirt and panties even quicker. All the while, Janelle was doing the same undressing trick to him. He cried out with joy when she gripped his throbbing hard love, sliding her hand around its length and thickness.

Soon lying on the bed, one of her breasts was covered by his mouth, while he squeezed her buttocks so erotically, Janelle couldn't help whimpering from the joy. He soon drowned her lips with more potent kisses, as he proceeded lower in delighting her stomach, teasing the flesh with maddening circles, and then delving lower to coiled hairs that led to the tight threshold of her love.

Stroking around her tiny bud that led to heaven for him, her pleasured moans urged him to bring his fingers inside. Caress after caress and her wild reaction to it, made him want to do more to please her. She raised her hips up from the agonizing joy, but he soon met her with a deep thrust of himself. Biting her lips from the unbearable joy, she was also treated to the taste of his tongue meeting with hers, pulsating wildly like the rhythm of his dance of love.

Losing her mind from the ecstasy that now shook her like her body had no control, Janelle held tight to Aaron. His pleasured moans and the quickening of his luscious movements, followed by convulsive motions revealed he was feeling the same. Then much too soon, it was all over, with the unutterably blissful feeling summoning their bodies to do it over and over and over. They didn't stop until well after sunrise.

Breathing heavily, Aaron brought her head to his chest and put his arms around her.

"Oh, I love you. And not because you can drive me crazy. But I just love you, Janelle."

Out of her exhaustion, she raised her head and smiled. "I love you too. And not just because we . . ." She laughed thinking of the right word.

He couldn't help smiling too. "I know just what you're thinking, we . . . we have a lot of *nature* when it comes to each other."

Both laughed.

Playing with the rugged hairs on his chest, Janelle felt as dreamy as she looked to him. "To think I almost missed out on all this." He didn't know it, but she was referring to a loveless life with Mitch.

"We just have to be determined not to let anything, or *anyone* separate us."

"We won't." She pecked his lips.

"And speaking of separating, I'm going to have to separate from you beautiful lady for a few days."

"Oh, no." Her heart sank. "Business?"

"No, my little man. I took him to this basketball camp last year and we're going again this weekend."

"A whole weekend without you?" she said playfully. "What on earth will I do?"

"Think about me every second I hope." He kissed her cheek.

"Will it be just the two of you going?"

"Well, my brother and his kids came last year, but they can't make it this year. And Brett is going to hold down the fort at the office here in Phoenix, but Demarre and his son are going to hang out with Kyree and myself. So you won't be the only lonely lady around here. Chantel can keep you company."

* * *

Camp Newhauser set on a grassy hill in Atlanta, Georgia was a basketball lover's dream. There were lessons on basketball, basketball practice, basketball contests and simply basketball twenty four hours of the day.

After solely three exhausting days, Aaron and Demarre found themselves sitting on the sidelines watching kids play instead of playing themselves.

"Man, I thought you were about to go pro," Demarre teased Aaron. "Look at you sitting here tired."

"You're sitting right with me," Aaron joked.

"Because I'm just humoring you."

"Yeah, right."

"I am."

"Well both of us must be getting old in our young age." Aaron snickered.

"Maybe you're using your energy for other activities?" Demarre nudged him on the arm.

"Are you trying to get in my business?" Aaron asked with a smile. "I'm not telling you about my baby. A gentleman never tells."

Demarre sucked his tooth. "The so-called gentleman I'm looking at doesn't have to. I can see what you've been doing. It's all over you. You're just smiling all the time. You have a new bounce to your walk too."

Aaron was tickled. "Cut it out, man. You're embarrassing me."

"No, seriously," Demarre went on, the amusement fading from his face. "It's nice to see you so happy. I'm glad you found a beautiful young lady after a broken marriage. And Janelle is very easy on the eyes and she's real cool people too."

"She is the best. I lo—"

Demarre's son racing over to his father and Aaron with a frantic expression halted his words.

"It's Kyree!" the boy yelled between deep breaths. "He's

in the basketball court in the back! He fell! This guy pushed him, trying to steal the ball and Kyree fell backwards and hit his head on the concrete! And he won't get up! And he won't wake up!''

Aaron, Tess, Demarre and Demarre Jr. stood outside Kyree's hospital room as the doctor approached them from the other end of the hall.

"So far he seems all right," Dr. Davidson informed them, sliding his glasses higher from the middle. "The impact of the fall made him unconscious for a few moments. But all our tests show no damage."

"Thank God," Tess declared.

"But why is he sleeping like that?" Aaron asked. He peeked in the room at the motionless boy, then addressed the doctor. "He hasn't woke up since we came here. That was five hours ago."

"Oh, the nurse didn't tell you," the doctor stated. "I apologize for that. He did wake up, when he was in the examining room with me. I've just given him a sedative so he can rest. That's why he's still sleeping."

"Oh," Aaron remarked. "Whoa, that was close."

"It was," the doctor agreed again sliding his glasses up by the middle. "But like the lady said, thank God he's all right. I'd just like to keep him overnight for observation."

"Thank you, Doctor," Tess said.

"Yes, thank you," Aaron added.

"You're all welcome," the doctor said. Shortly after, he headed in the direction where he'd come from.

Tess and Aaron were expressing their grateful sentiments and Demarre had just sent his boy off to the candy machine, when he looked up the hall and spotted an unexpected sight. Uncomfortably, he glanced at Tess, before calling to Aaron. "Aaron, look." He pointed up the hall.

Janelle was hurrying toward them. Aaron met her halfway, giving her a big hug. Looking on, Tess faintly smiled.

After Aaron updated her on the good news about Kyree, they walked toward Tess and Demarre.

"Hello," she spoke to Demarre, then smiled at Tess. "Hello, I'm Janelle. It's nice to meet you. Your son is so beautiful."

"Thank you," Tess returned with a smile. "I'm Tess. Thank you for coming."

"Oh, when Aaron called me and told me what happened, I had to come. Your son means everything to him."

Tess nodded. "I know."

When Tess and Janelle both mentioned wanting snacks, but neither felt like trampling through the huge hospital to get any, Aaron volunteered to get some munchies from the cafeteria. He asked Demarre to accompany him. Demarre wanted to take the stairs.

"So are you crazy man?" Demarre asked, stepping down the secluded stairwell.

"No more crazier than you are."

"No, seriously, Aaron. You called your girlfriend to come to the hospital where your ex-wife is. You better expect a serious showdown."

"No way," Aaron said, stepping around a corner to the next staircase. "Everything is cool."

"That's what you think. They were all nice in front of us, but wait until they get alone. There's going to be some hair pulling up there."

"You're wrong."

"I'm right. And I'm also really surprised you called Janelle. I knew you two were getting close. But *that close?*"

"Yes, we are close."

"How close?"

"I love her."

Janelle lounged in the tiny, waiting area with Tess and three other visitors. When the three visitors were called out by a nurse, leaving the two alone, Janelle felt awkward.

On one hand, she disliked Tess for what she'd done to Aaron. On the other hand, she didn't seem at all like the sort of woman to commit murder.

"I know Aaron must have told you about me," Tess spoke unexpectedly through a silence.

She glided by several chairs to sit next to Janelle.

Janelle sighed. "Yes, he did tell me about you."

Tess's bare lips half smiled. "Guess you must be thinking I'm crazy for hiring someone to kill him?"

"I have been wondering how you could do something like that," Janelle said, looking at her. Her pretty, delicate features and modest style of dress made her look more like a school teacher than a killer.

"I've been wondering the same thing myself," she divulged, her hands fumbling nervously around each other. "It seems like so long ago. And it seems like that wasn't even me that did that. Sometimes I wonder who that woman was."

"So you're saying you've changed?" Janelle swerved in her chair to view her better.

"Totally. I'm somebody else now. I have God in my life."

"Can't have a better person than Him in your life," Janelle agreed.

"No, I can't. But back then I was so screwed up. I loved Aaron so much it made me crazy. He was and still is the most beautiful man I've ever seen."

"Yes, he is one of the most beautiful creatures I've ever seen," Janelle concurred, and couldn't help scrutinizing Aaron's ex. Did she want him back?

"But I see him as only a friend now," Tess admitted. "But back then . . . back then I thought my gorgeous husband was playing around on me. Plus, I had all these friends encouraging that wicked thought. 'Don't trust a man that looks that good,' they used to tell me. It just goaded on all that jealousy that was pent up in me. So when he was working all the time, I thought he was working on women's bodies. Too late, I found out I was wrong. The man was just trying to give me and my son the world."

"Didn't you think you would go to jail after doing something like that?" Looking at her, Janelle still found it hard to believe she would have done such a thing. "Or did you truly think you would get away with it?"

"My insanity had it all reasoned out. I would have Aaron killed and go right on with my life. Go right on with it, with the satisfaction that I had gotten him back for cheating on me. What a fool I was."

"Well at least you did come to your senses."

"And don't you lose yours," Tess warned Janelle. "Don't ever not trust Aaron. That truly hurts him more than anything."

Underneath the moonlight, Janelle encircled her warm, silky arms around Aaron's waist. They stood near the bannister on the terrace of a cozy suite in Atlanta's Crystal Plaza hotel, peering out over the exhilarating nightlife of the sleepless city. From the high altitude of the suite, the sounds of the city's bustling activity was lost in the distance and much quiet surrounded them. It fit perfectly with Aaron's introspective mood, as he caressed Janelle's soft hands clasped together in front of him.

"What are you thinking, baby?" she asked. She curved her head around his shoulder so that it rested against his cheek.

"About what happened."

"He's going to be fine. You heard the doctor say that." She clasped her arms around his waist tighter and planted a kiss on the side of his face. "And he's going home tomorrow."

"And I'm so glad for that." His caress of her hand grew to a powerful grip. "I could have lost him."

"But you didn't."

"I don't know what I would have done if that would have happened."

"It didn't happen."

He eased around, facing her. Her exotically beautiful eyes always captivated him, but in the moonlight tonight, they didn't look real. They were something of a fantasy, a dream, and maybe he had dreamed her. "Thank you for coming. You're incredible."

Perusing the breathtaking portrait that was his face, she held it by the sides. "I wouldn't be anywhere else at a time when you needed me so much."

"Life is so short, Janelle. That's what this experience has taught me. It's short and we have to make the most of it. We have to cherish the good times and hold on to them as if they might pass away. We have to hold on to all the sweetness." His finger glided torpidly across her lips.

Feeling her body's need for him, she stared in his eyes, while accepting his finger in her mouth. "We have to be thankful for those things that are so good in this life." She was whispering.

His eyes never leaving hers, Aaron nodded. "You're good." His gliding finger, wound down from her lips and stroked her neck. "You feel so good."

Closing her eyes, she tossed her head back, aching for him to touch more. "I haven't felt . . . His finger sliding down past her neck, nearing her full breasts made her whimper. Before long, her blouse was unbuttoned, her bra removed, and the sweet stroke of his fingertips on her nipples made her struggle to speak words instead of moans of her delight. "I haven't . . . I haven't felt you in so long."

"I know, baby," he said, playing with her nipples. "I know." He bent his head, pressing his lips against them.

"Oh, Aaron," she moaned, anxiously raising the T-shirt he was wearing, until her hands roamed madly over his broad, hairy chest. "I want to feel you."

He lifted the shirt over his head, and returned to what he found so delicious. Swirling his tongue around her nipples, he soon ventured further to the fullness of her large breasts. "I want to be inside you, Janelle. I need you tonight."

"I need you tonight."

A blanket was spread on the terrace. Gently, Janelle was laid on her back. Afterward, Aaron leaned over.

Kissing her lips, her neck and her breasts again, he proceeded to kiss her skirt, hosiery and panties away. Raising back up to simply admire her beauty, she again didn't look real.

"I can't believe you're mine." His tongue thrust past her lips, tasting her nectar until both of them craved for air. Breathlessly, he raised up again, staring at her again. "You're so beautiful. I just want to do everything to you. Everything and anything to make you happy. Can I make you happy? Can I make you so happy tonight?"

"Yes," she said, fumbling with the elastic of his sweat pants. Sliding them past his hips, she was soon delighted to behold his firm love for her.

"Do you want it, Janelle?"

"Oh, yes," she said, stroking him, easing off his under-pants.

Closing his eyes and frowning, he moaned, "Now. I want to be inside you now."

"Give it to me, Aaron. Give it to me now."

With his head thrown back, and his palms flattened against the blanket, Aaron felt her hands guiding himself to her moist love.

"Yes," he cried, simply savoring the pleasurable heat of her before swaying his hips gently. "That's it. Oh, baby you feel so good. Nothing feels this good."

His mouth soon crushing against hers hungrily, Aaron sped up his thrusts. Overcome by the taste of his honeyed tongue, Janelle met his feverish grind into her love with a provocative sway of her limbs that soon made him quiver. Her own desire mounted. Her lower body felt a rush of sensations so pleasurable, she couldn't get enough of them. Her seductively wavering hips only beckoned for more.

Aaron cupped her buttocks, deepening his movements and kisses. Then moving his mouth over all of her face, he carried it lower to her breasts again. Sucking, licking, tasting them, he heard her whimpers growing. With each taste, he pounded his love harder, soon hearing her screams fill the air. Never had anything felt so good. It seemed that each time he made love to the woman he loved, he soared to new heights of ecstasy.

Wanting to give as good as she received, Janelle also couldn't help deepening her kisses and thrashing her hips wilder.

"Don't stop," Aaron cried. "Oh, don't stop."

But the love was too good, soon transporting them to such bliss it couldn't be held on to any longer. Each uttered, "I love you," as they let go.

CHAPTER NINETEEN

The morning sun blazed against Mitch's skin as he jogged around Fairmount Park for the fifth time. He was hoping the run would relieve the tension he was weighed with over the last few days. By the time he made his seventh trip around the jogger's path, he decided to go home. What was bothering him wasn't going away. Nothing could help. Nothing could stop the guilt he was burdened with whenever he envisioned Janelle. He had treated her so wrong.

Taking the elevator up to his penthouse, he asked himself the same question he was asking since George confirmed what Janelle told him: If Janelle was deceived by Lawson, why did the letter say otherwise? Stepping off the elevator, strolling to his suite, his head held down, he kept returning to the same answer. The one he didn't want to believe.

"Hi, Mitch." A familiar voice raised his head and his heart rate.

Roxanne was standing by his penthouse door with some papers.

"What are you doing here this early?" he asked, walking past her, unlocking the door.

There was something in his tone with her, an edginess. Roxanne had noticed it for the last few days. She shook it off with a provocative twirl of her lips. "I thought I'd bring by the proposal you were waiting for and we'd have a little breakfast."

He unlocked the door. Both strode inside. Automatically, she sat on the sofa, crossing her bare legs.

Mitch sat across from her. "Today is Saturday, Roxanne. The proposal could have waited for Monday morning."

"But I had stopped by the office this morning to pick up something and I saw that it had been delivered. So I thought why not bring it over to you. I know you were anxious to read it."

"I am." He stared openly at her.

The look she'd never seen before in her brother-in-law's eyes made her glance down at herself. "What? Do you like what I'm wearing? What is it?"

"It's you, Roxanne." Mitch steadied his small eyes on her large, hazel ones.

"What about me?"

"What if I told you I wanted you?"

"Wanted me?" A devilish lift of her lips assured him she knew what he meant.

"I'd say that's intriguing, considering . . ."

"Considering that we're relatives," Mitch finished her sentence. He then arose from the couch, walking forward until he was standing above her.

Looking up at him, her lips uncurled with her intense expression. "The Mitch I know always gets what he wants." She stood and gazed in his eyes, dividing the attention with his lips she was moving toward them.

Mitch moving back was all that prevented the kiss.

Roxanne was astonished. "What's wrong?"

"You. You make me sick!"

"You said you wanted me."

"I was lying! I just wanted to see how far you would go. And you would go far! Sleeping with your husband's brother. You're disgusting."

Roxanne's pride and anger forgot about her plans. "You have no right to call me that. You started this!"

"I was just testing you. I could never sleep with Lawson's wife."

"He slept with your girlfriend," she reminded him with a smirk. "Many times in fact."

"Now, that's where you wrong. I know the truth Roxanne."

"The truth?" Her face felt flushed.

Mitch saw her fear of being caught in a lie. "Yes, I know the truth. A friend of Lawson's confirmed that Janelle was telling the truth. Lawson tricked her, pretending he was me. That's how they slept together. The rest about the sizzling hot affair they were having was all made up. Made up by *you*."

Roxanne was shaking her head. "You don't understand why I did it. I cared about you. She would have ruined your life. She didn't even tell you what Lawson did to her."

"Get out of my sight."

"But—"

"Now! And clear out your desk before Monday morning. You're fired. You're also dead as Lawson is to me."

Days later, when Mitch asked Sherry's husband and his employee, Chris, about Janelle's whereabouts, along with her mother, Maya, the conversations turned up useless. With both of them refusing him, he turned to a private investigator. Three days passed when the investigator informed him by phone that Janelle was in Phoenix, the owner of her own successful dress boutique. He further questioned if Mitch had seen the latest issue of his fraternity's quarterly magazine. Via his research the investigator discovered an interesting piece about Janelle.

Curious why Janelle would be highlighted in his fraternity's magazine, Mitch located the issue, one in a collection he never read. He was floored seeing not only Janelle in a feature story, but his fraternity brother, Aaron. Aaron with his arms too closely around her. Forging beyond the shock, he read further into the piece. A new, prosperous dress boutique in Phoenix bound their business partnership. Not at all happy she made her dream come true without him, he perused further.

Immediately after finishing, Mitch tossed the magazine aside, and eagerly flipped through his Rolodex for Aaron's number. Under the pretense of finally coming in on a business deal, he would arrange to see him. Thereafter, it would be easy for his path to cross with Janelle's considering his old friend and his old love were business partners. But he hoped not more. Certainly Janelle wouldn't accept an invitation to see him simply from him. Not after how he treated her. And tracking her down at her boutique wasn't his style. What's more, Mitch didn't even want to see her alone the first time they met again. He wanted Aaron to be present and witness Janelle's strong reaction to him. If Aaron was involved with her intimately, Mitch wanted to let him know that that was all about to change.

An airplane ride later, Mitch was sitting in Aaron's office, reminiscing about their college days.

"You were a virgin up until your senior year," Aaron teased, as he always did with one of his dearest friends. They saw things differently on so many issues. Still, he felt connected to Mitch, if only by their drive to succeed and the experiences of their youth. Other than that, Aaron profoundly admired Mitch for the way he climbed his way from the middle class to become one of the most brilliant executives in corporate America. Additionally, he was impressed with his genius in the stock market. Mitch's business savvy was exactly what Aaron felt was needed in a new project he was formulating with their other college buddies, Demarre and Brett.

"I wasn't a virgin," Mitch countered with a grin. "You're just saying that because you always thought you were the ladies' man."

Adamantly, Aaron shook his head. "I didn't think that. You guys were always putting that label on me."

"Because you were always trying to be a player. Always had some woman drooling over you." Only now Mitch could say that without getting jealous about the opposite sex always swarming around his old friend. It was only thinking of him with one particular woman, which made the chair he sat in a little uncomfortable. "Bet you're still trying to be a player? Especially after being divorced? You're probably doing *the dunk* everywhere."

Tickled, Aaron threw his hand at him. "Get out of here, man."

"No, really," Mitch pressed. "How is your personal life?" He had to be skillful about getting to what he wanted.

Aaron's face lit up. "Beautiful." Shaking his head, Aaron closed his eyes and opened them emphasizing the point. "It's hard to describe man. As Brett tells Demarre, all the time, I'm whipped."

Mitch laughed. "Is that right?"

"Brother, I've been hit real hard with cupid's arrow. Real hard."

"Good for you. Who's the lucky lady?"

Aaron couldn't pry his smile away. "Her name is Janelle Sims. She owns a dress boutique here. Designs her own stuff. Bad stuff. And she's so fine, and that's inside and out."

Mitch continued smiling, above the thousands of curses and regrets screeching so loudly in his mind. "When will I get to meet her?"

"Matter of fact . . ." Aaron glanced down at his watch. "Matter of fact, she called right before you arrived and she should be coming by any minute now to drop some spreadsheets off to me. I'll tell my secretary that it's okay for her to interrupt us."

Mitch couldn't have asked for a situation to turn more in his favor. "Can't wait to see her."

"Just don't drool," Aaron warned.

However, as Aaron buzzed his secretary, he learned Janelle had just arrived.

"Tell her to come in please," he said.

Within seconds, the door opened slowly. Mitch didn't turn around. Instead, he inhaled the scent of coconut and heard steps thumping in the carpet approaching him. A calm countenance painted his face.

But opening the door to Aaron's office, calm was the last thing Janelle felt seeing the back of a man who looked disturbingly familiar. Her heart, ears and blood pounded with alarm. Faster and faster, she stepped toward the two men. The man sitting in front of Aaron couldn't be . . .

CHAPTER TWENTY

"Mitch?"

"Hello, Janelle." So glad to see her, Mitch rose slowly from his chair, taking in the beautiful features he couldn't forget. He must have been out of his mind to let this woman go.

Aaron looked bewildered. "You two *know* each other?"

"Yes, we do," Janelle acknowledged bitterly. Astonishment covered her expression as she strolled further into the room. "I know him from Philadelphia." Suspiciously, she eyed Mitch. "What are you doing here? In Phoenix of all places? And what business do you have with Aaron?"

Aaron was becoming more and more confused. It lured him from his chair and to a position between the two. "We were talking about Mitch coming in on a deal."

"A deal?" Janelle echoed. "Only a deal?"

"Yes," Aaron paused, his attention switching from face to face. Mitch and Janelle were looking at each other with a familiarity that made him uneasy. Aaron could hardly get out his next words for studying them. "Mitch . . . he's my frat brother."

"Your frat brother?" Janelle leered at Mitch. "Is this a joke? If it is, please let me in on it."

Returning a fonder expression to her, Mitch nodded. "Yes, Aaron and I went to Wharton together."

"Small world," Janelle remarked. She couldn't get over Mitch actually being in a room with her again after he treated her so horribly. The pain of those days instantly resurfaced. Sherry and her mother had called her, telling her he was demanding to know her whereabouts. "I don't believe you're here on just business."

"But I am."

"No, you're not."

"Why wouldn't he be?" Aaron asked.

Watching them, he knew something strange was going on. More than met the eye. "What exactly was the nature of your relationship in Philadelphia?" He searched both faces for the answer.

Mitch smiled at Janelle. "Should you tell him or should I?"

"Tell me what?" Aaron said irritably. He felt like the child everyone was hiding the grown-up secret from.

Janelle wrenched her stern gaze from Mitch and softened it on Aaron. She took a deep breath before revealing, "Mitch and I were seeing each other. We were involved before I came here."

Stunned, Aaron's eyes widened.

"We were living together and then engaged," Mitch elaborated. He stared at Janelle tenderly.

Disbelieving what he was hearing, Aaron was frozen absorbing it all. After a moment, he glared at Mitch. "So you're not really here about the deal after all? You're here to see Janelle?"

Mitch's expression became intense. Aaron was one of his best friends in the world. Fraternity brothers, they had gone through many things together. Financially, Aaron had been instrumental in helping him attain his wealth, helping him out in many situations. However, when it came to the woman who belonged to him, friendship wasn't as important. "To be honest, I am here to see Janelle. Her family and friends wouldn't let me know where she was."

"And why is that?" Aaron asked. "Did they tell you she had someone in her life now?"

"They didn't tell me anything. They hung up on me. They hate me to be more blunt."

"And why is that?" Aaron was getting close in Mitch's face. "You hurt her something awful, didn't you?"

"Yes, I was wrong." Mitch didn't like his old buddy's tone. "I treated her in a way she didn't deserve."

"You mean you dogged her out in some way?"

Not knowing what to say, Janelle looked confused from one face to the other.

"What went on with us is our business," Mitch enlightened him. "What is the nature of your relationship with her?"

Janelle was looking from man to man, hating that they were talking about her like she wasn't there. "Both of you stop. The point is that Mitch is not here for business. He—"

"You're right, Janelle," Mitch cut her off. "I have ulterior motives. And that's to win you back."

Aaron's nostrils flared. "You have some nerve! I don't know what went on, but you definitely didn't do something right, and it's over."

"It's not over," Mitch argued. "I—"

"Oh, but it is over," Janelle silenced him. "You treated me so wrong before I left. You humiliated me. Threw me out in the street like garbage."

"He did what?" Aaron restrained his fists from flying.

"You insulted me in your office." She still couldn't stop hearing what he said about her father. "I couldn't believe how cold you were."

"But I know the truth now," Mitch defended himself. "I know how Lawson deceived you. His friend George told me everything. The whole ugly story."

"I don't care. It's over. I have a new life now, and a new man that I love." She shifted toward Aaron. Standing in back of her, he put his arms around her waist. Both stared at Mitch. "Aaron is my heart and he's all the man I need and all the man I'll ever want."

Mitch refused to show defeat. "If that's the way you want it."

"That's the way it is," Aaron informed him.

Mitch nodded and shuffled toward the door. Before he opened it, he looked over his shoulder at Janelle. "So long, Janelle." He then brought his gaze over to Aaron. "Good bye old friend."

On the door's closing, Janelle spun around in Aaron's arms, gazing up at him with begging eyes. "I should have told you about my ex. Maybe we would have found out earlier you two were friends and avoided all this."

"You couldn't predict this. And I understand your not bringing up a painful past relationship. You wanted to leave it in the past where I also left mine."

She hugged him tightly for being so understanding. When she released him, she stared up at him again. "I want to tell you why we broke up. I want to tell you everything. Maybe it all isn't Mitch's fault. But I want to be honest with you."

After Janelle shared Lawson's betrayal, Aaron thought nothing less of her. He was more endeared to her knowing that Mitch had believed the worst of her so easily.

"They're gone now," he comforted her, planting a light kiss on her cheek. "Lawson, Mitch, the past. You and I are what matters. Our wonderful future together. We aren't going to let anyone get in the way of our happiness."

As the chauffeur drove him back to his hotel, Mitch couldn't enjoy picturesque sights of Phoenix passing by the window. The reason being, there was too much going on in his mind. He couldn't get over Janelle loving another man. Worst of all, it was his friend. He didn't like many people, but he had liked Aaron. How could she have gone on with her life and forgotten him so easily?

More questions badgered him. What's more, he couldn't stop replaying Janelle's parting words, or seeing Aaron's smug expression, and there was even an image of them making love. All crowded in his head, making him warm, and a little breathless. He couldn't let that little scene make him this upset.

Tugging at his tie and unbuttoning a few top buttons of his shirt didn't alleviate the distress. For some reason, Mitch's discomfort worsened. More than a little hot now, he was also dizzy, and soon gasping for air. Gasping like he did when he was a teenager. That was the last time it happened, he thought. Exactly like Lawson, he was having an asthma attack. He urged the driver to rush him to the nearest hospital.

As he was rushed inside its emergency doors, he had only one request. Since the oxygen mask was on his mouth, he scribbled it on a paper. It read: *Call Janelle Sims. Immediately. She's in the executive offices of Deverreau, Gracen and Hall.*

"Are you all right?" Janelle asked. Her alarm wasn't camouflaged at Mitch's bedside.

"Sure." Smiling, Mitch reached for her hand and squeezed it gently. "Don't worry about me. They said it was a minor attack and that I'll be released in the morning."

"And where will you be going when you're released?" Aaron asked. He shifted from beside Janelle toward the headboard to look Mitch directly in the eyes. There was no sign of sympathy for Mitch. Sure, he was grateful he hadn't suffered a serious attack. What he was unappreciative of was his calling Janelle to be by his side. "Do you have a flight scheduled back home already?"

"No, I don't," Mitch replied. "We both know I had planned to stay a while and do some business with you guys. But now that's off." He propped his back up on his pillow.

Janelle assisted him. "Easy does it."

"You shouldn't wait too long in scheduling a flight back," Aaron advised. "Tourists book them up quickly."

"Your concern is touching."

Janelle heard something in Mitch's tone that she tried to ignore.

Aaron refused to ignore it. "I'm just being straight because there's no need for you to hang around."

Nervously, Janelle glanced at her watch. "Maybe we should go now. It's getting really late."

"Fine with me," Aaron agreed. "But I am real curious about Mitch's plans."

"My plans?" Mitch echoed. "I'm going to rest in my hotel room for a while. Days, weeks, whatever it takes."

"Wouldn't it be better to rest at home?" Aaron inquired.

Janelle glimpsed at her watch again.

Mitch shook his head at Aaron. "There's no way I can rest at home. Everyone knows where I am. They'll be calling me about business. Yes, what I need is the peace and quiet of my hotel room. You see, the doctor said my condition could have been brought on by emotional strain." Pausing, he stared at Janelle. "I could have bit the dust just like my brother did. The physicians said his condition might have been brought on by emotional strain too."

At that, Janelle lowered her head. Afterward, she spoke her good-byes to Mitch, wished him the best and thought Aaron was following behind her.

"I'll be a minute, baby," he told her as she headed out the door. "I want to talk to Mitch for a minute."

Worried, they would feud, she was reluctant to leave them alone. "Please don't argue. It's not good for Mitch's condition."

"We won't," Aaron assured. "We're just going to have a quick civilized talk man to man."

The door closed. Aaron's head rolled back to Mitch. He

couldn't believe the hostility he was feeling for someone who was almost like a brother to him. "Are you going to throw our friendship away?" he asked him. "It's all in your hands."

"I'm not leaving Phoenix, right now. And it's not because I want in on some business deal with you. Does that answer your question?"

Inside Aaron's bedroom that night, he was so hot for Janelle he couldn't lie still. And didn't. In every way he could, he tried to make love to her. Whenever they were alone like this, they couldn't keep their hands off each other. Tonight, unfortunately, she was different. She expressed wanting to plainly snuggle, laying her head on his hard chest, with her body close to his. But with a kiss here and fondle there, Aaron was bent on making her change her mind.

His efforts were in vain. In fact, with her unresponsiveness, she was quiet. Far away she was. He prayed it wasn't so far that she was starting to lose sight of him.

"Don't you want me anymore?" he asked.

Frowning, she raised her face toward his. "Why are you asking me something like that?"

"Because you're just different tonight."

"Because I'm not in the mood for making love?"

"Maybe you just don't want to make love with me. Maybe your ex, and once good friend of mine is starting to get to you again?"

With a horrified look, Janelle sat up. "Oh, baby, no. I love you. I'm in love with you. Never, *ever* did I feel for Mitch what I feel for you. I guess I cared for Mitch. But we never had the passionate love you and I share. It's the kind of love I never dreamed I'd be blessed with and I'd die if I had to give it up."

Her words warmed his heart and his expression. "Sometimes you say things that just touch my heart."

"Because they come straight from mine."

He eased her back down against him. "So what's bothering you?" He began stroking her hair. "I know it's something. You're too quiet."

Loving the feel of his fingertips playing over her scalp, she nodded. "Something is bothering me. I guess it's seeing Mitch in the hospital having an asthma attack reminds me so much of Lawson. Sometimes I blame myself for his death. If I wouldn't have yelled at him like that and told him how much I wished he was dead, maybe he wouldn't have died." She turned her head away from him.

Aaron's fingertips on her chin gently curved her face back in his direction. He raised up, looking over at her. "Don't you ever feel guilty for that. Lawson did what could have amounted to raping you. You were angry and had a right to express what you felt. How he took it was all on him. No, Janelle. You are not the guilty one. And don't ever let Mitch manipulate you into believing that. I could have sworn he was trying to run that earlier."

CHAPTER
TWENTY-ONE

With all the urgency that his voice held when he phoned her boutique, pleading with her to come to his hotel suite because he was ill, Janelle entered Mitch's suite.

Wearing a blue satin bathrobe and a slight smile, he didn't look at all as sick as he claimed to be. "Mitch, I hope you didn't try to trick me over here."

"I wouldn't do that," he lied. "I really did feel like I was about to have an attack. But I do feel better now. Sit down." His small eyes pointed toward the sofa.

Hesitantly, Janelle obliged, resting her purse on the cushions. "What brought the feeling on? Emotional strain again? I thought you were at this hotel resting, getting ready to go back to Philly?"

Mitch lounged on a recliner across from her. "I was resting, but a person can still have stress. That's definitely what's causing my attacks you know. I don't want to wind up like Lawson."

Straightaway, Janelle hung her head. Looking back up, she scanned him over. "You look fine now. I think I better go."

She stood. He did too. Right in front of her. Close in front of her.

"Janelle, please don't go."

"Mitch, I'm in love with Aaron. You and I are over. Accept it and move on."

His jaw tightened at her insisting on such a ridiculous thing. "Do you know you nearly killed me doing that?"

Her eyes stretched. "What? Killed you? Me? Killed you?" Her hand clutched her chest.

"Yes you." He softened his expression. "By rejecting me. The way you did it. So coldly. That can kill a man. Being thrown away by the woman of his dreams. Look at Lawson."

Tension squeezed her eyes shut. She opened them with the same force. "I didn't kill Lawson."

"No, you didn't actually take the breath from his lungs. But the way you break up with someone is very important."

"I had a right to say what I said to him. He violated me."

"But I'm not asking to violate you. I'm just asking for your friendship at least. You've made it clear that you and . . . Aaron are involved."

"We're more than involved. We're in love."

Mitch's gut wrenched. "Yes, in love as you say. But that doesn't mean you just have to dog me like you did. I was so upset coming back to the hotel that I couldn't even breathe. You didn't even want to be my friend anymore. That's what I can't handle. I no longer have my friend anymore. It was really upsetting. Every time I think about it, it just makes me sick. Literally."

"I can be your friend, Mitch. Nothing else."

"Well, then be a friend to me. Stop by and see me while I'm here."

Leaving Mitch's hotel suite, Janelle knew Mitch was trying to manipulate her. Did he think she was that dumb?

Manipulate her back into his bed, back into his life. There was no way that was going to happen.

What she wasn't able to combat, however, was the guilt he sneaked into her consciousness. The situation surrounding Lawson's death. Was she really at fault? Thinking about it weighed on her so, Janelle could hardly concentrate at work. Worse, she was so stressed, she was never in the mood for making love. Much the opposite, Aaron was.

As long as Janelle wanted to be simply held, he would be there for her. Aaron thought this, as he watched her sleep in his bed one night. His eyes trailed over the exotic features of her face, before he raised the covers sheathing her luscious body to peek at what he wasn't getting tonight.

Feeling that all-too-familiar rigidity between his legs, he threw his legs over the side of the bed and stood. He didn't know what to do with himself to deflate his excitement. Except he was sure cold showers didn't work. He had tried that last week. Perhaps exercising would rescue him, he decided. Off to his gym in the basement he went.

There was weight lifting. He ran on the treadmill. Sit ups followed. Aaron also rode the stationary bike. By the time exhaustion froze him, his desire was quelled. Though, another emotion he would have to fight was strongly surfacing: insecurity. It drew him in front of the mirror.

What was wrong with him? Why didn't Janelle want to make love with him anymore? He knew she loved him. If she wasn't saying it fervently, she was showing it with the utmost intensity. That's why he couldn't understand this withholding of her physical expression of love. Did he need to work out more? Was it something else in his appearance that turned her off? Or maybe . . . maybe he just wasn't satisfying her.

* * *

"When he comes home tonight you just lay it on him."
Sherry provided her solution to Janelle's dilemma over the
phone one night. "Wham! Hit him over the head with it."

Janelle laughed. "You are still so crazy."

"I'm serious. What's happening with you is no joke."

"I know." Janelle sighed. "I guess laughing about it is
more fun than crying. Aaron and I were these wild tigers,
and now one of us has turned to a passionless poop."

"What's causing it? What do you think?"

"I don't know, Sherry. I went to a doctor the other day.
They said it's nothing biological. I'm in excellent health.
The doctor suggested it could be stress. He said that could
definitely take away a woman's desire. And I do have some
stress lately."

"Stress about what exactly?"

"Mitch for one thing. Every time I bump into him, he
has been talking about Lawson and then comparing his
illness with Lawson's. And he's always saying Lawson died
because he couldn't have the woman he loved—me. And
then he says that now, he can't have the woman he loves—
me."

"Don't let him play with your head. That's pretty pitiful
if he's trying to win you back through a guilt trip."

"That's what I say."

"But tell me this," Sherry went on, "did you ever think
of seeing a relationship counselor?"

"A relationship counselor?"

"That was some heavy stuff done to you—that Lawson
situation. It could have a lot to do with your sex life—
considering it was a sexual act he committed against you."

Chantel had a similar suggestion as Janelle chatted with
her on the phone later that night.

"So you mean to tell me y'all haven't done it in weeks?"

Janelle sighed. "And Chantel, I'm so attracted to Aaron. I'm just so blown away by his sexiness when I look at him, or even think about him. And his heart . . . he's such a good man, how can I not want to make love with him?"

"So girl, you have to find the answer."

"What can I do?"

"See a psychiatrist. A friend of mine did it when her husband cheated. It kept her from the loony bin."

"That seems so strange. I'm not crazy."

"No, you're not crazy, but not having sex with a man like Aaron is. Do you know how many women want that man? He just fights them off. But if you keep on holding back, I don't know how patient he's going to be. A man is a man now. Let's just be honest. If you don't give it to him, he's going to find somewhere else to get it. And for Aaron, he doesn't even have to go looking. Women throw it at him."

The possibility of some temptress weakening Aaron into having an affair did become a picture in her mind after she hung up from Chantel. Though her good sense faded it. Aaron wasn't like that. He didn't fit the stereotype of a man being such a sex-starved beast he would get it anywhere if the woman he loved was giving it. What's more, she already knew someone who was smarter than any psychiatrist or a relationship counselor—her mother. A woman who grew with the times, her mother was one she could talk to about anything—even sex. The only reason she hadn't talked to her lately, was because oddly enough, her mother was hardly home.

Luckily, she caught her this night. "Hello?"

"Mama, you're finally home. I've been calling you and calling you."

"Well, you didn't leave no message on the machine."

"You know I hate leaving messages."

"That I do know. So how's my baby doing?"

"How's the family doing?"

"Your brothers and sisters are doing fine. But you didn't answer my question about how you're doing."

"Oh, I'm . . ."

"You're what, baby?"

"I'm having a little problem."

"Please don't tell me it's with that wonderful Aaron you've been writing me about?"

"Yes, it is. And he's still wonderful. It's just me."

"What is it, baby?"

Janelle proceeded to fill her mother in on her problems, sharing with her even the details about the nightmare with Mitch and Lawson. When she broke up with Mitch, she had simply told her he had a case of cold feet at the engagement party. She was too embarrassed of the real reason, even to a mother who she could talk to about anything.

Maya Sims was livid hearing what was done to her daughter. Amid it though, she consoled Janelle, assuring her she had nothing to be embarrassed about. She also told her plenty more. Like she always had God to always bring her troubles to, no matter how embarrassing or silly they seemed. She also told Janelle she was feeling blameworthy for Lawson's death, when she shouldn't.

Equally, she was feeling she was at fault for him violating her—feeling as though she had brought it on herself. The most dramatic revelation her mother made was that Janelle wasn't facing the truth: Lawson had in essence *raped* her. That's what she hadn't really dealt with. And for hours, and hours she did just that. She dealt with it, her mother's wisdom and strength right with her in every tear, in every outcry, in every prayer they shared together.

Near the end of the conversation, Janelle felt like a weight was lifted off her. She could never thank her mother enough for her love, her strength and for always being there. Janelle wished so deeply a man had loved her mother like Aaron loved her.

"Anything else you want to talk about, baby?" Maya asked.

"Oh, Mama, I feel so much better. There's nothing else on my mind."

"Well, you can talk to me about anything. You know that, don't you?"

"I know."

"Even Daddy."

Janelle paused. Her heavy breathing filled the hush. "I don't want to talk about him."

"If you ever do, I'm here."

"But I don't."

Janelle hung up the phone, not letting the mention of her father break her spirit. She was too busy searching her closet for her sexiest outfit to wear over to Aaron's house. They hadn't made plans tonight because she had expressed wanting a night to herself to rest from a busy week at the boutique. In actuality, she merely longed for some time alone to figure out what was wrong with her. Suddenly though, all had changed. She felt like a wildcat and this wildcat was going to surprise her man.

Sticking the key Aaron gave her in the lock of his home, Janelle's body flooded with warmth. She couldn't wait to get to that man inside. Pushing open the door, she just wasn't prepared for what greeted her. A fortyish woman with her hair in a bun stood in the midst of Aaron's living room clad in her bra and panties. Her clothes were nowhere in sight.

"Are you Mrs. Deverreau?" she asked.

Janelle could hear her heart's loud roar deafening her. "No, I'm not. Who are you?"

"I'm the temporary maid. Mr. Deverreau's normal maid is out sick." She glimpsed down at herself. "I spilled something on my uniform and it's hanging to dry in the bathroom. I knew he wasn't coming back anytime soon. So that's why I'm doing my work like this. It should be almost dry."

Wildly, Janelle started shaking her head. This was not happening. This was not happening. Too bad the half-naked seductress standing in front of her screeched it was. Another woman was standing in Aaron's living room and he was probably upstairs. And they had rehearsed what they would do and say in a predicament like this. Like Chantel had cautioned, the lack of sex from her had made him turn elsewhere. Janelle bolted out the door.

Three hours later, Aaron returned home from the office to an immaculate house, but a jittery, appropriately attired maid.

"Is something wrong, Geri?" he asked. He laid his briefcase on a lamp table.

"Uh, uh, yes it is, sir."

Aaron smiled. "It's not, sir. It's Aaron to my friends."

Awkwardly, she smiled. "Well, Aaron. There was a young lady that stopped by. Very, very pretty. Smooth dark skin, shiny dark hair and these movie-star-looking eyes."

Aaron grinned at the description of his love goddess. "That was my girlfriend, Janelle."

"Uh, uh, she didn't look too happy. Not to see me."

"Didn't you tell her you were the temporary maid?"

"Yes, I did sir—I mean, Aaron. But uh, when she walked in I had my bra and panties on."

Aaron's curled lips unfolded into a straight line. "And why was that?"

"Because I had spilled something on my uniform. It was upstairs drying in your bathroom."

"Oh, no," Aaron thought aloud. Shaking his head, he headed back toward the front door.

Geri tracked his steps. "I explained why I didn't have anything on and I told her you were expected back much later. I let her know I wouldn't walk around you like that. But she ran out."

CHAPTER
TWENTY-TWO

In a state of disarray, Janelle answered her ringing bell without checking to who it was. When she opened the door and saw Aaron, she tried to shut it in his face.

His hand grasped the knob, stopping her. "No, you don't. You will let me explain."

"Go away, Aaron. A half-naked woman is at your house waiting for you. Go back to her."

Aaron brushed past her, making long strides into her living room. "That woman was a temporary maid. My normal maid is out sick."

"You expect me to believe that?" She glared up at him, placing a hand on her hip.

"Of course I do. You're supposed to trust me." But he could see from her entire demeanor that she didn't. That infuriated him. Once again, he was being found guilty when he was innocent. It was the most horrible feeling in the world. When would he stop paying for a crime he didn't commit? Never, ever. Especially with Janelle and her delusions about him being unfaithful.

Her chest rose and fell with her anger. "You couldn't

wait for the perfect excuse to cheat, could you? Since I wasn't making love with you, you had to go elsewhere?''

"Do you really think that little of me?" The pitch of his voice rose with his anger. "Do you?" He couldn't believe the love of his life was actually saying this to him.

"I know what really goes on in the minds of men like you."

Aaron sighed, clutching the side of his head. "This is unbelievable. You really, really don't trust me. After all this time."

"You want to take all the candy you can get—all the candy that's offered to you."

"And you want to forget a promise you made."

"What promise?" She spat the words out.

"The promise you made to me to never let anyone break your spirit."

"My spirit isn't broken. Not even you can do that."

"Your spirit is broken. No, not the one that holds your career dreams or that kind of purpose. But your spirit to *fully* love a man. Love him with trust. That's more than broken. That's dead and you let your dad do it to you."

"My dad didn't do anything to me. Matter of fact, he did me a favor by getting out of my life when he did. Look at me now. I don't need him."

"You do. You need him to tell you every man doesn't drop his pants for every skirt like he did. He needs to tell you he was wrong—that he wasn't a real man, leaving a wife and children to fend for themselves all in the name of chasing something meaningless. He needs to tell you every man is not like him—and that you sure messed up a good thing by thinking that Aaron Deverreau was."

On that note, he stormed out of her house, slamming the door behind him.

On the following day, Saturday, Aaron boarded a yacht with Brett, Demarre, Chantel and thirty or so other guests in celebration of Brett's thirty-eighth birthday. The yacht named *The Tall Man* was Brett's gift to himself. Aaron's three friends wondered aloud why his beloved wasn't by his side. In answering, Aaron decided to lie, claiming Janelle was busy with work. It was better than explaining the agonizing truth—they had an argument that might have ended their relationship.

Despite it all, he was determined to have a good time. Dancing, talking, laughing, playing cards as the yacht wafted out to sea, Aaron attempted to live in the moment. Fortunately, he had always been a master of masking his pain. He had always thought it was a selfish thing to do, letting his wounds bleed onto others, for the relief of himself.

When he returned home, Aaron had hardly been in his house a minute, when he played back the messages on his answering machine. He hoped Janelle had called at least a dozen times, apologizing for accusing him of such a thing. To his disappointment, there wasn't one call from her. He went up to bed.

Against the silken sheets where they had so often laid together, he was haunted by her again. There were memories of the way they so passionately made love. There were also erotic fantasies he'd yet to experience with her. Longing them so desperately, he soon transferred them to his dreams. They were so sensual, when he awakened he found himself touching himself like she had often touched him. In his seductive mist, he also reached for her side of the bed. It was empty. So was he.

How was he going to survive until the next time she called him or appeared before his eyes? He missed her like a thousand days had passed without being near her. He couldn't even imagine what one more day without speaking to her would do to him. Maybe he would call her tomorrow. Nonetheless, he thought again. Yes, it looked incriminating for a stranger to stand in his home in her underthings. Regardless, what was so unbelievable about the woman being a maid, who happened to be letting her clothes dry? Why was it so hard to believe if Janelle had once claimed to trust him? He started to phone Janelle and tell her to call the maid's agency to confirm who she was. But then, he thought again. He wasn't about to call her. She was supposed to trust him. She was wrong. He had to get her off his mind with something that would really uplift his spirits. And he knew what that something was. He would visit Kyree for a few days. Just seeing how miraculously his son had recovered from that accident would remind Aaron of what he had to be grateful for.

Needing something to help get her mind off Aaron and, knowing that she now had the time to spend with those girls, Janelle entered the doors of the Good Girls Of America. The day was spent participating in various activities as well as giving the girls inspirational talks. Observing Janelle's interaction with the young women, Ms. Jamison thought she was a natural motivator.

Except Janelle didn't feel so successful when she was first alone with Gretchen. The thin girl sat to the sidelines watching everything and Janelle decided to sit with her.

"So why aren't you playing with the girls?" Janelle asked, pulling Gretchen's long braids behind her shoulders.

Gretchen shrugged her shoulders. "I just don't feel like playing."

"Why?"

She shrugged her shoulders again. "I just don't."

Janelle slid closer to her. "You know, I heard about your dad."

"What did you hear?" Gretchen said almost angrily.

"That your dad left."

"Oh, brother. People really blab your business."

Janelle would have laughed at her spunk, if she hadn't felt so sorry for her. "They weren't blabbing about you. I asked what was wrong because I wanted to help."

"You can't help. He's gone."

"You mean your daddy."

Her mouth balled up angrily, Gretchen nodded.

"Maybe he'll come back."

"My mama said he won't. She's said he's a no good, low down, skeezer."

Janelle wanted to laugh again. "Oh, yeah. Mamas will say those things. And sometimes they are true. Some daddies need some sense knocked in their heads."

A grin broke through Gretchen's lips.

"But Gretchen, whether your daddy comes back or not, that's not going to affect your life."

"We don't have no money."

"That's all right. You don't have any now. But that doesn't mean you're not going to get some. I didn't have any money."

Gretchen looked surprised. "You? How did you get a dress store without money?"

"By working hard."

"Oh."

"And I didn't have a daddy either."

Gretchen looked surprised again. "You didn't have a daddy? I don't believe you. You're just saying that to make me feel better."

"No, I'm not saying it to make you feel better. It's true Gretchen. My daddy left when I was a little girl. My parents had five children and my mother had to take care of them all by herself. We were so poor sometimes we didn't have enough food."

"Not enough food! My stomach would have been growling."

"Well, mine growled many times."

"And this was because your daddy left."

"Well, a man should take care of his children."

"My mama said Daddy don't do nothing for us."

"Well he's supposed to."

"What didn't your daddy do?"

"Well for one thing my daddy didn't call . . . didn't write. Didn't care." She blinked away a tear that formed in her eye. "The next time I saw him, he was dead."

"Oh, my God. That's terrible."

"It was. But my point to you is don't let what your daddy did make you unhappy."

"Sometimes I can't help it. I just feel so sad."

"Don't! Don't let him stop you from enjoying your life. You can be anything you want to be. As happy as you want to be. It doesn't depend on him. It depends on you." But why, when she said those words, did she hear what Aaron said to her.

Was she letting her father ruin her life?

Pampering. It was what Janelle believed she needed after it had been three days since her big argument with Aaron. The torture of seeing that unclad woman in his house was unbearable enough. What made it worse, was that he wasn't even trying to call to plead his case again, or at least admit the wrong he'd done and beg for another chance—one which she wasn't about to give to him. Her mother had made that foolish mistake, but not her. So she tried to ease her suffering that day with a facial, massage, manicure, pedicure, an herbal body wrap and a new wavy hairstyle.

Much later, when Janelle returned home, she immediately slipped off her sandals with one hand. From the opposite hand, her finger pressed the answering machine button. Myriads of messages played. Conspicuously, one masculine voice was absent.

Fighting the sudden creep of a sickened feeling she had victoriously pushed aside all day, Janelle went up to the bathroom, shed her clothes and dipped her limbs into a hot bath. Laying her head back, she closed her eyes and tried to let all the moisture soothe her. It coated her skin, mingling with the tear that soon made a *plop* sound into the water.

But all the pampering in the world couldn't curb the sickness when it grew strong enough to leap up in her throat, making her scream out, "Oh, God what am I going to do without him! God, what am I going to do! Why does it hurt so much! I'd rather die than feel like this! Why did this happen to me! Why did you make love feel so good and then make it hurt so bad? Why? Nothing has ever felt like this. Nothing!"

CHAPTER
TWENTY-THREE

Mitch strolled through the Heard Museum, venturing to enjoy something entertaining since he couldn't enjoy what he really wanted. When someone tapped him from behind, he never expected to look into the face he beheld.

"Hello, Mitch?" Roxanne beamed at him.

His eyes narrowed. "What are you doing here in Phoenix? Stalking me?"

"I'm not stalking you. I'm here to apologize and make up for the wrong I did. I want to be your sister-in-law again. Your sister-in-law and nothing more."

Mitch almost yelled, but scanning the people near them, he ushered her into a secluded corner instead. "Being my sister-in-law is out of the question," he spat. "You're dead to me. Just as dead as my brother is."

"Mitch, have some compassion in your heart. I need your help."

Mitch's lips twisted in amusement. "At last the truth comes out. I knew it was something. How much?"

Roxanne swallowed. She might has well have come to the point. She was desperate. Her bank funds were depleted.

Creditors were hounding her. She'd lost her house. "I need a job."

"Your old one has been filled."

"Can you recommend me to someone else in the company? I can even assist you here in handling your affairs. I'll relocate. I have nothing to lose."

"Assist me? After what you did?"

"Mitch, I'm destitute and I'm your brother's widow. I haven't been able to get a job since you fired me. It's hard out there."

"Because you're a lousy secretary. Obviously, a lousy wife, too, since Lawson went elsewhere."

She wanted to smack him for saying that. Rather than succumb to the urge, a pitiful countenance masked her growing hatred of Mitch. "I'll do anything for a job. Even a small loan." Her eyes pleaded with him.

Mitch was about to say no. What stopped him was viewing this opportunity for what it was. Roxanne could do something to make him look better in Janelle's eyes.

"You can do something for me," he declared.

"What? Anything?"

The following afternoon, Janelle sat impatiently in the posh eatery Top of the Mountain. She was thinking of Aaron, but waiting for Mitch. He convinced her to meet him, pertaining to something crucial about Lawson's death. It was about the mysterious letter that ended their engagement. She had avoided contact with Mitch. However, her curiosity about that letter was piqued. Hence, she sat waiting.

Approximately ten minutes later, she saw a host escorting Mitch to her table. Who she didn't expect to see was the person striding behind him—his sister-in-law, Roxanne.

After they were seated, there were greetings, along with Janelle's shock at seeing Roxanne in Phoenix.

"What brings you out to Arizona?" Janelle asked.

Roxanne's large, hazel eyes fell on the table, before meeting Janelle's gaze. "I'm out here to visit Mitch, get a job if possible, and . . ." She hated to say what she was about to. Nevertheless, Mitch had promised her money and a job for telling Janelle the truth.

"And what?" Janelle prompted. Leaning forward, she propped her elbow on the table and her chin against her palm.

"Tell her," Mitch ordered.

Roxanne felt knots in her stomach. Doing this was so humiliating. "I . . . I came to apologize to you. I felt guilty."

Janelle frowned and sat back. "Guilty about what?"

"About that letter I showed Mitch."

"You had something to do with that?" Janelle looked amazed. She knew Roxanne disliked her, but to stoop to such a low level.

"Yes, she did," Mitch answered, and shook his head at Roxanne. "Tell her all of it."

Roxanne could have spat in both their faces. Restraining the impulse, she imparted, "I made it look like you and Lawson had an ongoing affair, after I read the letter. I was upset. So I did something stupid. I apologize." She then eyed Mitch, as if to ask, *are you happy now?*

But Mitch was too busy studying Janelle's dispirited expression. She looked at Roxanne. "What you did was wrong. But what I kept from everyone was wrong also. I just want to forget it all. I don't want to hold any grudges." She then glanced at her watch. "I have to leave soon."

Her reaction wasn't the one Mitch hoped for. He wanted Janelle to long to kill this woman for wrecking her life. Afterward, he and Janelle would sit at the table, sharing venomous remarks about this woman who had torn them apart. Thereafter, Janelle would realize she couldn't let her ruin what they had.

"Well, I do hold a grudge," Mitch countered. He was furious that his plan hadn't worked and glared at Roxanne.

"You ruined my relationship with Janelle. Now that you've apologized, I don't ever want to see your face again."

At first, Roxanne thought he was kidding. The plan was for her to apologize and Janelle would leave. After that, when they were alone, he would discuss giving her a loan and a job. However, from the rage in his eyes, she knew he wasn't acting.

"What about a loan? And a job? You said that if I apologized and told the truth, you would help me."

"Get out of my sight," Mitch demanded.

After hitting him on the head with a spoon she did.

Janelle watched her until she disappeared into the vestibule, then switched to Mitch.

"So she didn't apologize on her own. You tricked her into doing so."

"It worked didn't it?"

"But too bad it didn't work on me."

He leaned forward. "What do you mean?"

"I mean you thought this little episode was going to get you somewhere. But I tell you it didn't. I don't want to be with you, Mitch."

"Why? Aaron isn't standing in our way now."

She stiffened. How did he know they weren't seeing each other? It had only been two weeks. "What are you talking about?"

Mitch grinned. "Come on. I know you two haven't been seen together in a few weeks. I have money remember. It can buy spies."

"You make me sick! You think you can buy everybody. Well you can't buy me." She rushed up from the table and headed toward the entrance.

Mitch caught her arm in the foyer, spinning her around. "Don't be a fool. Don't give up the best thing that ever happened to you."

She jerked his hand off of her. "I was a fool to even

speak to you after you dumped me without even listening to my side of the story.''

"We can start over."

"Why Mitch? What did we really have anyway? I was just a possession to you. You never told me you loved me. I never heard those words from your lips.''

"That's not my style. I'd rather show it.''

"I don't care. I don't want to be with you whether I'm with Aaron or not. I don't even want you to love me. Because looking at you right now, I don't even like you. Look at how you exploit people. Look at how you exploited Roxanne.''

Mitch stretched his eyes. "You're defending her after what she did to you?''

"Not at all. She was wrong. But you were also wrong in promising her something you had no intention of giving. You love to play God with people's lives.''

"Oh, she can find a job. She just wants me and my money. She can find a job anywhere, even at Deverreau, Gracen and Hall Development. I heard through the grapevine that even your millionaire, Mr. Deverreau needs an assistant. Or should I say your ex-millionaire?''

"Say what you want. But it won't be to me.''

With that, Janelle sped out of the restaurant. Mitch hurried behind her. And when she knew they were a safe distance away, Roxanne came out from behind the door she was standing behind. They were near the phones. She had been trying to call some family to see if they could help her out. However, Janelle's and Mitch's conversation intrigued her.

Where was this Deverreau, Gracen and Hall Development located? And who was this millionaire that Janelle wasn't involved with anymore? And what were the qualifications for being his assistant? Sure as she was standing there, Roxanne would find all the answers out. Maybe things weren't so bad after all, she thought with a smile.

* * *

Aaron left the office early, grateful that his new assistant, Roxanne, was working overtime so that he could enjoy some leisure. So he headed for the road. Aaron hoped a long drive would make him stop reminding himself that it had been two weeks and three days since he'd spoken to or seen Janelle. They weren't even communicating on business issues concerning the boutique. His secretary was handling it.

He still couldn't get over the hurt of her not trusting him. Not even the evil his wife did to him had hurt as much. Because he hadn't loved her as much as he loved Janelle. He'd never loved any woman as much as her.

She was so absorbed in his consciousness, he was led to a place that would make him close to her. It was paradise— the lush land where he had brought her to on the day of the fair. It was the first place they kissed. They had almost made love there.

Hands in pockets, sauntering around the ravishing surroundings, Aaron wondered what she was doing at the moment. Who was she with? Had she started seeing anyone? Did she happen to lose her mind and rekindle the fire with Mitch? He couldn't even imagine it. He hated imagining her with any other man. Forget what people said about the one they broke up with: I just want him or her to be happy. Selfish as it was, he didn't want her to be happy with anyone else.

Laying back on the ground, folding his hands behind his head, letting the afternoon sun warm his face, he imagined her with him right then. They were making passionate, hot love—the love she denied him those last times they were together.

More than an hour later, when Aaron was driving along the highway heading home, his mind was too filled to notice the car passing in the opposing lane. It was a red Porsche. Moments later, after Janelle parked it, she had no idea Aaron had been so near either. Something had drawn her up to his land. The paradise where they had first kissed and nearly made love. If she couldn't be with him, at least this place would make her feel close. Sitting, resting her head back against a tree, she closed her eyes, and it was that day all over again.

CHAPTER
TWENTY-FOUR

"You're some interior decorator," Aaron complimented Roxanne as he strolled in her home.

She glowed. "All thanks to you."

"No, not thanks to me." He was turning around, examining the cozy art deco furnishings mixed with antiques. "You're the one with the decorating skills."

"But you're the one who advanced me months of salary to get a place and make it look decent. I was down to nothing, Aaron. You don't know how grateful I am." Captivated by his handsome face, and feeling so truly indebted, she longed to hug him.

"It's my pleasure," he said, making himself comfortable on a leather sofa cushion. "Now what did you want to see me about? It must be something big since you swore you couldn't tell me over the phone."

Her hazel eyes suddenly sparkled like her smile. "Oh, I hope you won't be angry. But it wasn't anything urgent. I just wanted to surprise you with a thank you. Come with me." She lifted his hand, leading him to her dining room.

Once inside it, he gasped, "Wow." There was a soul

food feast comparable to the ones his grandmother used to make. Although as delicious as it looked, and nice as she was, he really wasn't in the mood for dining with her. He debated a way to get out of it, but realized he couldn't hurt her feelings. Certainly, it had taken hours for her to prepare this meal. At least, this would be one evening, he wouldn't be moping around the house thinking about Janelle.

"This is my way of saying thank you for all you've done for me," she nudged him from his thoughts.

"I didn't do that much."

"Yes you did." She took him by the hand, steering him to a chair. Hurrying around to the one facing him, she added, "You helped me get this place. You hired me when no one else would. You advanced me salary. You've been a real dream to me."

"You're a great assistant," he praised. "I don't know why Mitch fired you for merely being late a few times. His own sister-in-law. But on the other hand, nothing surprises me about him anymore."

"Well, he did," Roxanne lied, then cleared her throat. "But enough about him." She picked up a glass brimming with champagne and handed one to Aaron. "To new friendships." Her glass tapped his.

"To new friendships," Aaron echoed, then scoured the table of steaming delicacies. "This food looks really good, Janelle—I—I mean, Roxanne."

When Janelle received a call from Sherry, claiming she was coming for a visit, Janelle was extremely grateful to see her good friend. After her arrival, Janelle took her on a tour of the boutique. Sherry was ecstatic that her friend's dream had come true. Thereafter, the two were determined to indulge in all the wonders of Phoenix. One day they went sightseeing, exploring all the picturesque landscapes.

Another day, they treated themselves to the Heard Museum and eating at a fine restaurant. On another day, they shopped until exhaustion stopped them. On another occasion, they attended a book signing of their favorite romance authors. Later that night, they shook their hips in a club. Sherry's final day, they decided to take in a movie. *Eve's Bayou* stood out on the marquee as they stood in a long line.

"I heard that this movie has an excellent story line," Janelle told Sherry. They were moving forward a few steps. She turned back toward her. "Some of my customers were talking about it. They call themselves film connoisseurs instead of movie buffs."

Sherry scratched the corner of her mouth. "I heard it was real good too. Can't wait to see it. Some real good actors and actresses are in it too." But just then Sherry's eyes widened. She was gazing ahead of Janelle.

Janelle turned around, following her line of vision to see what was so interesting. Her heart jerked. Aaron was standing on line far ahead of them. Though it wasn't merely seeing him that shook her up. It was who he was with. Roxanne was waiting on the movie line with him. "I don't believe this," she uttered. "I thought she went back home. What in the world is she doing with Aaron? How do they even know each other?"

"Oh, it's nothing," Sherry blew off. "Probably just two friends hanging out at the movies."

Nevertheless, Janelle could see from the look Sherry couldn't hide that it was something.

"I can't go inside the movie," Janelle announced. "I can't see him. And with her."

"You sure?" Sherry asked. "Maybe this would be a good chance for you to talk and work things out."

"Work what out, Sherry? He cheated on me. There is nothing to work out. And the way he has moved on so easily proves I was right." She glared at Aaron and Roxanne, then removed herself from the line. She made fast quick steps toward her car. She didn't want Aaron to see her.

Trying to catch up, Sherry was losing her breath. "I think you should go back there and lay claim to your man."

"He's not my man! He's everybody else's."

"Not by embarrassing yourself of course," Sherry continued. "But just having a talk."

"No way."

When they arrived home, they became comfortable in their pajamas. Bowls of popcorn, pretzels, chips and cans of soda lay on a table near the bedside. Though the relaxing comforts didn't breed a relaxed atmosphere.

Lines crowded between Sherry's brows with her belief that Janelle was wrong. "What harm would it have done to walk up in the line and say hello to him? Something might have been rekindled from there."

Wildly, Janelle was shaking her head. "You don't get it, do you? I don't want to rekindle something with a man who can't be faithful. I thought we were in a committed relationship. He broke my heart, Sherry. I don't have to tell you that. How many nights in the last month have I called you crying? Why would you want me to put myself back into something so painful like that? He'll just do it again. He never really loved me."

"I don't believe that." Sherry was crunching a pretzel as she talked. "Not after what you told me. That man seemed like he could kiss the ground you walked on."

"I thought that too," Janelle admitted, with a heavy feeling in her chest. "But I was wrong. I was one among many. Just a good piece, who happened to not want to give up the goods anymore."

Sherry grimaced. "Don't talk like that. I, for one, have never been convinced that he cheated on you. If I did, of course I wouldn't want you to go back to him."

"But he did. The woman was in his house nearly naked." Janelle picked up some popcorn, but put it back suddenly not hungry anymore. "And he knew I wasn't coming by. He also had to put up with my not wanting to have sex. It was just too much for a stud like him."

"That woman could have been a maid." Sherry bit into another pretzel and chewed. "And something really could have spilled on her dress and she was letting it dry."

"Yeah, right. And I can buy the Grand Canyon." Janelle twisted her lips sullenly. "Chantel was right."

"Who's Chantel?" Sherry asked between sips of soda.

"One of my friends here. She said if I didn't give Aaron what he wanted, he'd go elsewhere. And that's what he did." Janelle laid down, turning her back to Sherry. She felt like she was about to cry. If she couldn't hold it, she didn't want Sherry to see her crying.

"Well, I'll tell you this," Sherry said, hearing Janelle sniffle. "Chantel may be a wonderful friend to you. She also probably thought she was helping you by telling you that. But your friends will always give you their two cents. Sometimes I give you my two cents. *But I'm not always right.* Because I'm not God. Her opinions are based on her life's experiences and so are yours." More to the point, Sherry wanted to tell Janelle this was about her father. Though, she could hear Janelle's sniffles becoming more frequent. She didn't want to upset her anymore.

The sniffles grew to soft cries during the night, which didn't wake Sherry. Janelle couldn't stop thinking about Aaron. She couldn't stop wanting him. She couldn't help feeling so much hurt, questioning herself again and again about him really loving her. Most of all, she couldn't stop seeing them—Aaron and Roxanne. After the movie, would he take her home? Or would she come back to his place and do all the hot sexual acts Aaron's body had been starved for in their last days together? Roxanne was probably getting her greatest revenge for what had happened with Lawson. Over and over scenarios played in her head. It was torture like she had never known.

* * *

On another side of town, Aaron walked Roxanne to her doorstep. He was uncomfortable when she turned back toward him. Her face was void of the smile that had lived on it throughout the night. An intense expression replaced it as her face neared his.

"I had such a good time, tonight, Aaron," she said breathlessly.

"Me too. The movie was great."

"The company was even greater." She gazed at his lips, then looked back to his eyes.

"You were lots of fun too."

"Would you like to come inside?"

He felt uneasy. "Another time. I'm tired. It has been a long day and I just want to hit the sack."

She was disappointed. Even so, it didn't stop her from moving closer. She was bewitched by his lips again. "I've been wondering how you taste?"

Aaron laughed off his discomfort. "Probably like popcorn," he said, trying to lessen the tension.

Roxanne wouldn't budge her lips or intentions. "Can I kiss you?"

Aaron merely looked at her a moment, debating how to handle a situation he hoped wouldn't come. "You're very pretty, Roxanne. And very sweet. But right now, I just need a friend. Which you have been to me, as well as a wonderful assistant."

She smiled, despite the stab in her heart. "All right. But I know why."

"Why?"

"It's Janelle isn't it? Janelle Sims. I know you were involved with her before I started working with you. I can understand it's hard to get over one relationship and jump right into something else."

He took a deep breath. "It is hard. And right now I'm

just not ready. But as far as friends, I can never have enough of them.''

''Neither can I.''

Pulling her kitchen curtain aside, Roxanne watched Aaron heading back to his car. God knew she wanted that man. *Really* wanted him. Not for his money like she wanted Mitch. No. She would have wanted Aaron even if he was penniless. Not only because he was exceptionally attractive either. But he was warm and so wonderful in ways she couldn't describe. He treated everyone in his presence special. She could hardly wait to get to work in the mornings and loathed having to come home at night. She didn't know how Janelle could have let such a man go. If she ever had a chance to be the lady in his life, he would never get away from her.

CHAPTER TWENTY-FIVE

On Janelle's emotional parting with her best friend at the airplane gate, Sherry made her promise she would get out and enjoy herself. Get back into the swing of things and start living again. For Sherry expressed that it seemed to her, that Janelle wasn't. Slowly her friend seemed to be dying.

A black-tie fund-raiser was the perfect opportunity to indulge in what Sherry suggested. One of Janelle's best customers was the wife of a senator, who was running for office. So on the night of the gala, Janelle had her mind made up that she would start living again. In her green and black taffeta evening gown, she danced with numerous admirers, exchanged numbers with a few, drank champagne, managed to do some networking and even convinced the senator that assisting underprivileged children should be his top priority.

After having too much of one admirer's attention, she managed to slip from his presence and out onto the balcony. It was a beautiful night, the sky full of stars and such beauty for lovers.

When she heard someone come up behind her, something in the air told who it was even before she turned around.

"How are you, Janelle?" Aaron asked.

She tried to look collected, not at all like her heart felt like it was suddenly ripping out of her chest. "I'm fine. How are you?" She really hadn't expected to see him here.

"Good. I'm hanging in there."

An uneasy quiet trailed his words.

"Nice party," she said, noticing he looked more handsome than ever. Something must have been making him happy. Or someone.

"Yes, it is a nice party," he agreed, trying not to look down at her body, trying not to feel as warm as he did, trying not to want her as much as he did. "I hope tonight is a big success. And speaking of success, in handling your affairs with the boutique, my secretary has informed me that it's doing exceptionally well."

Pride brightened her face. "Yes, it is. Profits are nearing seven figures."

His face beaming with boyish excitement, he held back the need to hug her. He was so proud of all she'd done. He wished so deeply he could have been sharing these days of glory with her. They would have had so many exciting things to talk about at the end of the day. The nights would have been capped with the most erotic lovemaking.

"Congratulations," he told her. "No one deserves it more than you." His eyes lingered on hers.

Warmth rippled through her at his words. She knew he meant what he was saying. He had always been so positive about her success. More attuned to her need for it than anyone else. So wonderful it made her feel. So wonderful he made her feel looking at her in that way—that way he used to look at her, as if she was the air he needed to breathe. It made her melt inside. The look was so intoxicating, she had almost forgotten how deeply he hurt her. For that moment, she almost wished he would reel her into his arms and kiss her senselessly. Thereafter, they would start all over again.

"There you are," Roxanne pierced the dreamy mist with her voice and presence. She was smiling at Aaron. "I was looking for you. How did you manage to get away from me?" She switched her attention to Janelle, not feeling in the slightest malicious. She was so happy being around Aaron, his good naturedness was rubbing off on her. That was an even bigger surprise to Roxanne. "How are you? Haven't seen you in so long."

"I'm well," Janelle answered, making herself smile.

"Good."

"How do you like Phoenix?"

"I like it," Roxanne answered. "I have a great job and a great boss." She then turned to Aaron. "And speaking of great people, the senator wants to see you. And I think he's gunning for your checkbook."

Aaron laughed dryly. He didn't want to go. He didn't want to ever leave Janelle again. Despite his wants, it was awkward talking with her the way he wanted with Roxanne there, even if they were only friends. "I'll call you later," he told Janelle. God he hoped that maybe, just maybe there was a chance for them again.

"Okay." She nodded, surprised that he would say such a thing in front of Roxanne. Then again, maybe he wanted to talk about business. Because she didn't know what she would say if he wanted to talk about anything else. She was so confused. What she was certain about, was that she could never ever stop loving him.

"And that's a nice ring," Roxanne pointed out, drawing all eyes to a huge pear-shaped diamond on Janelle's ring finger.

"It sure is," Aaron said, taking her hand and examining the beautiful ring.

At his touch, her body flowed with heat. "Thanks," she said calmly, also admiring the gift she'd given herself.

Moments later, she watched Aaron and Roxanne walk off into the ballroom.

She had just turned back to admire the view of the sky when she heard someone approaching. Thinking it was Aaron again, she eagerly swung around. Seeing Mitch brought a stern expression to her face.

"What are you doing here?" she asked.

He joined her in admiring the view. "Attending a fundraiser for a well-respected senator."

"I thought you would have gone back to Philadelphia by now."

Mitch smiled over at her. "When I leave, I'm taking what's mine back with me."

His nerve shook her head. "I told you I'm not your possession. I don't want you anymore."

"You will again. You can't resist me too long."

"I see your ego is still growing."

"And now that Aaron is spending some heated nights with Roxanne, maybe you should forget him and get your fire ignited elsewhere. Didn't you see them together in there?"

Those words wrenched at her heart. "Get away from me!"

"The truth hurts."

"I'll leave then!" She started off into the ballroom.

Mitch grabbed her wrist, meeting her eyes with a hard gaze. "Face it that Roxanne is laying it hard on your exman and my old buddy every night!"

His ugly words were luring ugly thoughts to her mind. "Get away from me! No matter what happens between them, I won't retaliate by being with you—not intimately. Sleeping with you was horrible."

Amazed, Mitch eased his grip. "What?"

"That's right. I hated having sex with you. In fact, I had met Aaron before I started seeing you and he was all I could think about when you were trying to please me. Being with you was about as exciting as having a zombie lying on top of me! Why would I doom myself to a life of boredom again! Aaron was so different. So exciting I couldn't wait to rip his clothes off. He could really give you some lessons on not only how to please a woman—but how to be a man. A real man.''

The words were out before Janelle could stop them. She had never planned on saying such things to Mitch. Words like those normally wouldn't have come out her mouth. But she wanted him to leave her alone, and before she knew it, she was shouting things she had only thought before.

In a haze of astonishment, Mitch watched her walk off into the ballroom. He had never been so humiliated in his life. What's more, he wasn't going to take anymore. If she didn't want him, if she felt that way about him, he didn't need her. There were plenty of women who wanted him. Plenty. He was taking the first flight back to Philadelphia in the morning.

Although, as he was about to leave the balcony, he stepped on something. It was a striking diamond ring. It was Janelle's ring. He hadn't missed it on her hand when she humiliated him. It must have been too big. Debating whether to toss if off the balcony among the most distant trees, he thought of another idea as he caught a glimpse of Aaron inside the ballroom. Within a second, he walked over to him, twirling the ring between his fingertips.

He knew Janelle and Aaron were hardly speaking. Hence, he knew Aaron would probably believe him when he said, "Have you seen Janelle? She lost her engagement ring when we were outside.''

Aaron's mouth flopped open. "Engagement ring?'' He almost dropped the glass of wine he was holding.

"Yes, her engagement ring. Where is she?'' Mitch was looking around. He spotted her in a remote corner, but he pretended he didn't.

"Wait, wait one second,'' Aaron insisted, putting his

hand forward. "I know Janelle isn't getting married? You have to be kidding? I know you are?"

"You know wrong old friend." Mitch raised the ring higher between them. "She's engaged all right. To me."

Aaron felt like the floor beneath him had gone. "You?" The swell of breath in his throat hardly let him get out the word. "Not to you? She's not crazy."

"Ask her?" Mitch insisted, knowing Aaron's pride wouldn't allow him.

Aaron left the party earlier than he'd planned. He drove Roxanne home, all the while refusing to share with her what had happened. He was so quiet, angry and sad.

When he was finally alone, Aaron rushed up in to his shower. Letting the hot water cascade on his naked body, he wanted to scream. Yet, it just wouldn't come out. He wanted to die, but God wouldn't give him the honor. He wanted to go back in time and erase the situation that ended his relationship with Janelle. If only the past could be undone.

How could she marry Mitch? How could she marry so quickly after they broke up? Perhaps it was so easy to get engaged because there was nothing for her to get over. Perhaps she didn't love him as he had loved her. Maybe the love he believed he felt from her was all in his head because he wanted it so bad. She didn't even want to make love to him in those last days. Wasn't that some proof?

The mental torture of Janelle's engagement went on for hours. Water fell and fell and fell on him, until he was numb, not even feeling it. When finally, he stepped out and began drying himself, he realized something. There was no way he could stay in Phoenix with Janelle and Mitch flaunting their engagement. He had to get away. Had to or it all would kill him.

There was an overseas business project that needed tending to. Some property in Japan. He had been putting it off because it would be time-consuming. Moreover, he hadn't wanted to go too far from Janelle. Every day he had held the hope that something would bring her to his door. She would realize she was wrong and promise to always trust him. From that day on, his life would be filled with the warmth and passion that only her love could give it.

Fantasy aside, since that wasn't going to be, he would go to Japan. In fact, when Roxanne heard about the opportunity, she asked if she could accompany him in a work capacity. Now, the more he thought about it, the better that idea seemed. He needed someone to talk to now. Otherwise, he might have lost his mind.

Janelle had fallen asleep waiting for Aaron's call. When a restlessness awakened her with the darkness still outside her window, she turned on the lamp and peeked at the clock. It was almost three-thirty in the morning.

She should have known he was just saying something to end the conversation. And why was she waiting for his call anyway, she further admonished herself. He was dating Roxanne now. And even if he wasn't, how could she ever trust him again after what he did? The questions ran continuously until daylight finally arose.

CHAPTER
TWENTY-SIX

Three months later, Roxanne strutted into Janelle's boutique, trying on numerous stylish dresses before she brought them up to the counter for purchase. She had to admit, her designs weren't tacky like they used to be. Janelle happened to be the one ringing up her sale.

"My, my, you are in a shopping mood," Janelle said, trying to be friendly. Although, she couldn't help feeling sick about Aaron being with this woman.

"Oh, yes, I feel like shopping and shouting to the rooftops."

"Cash or credit?" Janelle asked, lifting the tag of one of the garments.

"Credit." Roxanne handed Janelle Aaron's credit card. Afterward, she noted her disturbed expression. "I just felt like buying out the place. I did the same thing in Japan."

"Japan?" Janelle echoed. She hadn't seen Roxanne lately, but she had no idea she was overseas. Sleepless nights had made her life miserable as she imagined Roxanne and Aaron on a Caribbean island somewhere.

"Oh, yes, Japan was so beautiful," Roxanne raved.

"Aaron loved it too." Roxanne had told herself she wouldn't rub taking Janelle's man in her face. Yet, it was too tempting to resist. Especially since her dislike for Janelle was rekindled. Yes, Roxanne was with Aaron, and she also had that big surprise to spring on Janelle, which would further bind her to him. Despite it all, she had sensed so often during their growing closer that he was somewhere else. Calling out Janelle's name last night when they made love confirmed it. He didn't even realize he did it, and Roxanne didn't tell him that he did. She wanted to forget it, just as she would make Aaron forget this woman before her. "Aaron was there on business," Roxanne went on, "and he couldn't bare me not coming along."

"Japan must have been nice." Janelle was ringing up each price, trying her best to concentrate.

"More than nice. It was a dream. Especially when Aaron proposed."

Janelle froze. A fullness grew in her chest as she looked up at Roxanne. "Aa—Aaron proposed to you?"

"Right in a boat in Japan. We're shopping for my ring today."

"Congratulations."

"Thanks. The wedding should be soon. You'll be one of the first to get an invitation."

The rest of the week, Janelle struggled to attend to customers with a happy face. And she did have something to be very happy about. She had been spending time at the Good Girls of America club and had made significant progress with Gretchen. Gretchen had become very outgoing, positive and excited about her future. However, even with that major accomplishment, behind Janelle's smile she ached with the fact that Roxanne was marrying Aaron. Late Friday afternoon, however, near closing, she learned there was something worse.

Two women entered the boutique, looking at dresses. One was someone she had never seen before. Unfortunately, the other face she would never forget. It was the woman she had seen at Aaron's house half dressed.

When she came up to the counter to pay for a dress she looked nervous.

"Hello," she greeted Janelle. She removed some bills from her wallet.

"Hello." Janelle removed her items from the hanger and proceeded to ring up the sale. She couldn't look the woman in the eye.

The woman touching her hand made her do so. "Ms. I'm truly sorry, for any problem I may have caused you and Mr. Deverreau by spilling the juice on my clothes. Thank God he didn't call my agency." She then took out a card and handed it to Janelle. "If you're ever in need of a maid, I give you my word I do good work. My husband and children claim I'm the best housekeeper in the world." She smiled and claimed her package. Afterward, she strode out of the store with the other woman.

Her mind reeling with the woman's words, Janelle glanced at the woman's name and agency. In a breath, she was dialing the number on the card.

"Magnificent Maids?" a woman's voice answered.

"Yes, my name is Janelle Sims. I'd like to inquire about the service of one of your maids. She said she worked for one of my friends, but I can't reach him right now. Could you confirm that."

"What's the name ma'am?"

"Geri Michaels."

"Geri is one of our best."

"Did she ever work for an Aaron Deverreau?"

"Oh, I don't even have to look that up on the computer. I remember when she worked for him. She was real upset because she thought Mr. Deverreau wouldn't request her services again. She'd taken off her clothes after spilling some juice on them and it caused a little tiff with his girlfriend.''

Janelle slammed the phone down, her cries soon shaking her shoulders. Aaron was telling her the truth all along. What had she done?

Aaron sat watching television while Roxanne stirred around his kitchen preparing him a meal. He hadn't asked her to, but she was so excited over the ring he'd given her, she claimed she had to do something special for him.

The show was one of his favorites, *New York Undercover*. He loved all the characters and would often make sure he taped the show if he was working late. Tonight however, the images were blurred by all the commotion in his mind. He was getting married. Married to a woman he didn't even love.

In Japan, she had been very comforting when he talked about his hurt over Janelle's engagement. The next thing he knew, he was forcing himself to get over it by lying within her eagerly awaiting body. Being with her was nothing like being with Janelle. Even when he pretended she was Janelle, the emotions he wanted to experience wouldn't come.

One night after he was feeling particularly down about Janelle marrying Mitch, she informed him that they were probably married already. The jealousy and hurt that welled inside Aaron was overwhelming. So the idea didn't seem too bad when he suggested, ''Why don't you move on too? With me. I can make you forget her. I promise. I can take all the pain away.'' And with pain so excruciating, with no medicine that he knew of for it, Aaron reached for anything, anything in this world to take it away.

CHAPTER
TWENTY-SEVEN

Aaron's wedding announcement was featured in all the society papers and even the local ones given away for free. Everywhere Janelle turned the quickly approaching date was slamming her in the heart. In need of escaping it all, she knew of only one place that could soothe her. Before she knew anything, Janelle took a flight out of Phoenix. Her destination was her mother's home.

Except when the old familiar door was opened, Janelle didn't see the woman she expected. Facing this person before her, it was hard to believe it was her mother. A glamour girl stood before her. The last time she'd seen her mother, she wore big housecoats all the time, absolutely no makeup, didn't care about hairstyles and was so thin she looked anorexic. Now the opposite, she wore a comfortable pantsuit, softly applied makeup, an adorable short shaggy cut, and had curves fit for *Players Magazine*. Most noticeable, were her eyes. That everlasting sadness in them was gone. Now there was a sparkle.

Maya Sims laughed as she hugged her daughter, then

reared back to check her out too. "You look cute as a button, baby. Beautiful as ever."

"And you look . . ." Pausing, Janelle looked her mother up and down at a loss for words. "You look like someone else."

"I know," Maya said with a laugh. "I've been told that often lately."

Maya closed the door. Janelle plopped in one of the dining room chairs. Her mother sat next to her. On a tray a teakettle filled with chamomile sat between them, sweetening the air.

Speechless, Janelle was still gawking. "Mama, you really do look so good. So, so good."

"Because I'm happy."

"Happy about what? Are you involved in a lot of activities? Every time I call, you're sure out."

"How many times have I told you to leave me a message and I'll call you back?"

"I hate leaving messages. And why haven't you come out to see me? I can't believe you still haven't seen my boutique."

"I was waiting until Winston went on vacation so we could come together."

"Winston?" Janelle echoed and thought back to when she heard that name. Before Maya could answer, Janelle remembered. "Isn't he that man that came around after Daddy left?"

"Sure is."

Janelle noticed her mother was glowing even more. This man was in her life. This was the reason she looked like she did. "What is going on?"

"Winston and I are getting married."

Tears rose in Janelle's eyes. "Mama, you've found someone?"

Maya's eyes reflected her daughter's. She dabbed at her wet lash. "I sure did. And baby, he is the most wonderful man in the world. I feel so blessed. Never has a man treated me so well. We can talk for hours. We love to listen to romantic ballads and slow dance. We laugh. We say and do such wonderful things to each other and for each other. And there is just so much more. He understands me. He's supportive of me. He showers me with gifts. He makes me feel so loved. And when he holds me in his arms, it's like I'm lying in heaven."

Janelle nodded, totally understanding what her mother was talking about. Aaron had made her feel the same way. She was so grateful someone had finally loved her mother the way a wonderful woman should have been loved. "I'm so happy for you, Mama."

"I'm happy for me too." Maya rocked a little. "I guess it all goes to show you that if you're a good person and you keep on doing the right things, God is going to bless you. You just have to stay strong in the hard times."

"And it was hard . . ." Janelle said aloud, and saw an anguishing flash of her childhood. Her father had kissed her and walked out the door.

Maya saw her daughter's disheartened expression and gently held her hand. "Janelle, I asked you this before. And you told me no, but do you want to talk . . . about Daddy?"

"I hate him. I don't want to talk about him." Her chest heaved with her adamancy.

"That's why you should talk about him."

"Mama, why do you want to talk about him after what he did to you? You're happy now, but he hurt you so bad. How can you stand to even think about him? For years, I've looked at your eyes and seen that pain that he put there. Thank God, it's gone."

"He didn't put pain in my eyes."

"He did! He hurt you. That's why you looked so down and out."

"I'm telling you, baby. It wasn't that."

"It was. You loved him so much and you couldn't get over it."

"Wrong. I did love him. But I did get over it. Long, long time ago. What made me sad, was something else."

"What?" Janelle looked confused.

"It's what I gave up that made me sad."

"What did you give up?"

"A man who loved me."

Janelle was more confused. "I don't understand."

"You do remember Winston coming by to see me after your daddy left?"

"Yes, but I also remember he stopped coming. And if I'm not mistaken you stopped him. You didn't want to see him."

"But I did. I fell in love with Winston. And he fell in love with me. He wanted to marry me and take the responsibility of my five children and take us all with him in his travels in the army."

Janelle looked amazed. "So why didn't you go? Why didn't you take us and go?"

"Because I was foolish, baby. Instead of listening to my own little voice inside me, to my heart, to my intuition, I listened to family and friends who were telling me that I shouldn't ruin my children's lives by breaking up the family. The people around me then were a little more tolerant of unfaithfulness than women are today. They said your daddy was going to get over this thing he had with other women and finally settle down at home.

"And that running off with this man, and having him raise my children wasn't going to work out. They said Winston could never love you all like your daddy could. That every time he would look at you all, he would be reminded of me loving another man. Worst of all, they told me children from broken homes had all kinds of problems. And I know how much you'll loved your daddy back then. Couldn't nobody replace him. I used to see your faces when Winston came around. And how you all wouldn't act right toward him.

"So for my children's happiness and well-being, I said

I would keep my family together no matter how much I didn't love your daddy anymore. I would have done anything for my children, even look at his sorry face every day of my life. But by the time I realized he wasn't coming back, it was too late for me and Winston. He had already left for the army. He says he never stopped thinking about me. And loving me. One day after he divorced a woman he married, he hired a private investigator to find me. And now here we are."

Janelle was in tears hearing what her mother gave up for her. They hugged and held each other, until Maya raised up to look in her daughter's face.

"Now what is on your mind, young lady? I know you didn't fly here for nothing."

"I wanted to see you. But I also needed you. Mama, I know that every time we've spoken lately, I've told you that Aaron and I worked everything out. But we haven't. I went to see him after you gave me that good advice and I jumped to the wrong conclusion about him."

Maya scowled. "What happened?"

"I thought he was cheating on me. But I've recently found I was wrong. Now he's going to marry someone else. Oh, mama, it hurts so bad. I can't stop loving him."

"Baby, you don't have to."

"But he's marrying someone else: Roxanne."

Maya frowned. "Mitch's sister-in-law?"

"Yes."

"My goodness. How did that happen?"

"I don't know. All I know is that it's my fault. I always thought he was going to cheat. I always thought he was just like . . ." Not wanting to even think of her father, she stopped herself.

"Say it, Janelle. You thought he was like your daddy."

She laid her head on Maya's chest. "Mama, I didn't mean to. I just couldn't help it sometimes. It just came out of me. Even when I first laid eyes on Aaron, I was thinking he was a playboy just because he was so good-looking. I guess even with all the love he showed me, it wouldn't stop."

"You can't let your daddy ruin your life. I nearly let him ruin mine. I will not let him ruin yours."

"I already let him ruin it. If I could just take it all back. If I just had another chance with him, for the rest of life I would love him with all my heart and soul, trusting him, trusting him so deeply."

Maya lifted Janelle's head, holding it before her face. "Baby, it's not too late."

"But he's getting married. She even sent me an invitation."

"But who says he's marrying her because of love? He could be marrying her all of a sudden because he's on the rebound. He could be marrying her to forget you."

"Are you telling me to go in there and try to steal a man who's engaged to someone?"

"Of course not. We're decent women. But you did say she sent you an invitation. So why not attend the wedding?"

"What?" Was her mother crazy?

"If he loves that woman and you're sitting there, your presence will mean nothing to him. But if he doesn't love her, and you're right there, he can't marry her. Not if your love was as deep as you say. The old people used to say 'if you love someone and they leave, if they really, really love you, they'll come back.' Look at what happened to me."

Beads of perspiration coated Aaron's face as he stood in the anteroom. One of his brothers had just left to see if it was about time for the ceremony to start. The other was singing a stirring rendition of "For You" by Kenny Latimore.

"Here comes the old ball and chain," Brett teased Aaron, punching him on the arm. You're trapped now, man. This is a life sentence."

"The car is outside," Demarre joined in the fun. "I can help you make the getaway right now."

Yet, both men noticed their friend found nothing funny.

"Lighten up," Brett said, his frown soon matching the one distorting Aaron's features. "Man, are you having second thoughts about this?"

Demarre studied Aaron too. "You don't look too happy, Aaron. You look like you're about to die instead of get married."

That's what it felt like Aaron thought looking down. What's more, he had been telling Roxanne for weeks that he didn't feel ready for such a big step and that he wanted to get to know her a little better before sending out wedding invitations. She sent them out anyway. She made the other arrangements, too, all the while urging him, that what he was feeling was normal for a man about to get married. Finally he met his friend's eyes. "I guess I just was expecting to marry . . ."

"Janelle," Demarre finished his sentence. He eyed Brett. Both of them had stayed clear of mentioning her name since the two broke up. For the simple fact, that Aaron had insisted on not talking about her. He would get so upset. But seeing his friend like this, Demarre had to say something on this day. "Man, you can't marry the wrong woman. If you want Janelle, go get her."

"I can't get her. She's married or about to marry someone else."

"Who?" Brett asked.

"Yes," Demarre echoed. "Who is she going to marry?"

"Mitch!" he spat out.

Brett and Demarre thought that was funny.

"Since when?" Demarre asked.

"Since I saw him at the fund-raiser. He showed me the wedding ring."

Demarre started shaking his head. "No way, man. Mitch is gone."

"Gone?" Aaron echoed. "Gone where?"

"Back to Philly," Brett answered. "He called me the other day. He's thinking of buying some property in California and was asking my advice. Said he might relocate there."

"Is Janelle going with him?"

"No," Demarre answered. "They're not even speaking anymore."

Aaron's eyes widened. "How do you know?"

"Because of Chantel. Her and Janelle chat sometimes on the phone. Mitch left a long time ago. She said Janelle dismissed him. Really dismissed him. Told him that he didn't have any skills." Demarre glanced down at his pants. "Now you know Mitch's ego couldn't take that."

A smile broke through Aaron's gloom. "I guess she really wanted to get him out of her life. Otherwise, I don't think she would have gone *there.*"

All the guys laughed. It was only the introduction to the wedding march summoning Aaron, that dried his smile away.

A few steps out of the anteroom, and Aaron dressed in all white, stood before the minister. More than three hundred guests crowded the room, smiling and looking up at him. Before long, the bridal march played. The flower boy and girl passed. In yellow chiffon gowns, the bridesmaids followed. Through it all, Aaron tried to feel joy. Yet all he could feel was that he was looking down watching a man in a church. This didn't feel at all like his life. It felt like his death.

Within moments, the admiring gasps of the crowd drew him around to the bride entering the church, who wore a form-fitting taffeta gown with a lengthy train. Slowly, Roxanne began to stroll toward him, the biggest smile imaginable stretched across her face. She looked pretty, he thought, but when his eyes caught someone in a row she passed, he thought she was beautiful. It was Janelle. Their eyes met and all else was blurred away in the church. Aaron couldn't keep his eyes on his bride, even when

Roxanne stood by his side. He constantly looked back. Once or twice, Roxanne looked back to see what was distracting him.

The minister began reciting the wedding vows. And as each word, drew him further and further from the woman he really loved, Aaron began to feel desperate. She loved him. She didn't marry Mitch. She sent him away. And what were her eyes saying to him now? Every fiber of his heart knew it was love. Maybe, just maybe she could trust him now. And if she couldn't, wasn't her fully loving him worth fighting for.

"Aaron?" the minister jarred him. "Do you take this woman to be your lawfully wedded wife . . ." The words blurred with Aaron's racing thoughts. So much so, he held up his hand. "I have to speak to Roxanne in private," he whispered.

But at this point, and standing before the altar, Roxanne knew he could only want to talk about one thing. She wasn't having it.

"No, we have to continue." She bowed her head to the minister.

He began reciting the vows again.

"No," Aaron stopped him. "We have to talk." He looked back at Janelle.

Roxanne looked around too. Seeing what he was looking at, she turned back around, ignoring the knot in her stomach. "No. We have to go on." Her tone was low.

"Please," Aaron begged. "Let's go in the anteroom."

The guests began leaning toward one another, murmuring.

Hearing them and knowing what was happening, Roxanne held back her tears.

"Please," Aaron pressed in a whisper.

"Not now!" she yelled out before she realized it.

"Then I have to tell you right here."

"No!" she screamed, and suddenly became hysterical. "No! No! You can't do this to me!"

"I'm sorry."

"We are getting married today!"

The guest were in an uproar.

"But I love someone else." With that, he gazed into the stunned guests until he saw the face he sought. Without even realizing she was doing it, Janelle stood.

A hush went over the crowd as Aaron walked away from Roxanne's side, stepped down the aisle and extended his hand to Janelle. "I . . . didn't want to tell you like this but I still love you."

Grasping his moist fingers, Janelle's lips trembled. Tears strolled down her cheeks. "I love you too. I never stopped. Never."

They embraced tightly, hardly separating even as they ran into the limousine and Aaron gave the driver directions to a special place. In moments, they stood in the paradise-like place where they first kissed. With the daylight fading into the orange-yellow of dusk, it looked exactly like it did when they were there together.

Planting soft kisses along her face, Aaron thought he was dreaming. "Baby, I'll prove to you that I can be the man you want. I'll do anything to prove it. As long as you're in my life. Whatever it takes, I'll do. Life hasn't been the same without you."

"You don't have to prove anything," she said, returning soft kisses to his handsome face. "I trust you, Aaron. I will never, ever project my father's sickness onto you. You're an individual. And I'm the woman who was born to love you. And I'll be by your side forever."

"Oh, God," he said, his lips caressing downward on her neck. "You don't know what it means to hear you say that. I want to be with you forever too."

She raised her head as his mouth probed lower. "I love you so much, Aaron. I never thought a love like yours would be blessed into my life."

"I love you, too, baby," his voice husky with lust. "And no else can replace you in my heart." He was kissing her cleavage, while skillfully unzipping her dress from the back. It fell to the ground.

Kissing her, while stroking the rest of her clothes away, he felt her doing the same to him. In a breath, he lay on top of her, her breasts tingling against the hardness of his chest. Ravenously, his tongue explored the inside of her mouth, while his hands explored over her.

Stopping at the dewy heaven between her legs, he thrilled her with an erotic dance of his fingers, her whimpers of pleasure making him do more and more. Her heart thudded wildly, matching the rhythm of his.

His lips soon replaced his fingers in driving the cache of her love into a frenzy. Cries of her joy filled the air only muffled by his mouth returning to her lips. His kisses grew hungrier, punctuated by intense caresses that sent her body aflame. But no longer being able to be together without being one, Aaron took her erect nipple in his mouth as he thrust his own erect affection inside of her.

His tongue circling one breast torpidly and then the other, he moved his hips with the same careful precision. Biting her lip from the joy firing through her limbs, she arched her back, and raised her hips to feel more of what she couldn't get enough of. While she did so, Aaron cupped her buttocks, and with a maddening force brought them toward him. Writhing his hips wildly, and then in an erotic dance, he felt like he was going to explode from the pleasure. His groans from the sweet feeling only blended with her own.

But no longer able to take anymore of the agonizing joy, he succumbed to the rush that shook them uncontrollably. His erratic breath was barely able to get out the question, his raging heart needed an answer to, to calm itself down.

"Will you marry me?"

"Yes, oh yes."

Acknowledgements

I want to thank God for blessing me with another dream come true. My deep appreciation is also extended to those whose support meant so much to me. To my son, Brandon, who gave me a smile, a kiss on the cheek and an I love you whenever I needed one. To my parents and genius sister, Sharon, who gave me the warmth of family. To Norm who gave me encouragement throughout my career. To my beautiful cousin's, Diane and Marguerite, who are both inspirations to me. To Marvin, who has been an awesome friend; thank you for everything. To my editor, Karen Thomas, who is brilliant and a pleasure to work with. To Robert Johnson and Kelli Richardson, who presented such exciting opportunities with BET. To Monica Harris, Walter Zacharius and the Kensington family, who gave me my start. To my agent Denise Stinson, who is wonderful. To Kate Ferguson, who gave Love So True exposure in her fabulous publication. To Marcia Mahan of Black Romance, who published so many of my short stories. To all my friends and family, who I didn't have space to mention, my appreciation reaches from my heart to yours.

ABOUT THE AUTHOR

Louré Bussey is a graduate of Borough of Manhattan Community College. She wrote 56 short stories before her best selling novel Nightfall was published. Since that debut, she has written three other novels: Most Of All, Twist Of Fate and Love So True. A fifth novel, A Taste Of Love, will be published in August 1999. In addition to writing novels, Ms. Bussey is a singer/songwriter who is recording a CD based on one of her novels. She lives in Brooklyn, New York.

Dear Readers:

I hope you enjoyed Janelle and Aaron as well as the other characters in Love So True! I tried to create a heroine you truly cared about and a man any woman would fall in love with.

Thank you for all the wonderful letters about Most Of All, Twist Of Fate and Nightfall. All of them touched my heart. I hope I can continue writing stories that you enjoy. I'd love to hear from you at:

PO Box 020648
Brooklyn, New York 11202-0648
or
Email me at: LoureBus@aol.com

You can also find out what I'm doing so that you can enjoy these stories even more at my author homepage at: www.Arabesquebooks.com

I wish you lots of love!

Sincerely
Louré Bussey

COMING IN FEBRUARY ...

ONE OF A KIND   (1-58314-000-X, $4.99/$6.50)
by Bette Ford
Legal secretary Anthia Jenkins and Dexter Washington, director of a
Detroit community center, were good friends. But Anthia wanted more
than friendship. Once unjustly convicted of his wife's suicide, Dexter
didn't want to love again. But he couldn't control the passion between
them and now he needs to convince Anthia to believe in him and in
love.

TRUE BLUE   (1-58314-001-8, $4.99/$6.50)
by Robyn Amos
When her sister announces they've won the lottery, Toni Rivers is
off to the Florida coast and a new life. Blue Cooper is ready to sweep
Toni off her feet when she walks into his nightclub. But the powerful
feelings between them frighten Toni. She holds back more so when
a dangerous past surfaces. Now he must find a way to prove that his
love is true.

PICTURE PERFECT   (1-58314-002-6, $4.99/$6.50)
by Shirley Harrison
Davina Spenser found out that her father was actually the brilliant
painter Maceo James, who had gone into hiding for a murder he didn't
commit. She was determined to clear his name and take his paintings
from Hardy Enterprises. But the handsome new CEO Justin Hardy
was a tempting obstacle that could bring her delicious disaster or
perfect love.

AND OUR VALENTINE'S DAY COLLECTION ...

WINE AND ROSES   (1-58314-003-4, $4.99/$6.50)
by Carmen Green, Geri Guillaume, Kayla Perrin
February is for Valentine's Day, but it can also be a time of sweet
surprises for those who aren't even looking for love. Delight in the
joys of unexpected romance with reignited passion in Carmen Green's
"Sweet Sensation," with the eternal gift of love in Geri Guillaume's
"Cupid's Day Off" and renewed hope in Kayla Perrin's "A Perfect
Fantasy."

*Available wherever paperbacks are sold, or order direct from the
Publisher. Send cover price plus 50¢ per copy for mailing and han-
dling to Kensington Publishing Corp., Consumer Orders, or call
(toll free) 888-345-BOOK, to place your order using Mastercard or
Visa. Residents of New York and Tennessee must include sales tax.
DO NOT SEND CASH.*

BOOK YOUR PLACE ON OUR WEBSITE AND MAKE THE ARABESQUE ROMANCE CONNECTION!

We've created a customized website just for our very special Arabesque readers, where you can get the inside scoop on everything that's going on with Arabesque romance novels.

When you come online, you'll have the exciting opportunity to:

- View covers of upcoming books

- Read sample chapters

- Learn about our future publishing schedule (listed by publication month *and author*)

- Find out when your favorite authors will be visiting a city near you

- Search for and order backlist books from our online catalog

- Check out author bios and background information

- Send e-mail to your favorite authors

- Meet the Kensington staff online

- Join us in weekly chats with authors, readers and other guests

- Get writing guidelines

- AND MUCH MORE!

**Visit our website at
http://www.arabesquebooks.com**